AF194362

HEMIS

~ A Novel ~

Madhu Tandan lived for seven years in a remote Walden-like Himalayan monastery with a simple 'soil to soul' philosophy where every experience was viewed as an opportunity to grow. Her experiences in the monastery, inspired her first book *Faith & Fire: A Way Within*. Her second book, *Dreams & Beyond: Finding Your Way in the Dark*, explores the multiplicity of the dreaming mind from the perspectives of science, psychology, paranormal and transpersonal paradigms.

Madhu has presented papers on dreams at international conferences. She has also contributed short stories and articles to anthologies.

She lives with her husband in New Delhi and often goes to her second home in the Himalayas.

HEMIS

~ A Novel ~

Madhu Tandan

HarperCollins *Publishers* India

First published in India by
HarperCollins *Publishers* in 2018

Building 10, Tower A, 4th Floor, DLF Cyber City, Phase II,
Gurugram Haryana – 122002, India
www.harpercollins.co.in

2 4 6 8 10 9 7 5 3 1

Copyright © Madhu Tandan 2018

P-ISBN: 978-93-5277-913-0
E-ISBN: 978-93-5277-914-7

Typeset in 11.5/14 Adobe Garamond Pro at
Manipal Digital Systems, Manipal

Printed and bound at
MicroPrints India, New Delhi

To
the few who stole the fire,

and to
Rajeev, Purnima and Karthika,
the best of friends.

Author's Note

On 6 August 2010, shortly after midnight, a cloudburst over Leh led to flash floods, which paralysed a large part of Ladakh. The full year's rainfall precipitated within half an hour. This was followed by a second cloudburst the next day. Reportedly, 255 people died; 800 were injured and more than 200 went missing, perhaps washed away by the gorging rivers. Thousands more were rendered homeless. The actual toll may have been significantly higher. It was the worst flood ever in Ladakh.

The main telephone exchange and mobile network system were completely destroyed. The district's lone civil hospital was flooded and rendered dysfunctional. The runway at Leh airport, covered with debris, became unusable, leaving 5,000 tourists, most of them foreigners, stranded.

One of them was Ajay Kapur. This is the story of his twenty-nine days in the Hemis Sanctuary.

Calender in Ladakh

Aloneness

4 August: Morning

Lassitude suddenly struck his body, and his face creased with tension. He shifted restlessly in his seat, cramped for space. Each thought hurt, like a slap. Damn her.

Looking out of the window, Ajay took a deep breath and slowly expelled it. 'Breathing and thoughts have an intimate connection,' his yoga instructor had said. 'Slow down your breathing and your thoughts will become calm.'

They were flying high above the snow-covered peaks of the great Himalayas. The Zanskar range was directly below them, with its spectacular spread of jagged crests and ridges of hard blue granite paradoxically capped with the softest gossamer folds of snow. The rigid and the yielding had no difficulty in coexisting in the same space. So much beauty and desolation in the view, an impersonal grandeur that held up a mirror to his own insignificance. He leaned back and sighed.

Their last fight had been the epicentre. He couldn't stem the tremor in his thoughts, no matter how slowly he breathed. An inconsequential question; his feigned ignorance; shards of words flying between them. His knee-jerk reaction; her tearful eyes, pools of despair and bewilderment. The argument had a blind impetus to it, predictable and banal in its irresolution. Why is everything in the world about sex or, rather, the lack of it? A man is only as faithful as his options.

The landing announcement was a relief. A double range of mountains, brown, stark and shaped like a horseshoe, sprang into view as the plane descended towards Leh. Their two ends gradually sloped, seeking confluence with the river that had cut a wide bed for itself. The otherwise rocky landscape merged with green and golden fields. Strangely uplifted, he gathered his things together, preparing to disembark. Enough is enough. I am going to enjoy Ladakh and the trek, he told himself.

An hour later, Ajay walked into Omarshila, a charming little hotel, its garden lined with petunias, geraniums and hollyhocks. A tree, bent with the weight of green apples, the first blush of pink on them, stood sentinel at the edge. Willows watched their reflection in the small stream that meandered past, whispering over white stones and rocks as it made its way to the fields beyond. It was an oasis of green, crowned by snow-clad mountains. He had read somewhere that the melting snows were the only form of water that sustained the valley's pockets of green.

He knew he would have to stay indoors for the rest of the day to acclimatise before he ventured out again. But how was he to rest? The same bloody thoughts. He shook his head. No, sex was not the answer; sex was the question.

Leh

The air had a piercing quality to it. Breathing raucously, Ajay climbed to the highest terrace on the southern side of the Spituk monastery, which was located on the outskirts of Leh. He stood atop a precipitous crag, looking at the lazily meandering Indus shining under the cloudless gaze of an azure sky.

The thin, pure mountain air carried a feminine voice with a distinct American accent. Realizing he was not alone, he turned around. A woman in her thirties, with blue eyes and hair the colour of ripened wheat, stood next to a monk, who was waving what looked like a drumstick in the air. The woman's face was impassive but her eyes were alert. The monk waved the drumstick again. 'Do you know what this is?'

Ajay moved closer. It didn't look like a regular drumstick.

The monk said with a smile, 'It's a human thigh bone!'

Oh my god, it was! What was he doing with it? Ajay thought, aghast.

The monk flung his hands heavenwards and declared, 'It has great power. It belonged to my teacher. Last night he came to me in a dream.' He broke into a near chant:

'That which quenches but also drowns,
That which yields but also devours,
That which flows but also floods,
Is coming your way.'

This was bizarre. Ajay shrugged his shoulders dismissively. The woman's eyes showed interest as she enquired about the meaning of the dream. 'Water…something to do with water? It has been so dry. Even the usual two inches of rain has not fallen this year. Perhaps your dream foretells rain.'

She had fallen for the mumbo-jumbo, Ajay thought.

The monk paused before replying. 'Water cleans…gives life… If so, what is the dream telling me? Water also changes course to create new directions. Could it be warning us of big changes ahead?'

This is what happens, Ajay thought, when you lock up hundreds of able-bodied young men in a monastery instead of utilizing them to develop the resources of the land. They end up meditating on bones. But the woman surprised him. She displayed no signs of the usual credulous enthusiasm of foreigners in search of the spiritual elixir of the East. Yet she had an innate respect for the monk's ways. Something about her reminded him of Akanksha, the pensive look and her attentive way of listening, the same tilt of the head, with eyes and ears focused on the speaker.

The drive back to Leh was picturesque and lifted his mood. The road wriggled through the periphery of the town, round a last spur and up a steep ascent. The view of Leh then, dominated by the massive bulk of the nine-storeyed palace atop the hill, was stunning. A collection of flat-roofed houses with whitewashed walls and red-painted windows winked among the trees.

The main bazaar was broad, open and airy, shaded by a splendid avenue of golden autumnal poplars. Shops selling semi-precious stones, prayer wheels, wooden bowls, traditional Tibetan carpets and local herbs lined both sides of the road and spilled into the side streets. A man sat quietly turning the beads of his rosary. A lama passed by a Kashmiri squatting outside his shop, and they exchanged friendly greetings. An old bearded man in a loose pheran and a skullcap sat under a tree, smoking a hookah and staring at the water running in ragged stone channels near his feet.

People here seemed peaceful and content, far away from the terrors and strife of the competitive world. It was a life diametrically opposite to his own in Delhi. His success as a manufacturing specialist stemmed from the fact that he was never content. *Ne jamais être content* was what he advocated to all his juniors in the factories he had headed. If they were content with their product quality today, how would they improve it tomorrow? What he believed in was this: Let's do it now. Fix it, improve it. Don't go to sleep without a plan.

Ajay stopped and turned around as he heard a voice behind him say, 'Julley.' A Ladakhi woman looked at him with friendly eyes. He looked at his taxi driver enquiringly.

'She is saying hello. Welcome. God be with you.'

Ajay broke into a smile and returned the greeting. They stood in the centre of the marketplace, nodding and smiling at each other, while the stream glittering with snow-water splashed past them. It seemed to him that it was singing, 'Julley, Julley.'

His thirty-year-old guide Abdul chattered incessantly. 'Must go to Tibetan restaurant for lunch. Down the street. Everyone go there.'

The restaurant was a modest room with posters of Manjushri competing with a torn one of Michael Jackson and, in between them, a man on a motorcycle trying to bridge the irreconcilable chasm. The windows overlooked a street that had a small stream flowing past it. Leh was full of these streams of murmuring water.

Mama, the round-faced Tibetan owner, presided over the restaurant with a smile that crinkled around her eyes. She was abundant in presence and information as she told Ajay, 'You can have roasted barley tsampas like that Italian, the one strumming the guitar in the corner. Or you can have Lhasa chow mein like my German friend,' and she pointed to a blond, muscular man industriously writing in his notebook. 'Soup, you want soup, a hot bowl of spicy thukpa, like that man,' and her eyes pointed to a Ladakhi who had just been served the spiked dish and was noisily spooning it into his mouth. Perhaps the locals were familiar with this mix of people and nationalities. After all, traders on the Old Silk Route had plied their wares here for centuries. Trading then, tourism and trekking now. But Ladakh still remained Ladakh.

After seating Ajay at a table near the entrance, Mama appeared like a genie with a large copper kettle and asked him, 'Want tea?'

Ajay knew this was no ordinary tea and her question was a test. He nodded and took a sip. It was a strange brew of tea, butter and salt. Keeping his face impassive, he delayed looking up as Mama stood watching. Finally, he said, 'Different, but nice. In fact, very nice.' Oddly, he liked its strong, unusual flavour—butter instead of milk, salt instead of sugar. My world view is changing, he thought wryly.

'Good. If you not like our tea, you not like our land!' Mama said beaming.

After lunch Abdul was by his side again. 'They are simple people. Always drinking tea and turning their rosary. If not rosary, then prayer wheel. Not interested only in money. Ladakhis not like that. Have many gods. Maybe that is why not greedy.'

Ajay smiled, his mind gently drifting away. Suddenly he realized he had not heard Abdul's question.

'What?' Ajay asked.

'What you believe in?'

'Not in gods, only in work.'

He had told his factory supervisors and managers, 'You cannot change the dollar parity, a dysfunctional parliament or a stagnant market. That's not in our hands. But we can change what *is* in our hands.' And changed they had, altering the entire manufacturing process, allowing their exports to be ramped up by low costs and world-class quality.

'Why you not believe in anything?' Abdul's horrified voice cut into his thoughts. Then he shook his head and said, 'Perhaps, here you find answer.'

6 August: Morning

Early in the morning, Ajay set off for Pangong Lake. He had a few days to spare before the trek began. The road wound its way over small hillocks with ochre-red gravel on the slopes. His gaze swept the surrounding rocky mountains, carved by wind and snow into the most stunning and unexpected shapes, glinting in the early morning sun like timeless sentinels. Now and then, an outcrop of rock towered above the desert with a monastery clinging to its harsh vertical face, as if its inhabitants needed further toughening. It was not difficult to see how the belief of the Ladakhis informed the landscape, how faith fashioned stone in this last outpost of the Tibetan Buddhist way of life.

Everywhere was the calligraphy of the spirit. It was there in the long mani walls that lined the road with the sacred inscription *Om mani padme hum*, and in the white and grey mantra stones piled on top of each other, a sight he would often encounter as he drove through the desolate landscape. High above, on pinnacles of rocks, on flagpoles, on suspension bridges were colourful prayer flags, sighing and snapping in the fierce winds, breathing the Buddha's words over rock and stone, softening their contours with love and prayer. At every turn, he saw a limewashed stupa with a large square foundation. On top of that base were slabs, diminishing in size as they rose. Each stupa ended in a hemispherical dome with a long conical spire, holding at its pinnacle a crescent moon cradling a sun. Interred in these stupas were the relics of great kings, saints and teachers.

A solitary bird spread its wings and dared the ascent from mountain to sky. Ajay watched its flight, and felt himself opening and becoming as expansive as the mountains, as wide as the sky, and as free as the wind. Stunned into silence by such austere grandeur, momentarily, he understood why these people believed. Stripped of his usual armour, vulnerable to these lonely spaces, he finally opened himself to Ladakh.

They stopped at Thiksey monastery. Standing before the immense image of the Maitreya seated in the lotus position, he wondered what had brought him to yet another monastery when he did not believe in either god or ritual. Incense sticks and butter lamps burnt at the altar and the baritone chanting of the monks seated on the floor resounded in the two-storey hall. Nature may be godlike, he thought, as he got into the taxi, but that does not mean there is a god.

The Scorpio engine increased its whine, groaning under the severity of the climb as they gained in altitude. His attention shifted from his thoughts to the narrow road ahead that had been cut through a stony wasteland of loose debris and boulders. Now and then small pathways of melting snow had eaten into the road, making the ride rougher. The terrain had a savage grandeur to it. Barely any vegetation broke the grey and brown rugged sameness of the landscape. He thought it was ironical that this land through which flowed one of the world's greatest rivers, should be a cold rock-strewn desert.

Pangong Tso

6 August: Evening

Beyond man and monastery, beyond the endless stretches of mountain ridges, they drove towards Pangong Lake, a 160-km trip from Leh, with no settlement around once the valley had been left behind. Ajay felt the palpable heartbeat of fear as the road shot up abruptly and steep slopes were met by uneasy bends and chunks of ice on the way to Changla Pass. The wind was cold and strong. A few thousand feet below, the Indus gushed with unbridled enthusiasm. The rarefied air made breathing laborious, but a cup of hot tea with the army jawans at Changla and the urge to flee the emptiness reduced.

As they descended, Ajay was relieved to see some grassy flatlands where yaks and pashmina goats grazed under the vigil of the nomadic Changpa tribe. It was difficult to imagine that the dirty, matted hair on these goats would transform into one of the world's finest wool, feeding the flourishing shawl industry of Kashmir. No wonder successive rulers of that territory from Shah Jahan onwards were so keen to establish their hegemony over this otherwise inhospitable land—all in chase of these goats! Swati's face swam before his eyes, the longing in her eyes when she had first held a Kani pashmina shawl in her hands, so out of reach in the early days of their marriage.

By the time they reached Pangong Lake, six hours after leaving Leh, the flanks of the Scorpio were covered with dust. Ajay got out, stretched his legs and arched his stiffened back. Forty-three and ageing, he thought ruefully. An unimaginable age when he was at school in Sanawar or even at IIT, Delhi. He caught sight of his tall frame in the side mirror of the Scorpio and ran his hand through his tousled dark hair. Ahead of him was a long stretch of calm water cupped by seared brown mountains. It was difficult to make out if the water was blue or green as it shimmered in the sun. Nothing moved except the sunlight flirting with the surface of the lake and the snow on the mountains beyond.

He felt a pang of loneliness amidst such startling beauty. I wish you were here, Ati. You would have loved the fluid movement of blue, the cyan near the shore merging into turquoise, giving way to Prussian blue, turning purple-violet at the hem of the mountains. The cobalt blue of the sky canopying the stillness of the lake.

Why did you stop painting? One Sunday morning, your easel lost its place in the study to be replaced by a divan. One by one, all your paintings came down, their place taken by well-known artists. Why? Maybe I should have pressed you for an answer. Or maybe I never heard yours clearly enough. Did my growing success eclipse your abilities? I don't think you know how often and how proudly I showed your paintings to our guests. I had seen beauty only in the hum of machines but you showed me beauty in nature and other things.

I remember the time we drove to Meerut soon after our wedding. Suddenly you waved your hands excitedly and shouted, 'Stop! Stop!' Worried, I pulled to the side and you leapt out to photograph a herd of buffaloes!

Appalled that you had finished the entire roll of film, I asked, 'Why?'

'Aren't they beautiful?'

'Really?'

'Look beyond their lumbering bulk. See the interplay of light. How it catches their horns, softens the eyes. Notice how their blackness changes hues.'

You had smiled with glee at my expression. 'These aren't just buffaloes, Ajay. I want to capture their essence and how they impact my eye, the feelings they evoke.'

I looked at the buffaloes again. This time, with a little more respect.

A year later, while driving in England, I stopped to admire the countryside, and you said to me, 'Look! It's the light playing on grass that makes the meadow beautiful. Not the picket fence, gate and stone walls or the grazing cows.'

He took out his mobile and phoned her. From the corner of his eye he sensed movement and saw a flock of brown-headed gulls land gracefully on the water. Probably early migrants from the high plateaus of Central Asia wintering on the lake. Maybe they would fly further over the long stretches of water towards Tibetan China, unaware of boundaries and borders as they traversed two countries. The phone beeped and then disconnected. He turned to his taxi driver, waving his mobile enquiringly.

'Sometimes it comes, sometimes it goes.' Yeshe Tenzing shrugged as he began unloading the tent from the vehicle.

He tried Swati again, his eyes lingering on the uncluttered waterfront. No luck.

Half a dozen orange tents were pitched a little above the lake with three jeeps parked next to them. A few people clustered around them. Probably a group of foreigners with local guides. A pair of blue tents were pitched a little further down. 'Let's tent away from them,' he told Yeshe, and looked at his phone with the impatience of the denied. No connection still.

They pitched the high-altitude tent over a thick plastic sheet, hoping it would provide protection from the damp. Before rolling out his down sleeping bag, Ajay laid a thick blanket beneath it. Night temperatures could drop to near zero on the lake. He unpacked his powerful rechargeable torch and the hip flask of whisky, slipped on a windcheater and slung his camera around his neck, ready to walk on the shore of the lake again.

The clouds floated low, watching their reflection in the clear waters. One of them looked, to his enamoured eyes, like the Yeti, the Abominable Snowman, striding across the sky. The Tibetans called this the enchanted lake. Here anything was possible. The footprints of the Yeti could be traced in the sky instead of snow.

Ajay moved towards one of the three very basic stone-and-wood dhabas on the far side for a dal-chawal lunch. The dal was diluted and the rice a coagulated mass. He would have loved some hot fish curry, better still, fish in tomato and basil sauce. The memories flooded in, quick and strong. The taste of the fish at that first meeting with Swati at a Mumbai restaurant. She had walked through the door, wearing a bold maroon saree with a large matching bindi. He had watched her progress with interest. Her eyes sparkled, her earrings danced as she walked. Energy swirled around her, sweet and wild.

He had loved the way she knotted her long hair into a low bun as she chatted, her hands expressive, her speech animated. His blood would grow warm as he realized that every time her silver amulet touched the glass table, she was looking at him with her bright kajal-lined eyes.

It was instant attraction; they couldn't keep their eyes off each other. They met the next day and the next, each meeting an offering to the god of desire. For him, the world seemed bathed with thoughts of Swati and even the night sky held a constellation by her name. Heaven and Earth had confirmed his choice, and now only his mother had to. He took her home to meet his family and they warmed to her immediately. Wherever he turned, his love was affirmed.

He dialled Swati's number again. Unbelievably, it rang. Nothing is insolvable, you just have to persist, he thought with satisfaction. It rang and rang. Pick it up Swati, pick it up! I may not get a connection again. But she did not. Was she avoiding his call? Or was she having her usual, interminable conversations with friends?

The sun was fast losing its warmth, the clouds seemed heavier. His solitude turned from loneliness to a chill.

In the last three months, Ajay had been reduced to feeling like a visitor in his own home. Sometimes, after returning from work, he lingered outside the door, reluctant to enter. When he did, only their dog Frodo came bounding to greet him. Neha, their daughter, was away at boarding school, and Swati was often out. When she did return, their greetings were stilted and perfunctory.

When he left for work at 7.30 a.m., Swati would be asleep. What a paradox, he mused. At the office, people were ever keen to linger in his room, hoping to prolong contact with the boss, while he preferred to be left alone. At home, when he returned from work, he desperately wanted to prolong contact with Swati who, after the briefest exchange, would go upstairs to chat with her friends on the phone. He would be reduced to switching on the TV to fill the frigid silence of the evening.

Two hours later, the household help would announce dinner. By the time he made his way to the dining room, Swati would already be seated at the table, impeccably laid with its crisp white napkins with lace edging, Wedgwood grey and silver plates and soup bowls. Nothing was passed between them, nothing was said: everything was served and everything was left unsaid.

At least twice a week, they dined out. On the evening before he left for Ladakh, they were heading for dinner to a friend's house. Swati, sitting beside him in the car, had looked striking in a black-and-white kantha saree, the solitaires in her ears winking mischievously in the glare of an oncoming car's headlights. He took in her profile—pert nose, stubborn chin and eyes cold with the armour of indifference. He still clung to the hope that she would reach out and, miraculously, the nightmare of the last three months would end.

Knowing he was watching her, she turned her face towards him. Her look was one of accusation; in fact, it seemed as though she awaited his contrition. Much earlier he had realized that trying to convince her of his innocence only inflamed her, and his silence confirmed his guilt in her eyes. His jaw tightened as he turned his face away. What had seemed a half-open door now closed.

Swati's face transformed as she greeted their hosts animatedly. Ajay went straight to the bar to supervise her drink, just the way she liked it. He watched her as she glided around the room, attracting people with her vivaciousness. When he went across and handed her the drink, she flashed him a brief smile, but he couldn't help wondering if he had merely been included with everyone else. Neither was he certain whether he preferred this pretence of a truce to the earlier accusatory look.

Now, as he stood looking out at the lake, he reminded himself that Swati's love was as real as her anger. Her love was a force that had swept him away; she loved passionately, overwhelmingly, knowing no half measures. He paced up and down the waterfront, feeling the nibble of the pebbles beneath his feet, the ground mist licking his ankles. A low wind rose as evening slid on to the lake. Finally, he had to force himself to face facts. All he was doing was quelling his doubts by dredging up memories. Things are screwed up between us, he thought. Accept it. We live in the same house but not together.

But his mind would not still. How come the problem was always him? When he was stressed, she wanted him to talk about it, accusing him of not letting her in, never heeding her advice, always pushing her away. However, when she needed to vent about something, he was expected to listen quietly. Any comment he ventured would be met with a fiery tone of injury, 'Can't you understand, it is not what you say, but *how* you say it that hurts?'

He paused and swept his brow with his hand to clear his thoughts. This was not going to get him very far. He had to think differently. The first thing we need to do is analyse the issues, he told himself. The root of the problem is that she misreads my intent and believes I do not appreciate her. Perhaps I have been insensitive, too focused on work. The key is dialogue. We need to tell each other in no uncertain terms, 'This is what hurt me.' Without accusations. Pointing fingers never helps, pointing out issues does.

Swati would love this place where the freedom of colour to change from one to the next would surely make her eyes dance, her imagination take wing. In Delhi, they got caught in the same cycle of blame and self-defence. He would tell her that he had found the ideal spot for them to reconnect. It was so simple, why had he not thought of it earlier? He took a deep breath and felt better. He had a workable plan now. He reached for his phone to call her. Again and again, he dialled her number but was unable to connect. Despairing, he switched off the phone to preserve some charge and took a long swig of whisky from his hip flask to combat the growing chill of the night.

He looked up at the sky with its spray of bright stars, dazzling in the rarefied mountain air. The lake, now an inky blue, was lit by a waning moon. There was silence in the air, except for the gentle lapping of water against the shore. For an instant, his restlessness was overwhelmed by this night of a single colour.

Swati

6 August: Late night

Swati sat outside the ICCU, bone tired. An eerie hospital-night silence had settled in the corridor, the dim lights defying darkness and death. She rubbed her eyes, rested her head against the wall, arching her back instinctively against the metallic discomfort of the chair.

These had been days of loss.

Two days ago, she had driven with Ajay to the airport when his taxi had failed to show up. The rain had turned into a downpour, blurring the windscreen, and Ajay drove with silent concentration. She peered ahead attentively to warn him of anything he might miss. Unwittingly, they were working like a team again. He at the helm; she, his support. She could not forget the look on his face as he stood on the pavement outside the airport entrance with his luggage beside him, his hand half raised in a goodbye, his eyes blank, without hope.

Sitting in the car, her eyes had pleaded with him not to go, the terror of losing him all of a sudden becoming overwhelming. He had paused, uncertain about what he saw, and momentarily faltered. Despite the honking behind her, she had opened the door and stepped out. But, by then, he had turned away, wheeling his luggage, his jeans wet at the hem, his athletic frame moving without hesitation towards the entrance and away from her.

Slowly she had got back into the car and driven away, the rain drumming relentlessly on the windshield. Fifteen minutes later, she stopped the car at a curb and rested her head on the steering wheel, so reassuring in its solidity. Gradually, the rain relented outside, but her thoughts refused to calm, roving back many years to her childhood.

She was six, in a swimming pool, snug inside a rubber tube. Unexpectedly, the tube deflated and she began to bob up and down, gulping water. She saw her father throwing a rope towards her but she could not reach it. He shouted at her, 'Save yourself! Take the rope! Why don't you take it?' He couldn't see how frightened she was. I did make it back though, didn't I? Back to you, Dad. And that's exactly how I feel now. I want to be back with you, Ajay. For the sake of the love I still feel for you.

Swati picked her head up from the steering wheel and stared out of the window. Surely a water colour, she mused. Traffic, wet streets, potholes, muddy pools of water, a weepy grey sky. But one thought continued to dominate her mind. How could she reach him? She wanted to. Very much.

You are not wrong in wanting your space, Ajay, and I am not wrong in wanting to be close. But the space you are asking for is born from denial. There are no bridges to that land. Only ghosts, mist-dwellers and people of dreams exist there, forever coming between us as they seek vengeance for their banishment. Sometimes we went to bed angry, but at least we were together. But tonight, you won't be there. And that makes me feel empty.

Early that morning her phone had rung. It was her father. His voice quivered. 'Ati, Mama has had a heart attack.' Despite the shock, her father's use of her childhood name melted her heart. She drove directly to the hospital. The day was a blur of phone calls, doctors, friends and family. It was a day of looking at her mother's face in the ICCU and realizing she was mortal. A tear trickled down Swati's face. Why was life about loss, inevitable or created? It was late in the evening, after she had finished a long call to her anxious father, that she saw the missed calls from Ajay. When she called him back, his phone was not reachable. She sat on a bench in the hospital corridor, missing him with the longing of the lost.

The Flood

7 August

Ajay's plans for an early start that morning to Alchi and Lamayuru on the other side of Leh were met with anxiety by Yeshe. A cloudburst at Basgo-Nima, followed by flash floods, had washed away the road. Ajay looked up at the sky and saw that the white clouds of yesterday were now dark-edged, bloated and grey.

They would have been stranded had they returned the previous day. Regions to the west of Leh were severely affected and many people had sought refuge in Leh and its outskirts. Yeshe suggested that they abort their trip to Alchi and Lamayuru. Instead, Ajay could visit Chemrey monastery with the pretty belt of villages around it. It would be just the place for some innovative photography. And then there was Tangtse Gompa. 'That should be enough sightseeing for the day,' said Yeshe. His casual tone offset the gravity of the situation as he also suggested it might be better to spend the night at the first convenient place on the road, away from the disruption and panic in and around Leh. Reluctantly, Ajay agreed.

8 August

In the morning, on their way back to Leh, Ajay and Yeshe had barely driven for an hour along the river, a tributary of the Indus with its swirling muddy waters, when they encountered a roadblock at the Karo crossing on NH1D, the national highway that ran along the Indus. The sparse traffic on the road was being diverted. Another cloudburst over Leh had put the city out of bounds. Loose soil laden with moisture had cascaded down like an avalanche, sweeping away in its path boulders, trees, cars, the road, everything. The airport road was closed. Exasperated, Ajay tried to call the trek organisers in Leh but the mobile network seemed to have snapped. After many hours of waiting and periodic requests for information from the authorities, they abandoned the idea of returning to Leh and, crossing the Indus, headed towards the high ground that led to the Hemis monastery.

They drove through a bleak and barren wilderness where nothing grew, not the smallest shrub or blade of grass. As far as the eye could see, there was no habitation. The mountains were the colour of granite with crags of purple rock and loose scree on some of the flanks. Ajay marvelled, not for the first time, how the Ladakhis had made a life for themselves in this desert, where punishing cold winds alternated with an unrelenting sun. It was said that a bareheaded man sitting in the sun with his feet in the shade, could suffer from sunstroke and frostbite at the same time. Idly Ajay wondered, if Tibet shared a similar landscape, what had impelled Buddhism to travel from India, take root there and flourish for nearly a thousand years? And why had the Chinese bothered to invade it?

On reaching the Hemis monastery, Ajay and Yeshe found tents pitched outside the entrance gate to accommodate people displaced by the floods. The place was already overcrowded. They decided to drive ahead into the Hemis Sanctuary, whose southern boundary was formed by the Zanskar range.

Ajay couldn't help feeling apprehensive, driving on an unmetalled road that seemed to be going nowhere. After about twenty minutes, they turned alongside a stream with greenery along its banks. The small roadside chortens and mani stone-piles attested to habitation.

After an hour, they reached a small settlement beside a monastery. Nearby flowed a stream. Perhaps this tributary, too, fed the Indus. The sun had descended, suffusing everything with a golden light. The sky exhaled luminescence. Caught between the crease of day and night, the mountains grew sombre and still, the depth of their silence palpable. Then twilight slipped in, etching in charcoal the outline of the peaks that serrated the sky.

Yeshe pulled up on the side of the road and suggested that Ajay request the abbot for shelter for the night. Ajay walked towards the monastery, perched on top of the cliff, a carving in sepia. Its golden pagoda-like roof shimmered against the darkening sky. He was worried now that he wouldn't be able to reach the trekking campsite the following day. He would then have to forgo both the trek and the advance he had paid.

When he asked the monk at the gate if he could meet the abbot, he was guided past lightless passageways and up an equally dark staircase until they arrived at a door. The monk knocked on the door. The abbot stepped out. Ajay was struck by the grace of his movements, an odd mix of fluidity and stillness. The junior monk bowed and explained Ajay's predicament to the abbot in what sounded like Tibetan.

The abbot looked at Ajay and said in perfect English, 'What took you so long?'

Startled, Ajay stared at him. Surely they weren't expecting him. Perhaps what he meant was the inevitability of the spillover from Hemis, of travellers seeking shelter. But the abbot continued to look at him with silent attention, and this was no common scrutiny. His eyes held Ajay as though looking past the outer body to what lay within, and beyond him. Mesmerized, Ajay found himself incapable of breaking the silence.

'When the fork came in the road, between the gentler and the steeper paths, which one did you take?' the abbot asked.

'I beg your pardon.' Was the abbot referring to some bifurcation en route that he had missed?

'We believe there are no chance encounters. Without knowing it, we usually choose a way or a situation that makes us confront the very thing we are not acknowledging.'

Still uncomprehending, Ajay heard himself say, 'I think I took the steeper one.'

The abbot nodded and then said very softly, 'Usually, when you take the steeper climb, you are helped.'

This was absurd. What kind of place was this? Even the monk at Spituk had been weird. Maybe all of them were! Which steep road was the abbot talking about? Helped by whom? What was layering this conversation? Was something other than the obvious being implied? Baffled, Ajay continued to gaze at the abbot. His gaze was returned with a steady calmness, as though some strange initiatory rite was being performed.

Then the abbot whispered into the dark:

'Footfalls echo in the memory,
Down the passage which we did not take,
Towards the door we never opened…'

Ajay was taken aback. A monk who could quote Eliot? But why these lines about choices not made? Did he mean Akanksha? No, it couldn't be. How could a perfect stranger know anything about him? Perhaps the abbot was not asking about choices on a literal road.

'May I be permitted to stay the night in your monastery?' Ajay said, finally recalling why he had come to stand in front of this strange man.

The abbot nodded his assent as though that was the least important part of the conversation. 'Why did you come to Ladakh?'

'To trek in the Markha Valley.'

'Is that all?'

Silence followed, hiding the flash of turmoil Ajay felt inwardly at his inability to answer the rather penetrating question. The abbot moved and the floor creaked; the spell was broken. He nodded towards the monk, who motioned Ajay to follow him.

Ajay was led to a small room, its floor dark with age. Mud-plastered walls, a single bed, a small table with a pitcher of water, and a solar lamp on the mantelpiece were the width and length of the luxury afforded in this cold and forbidding room. A single window overlooked the mountains and the river below. The smallness of the room suffocated him and the night's primitive silence was discomfiting. He sat down on the lumpy mattress and mentally reached out for his comfortable Delhi life. He wanted the predictable. Not floods. Not being marooned in an unknown Tibetan monastery with a strange abbot who quoted Eliot and spoke of intangible choices.

All this is the result of my sudden decision to make the trip, he thought wearily. He lay down, mulling over the abbot's last question. Why had he not taken Ajay's reason for coming to Ladakh at face value, almost implying that he knew more about it? The more he thought, the more his mind became fertile, reaching back into the past and that last fight with Swati.

Swati had found the birthday card Ajay had written for Akanksha. Like hungry sharks, they circled each other. She waved the card at his face. 'So, you don't intend to let go of her, do you?'

In a knee-jerk reaction, he shouted back at her. 'Why have you been prying? This is the limit.'

'I was looking for the chequebook in your bedside drawer when I found this. Why, Ajay, why are you doing this to me?'

'It's only a birthday card! What's the big deal?'

She read the words out with a sing-song snigger, 'Thinking-of-you-and-wondering-how-you-are. Happy-Birthday-and-warm-wishes.' She paused before continuing, 'And pray, why were you thinking of her with such warmth?'

'For god's sake, that's only birthday card language, Swati!'

'Don't lie to me! You're in love with her but don't have the guts to admit it.'

'That's sheer imagination. My meeting Akanksha was accidental, and you know that,' he said.

'So I believed, but this card tells a different story.'

In triumphant anger, she slapped the card down on the table like the ace of trumps. A corroding silence filled the room. He felt violated, having to explain an innocuous card meant for an old friend, pushed to defend himself against a crime he had not committed. Anger coursed through him, burning up his chest. Would she ever understand that he did not love Akanksha, and never had?

That night, when the lights had been switched off, Swati turned on her side, as was her wont in the past few months, feigning sleep. Gingerly, he put his hand on her waist. There was no response, but neither did she recoil. Encouraged, he let his hand wander towards her navel. She stopped its further advance, lifted his hand from her body, and paused before letting it drop between them. There was no aggression in her action, only a chilling disdain.

The next morning, he had decided to leave town, and signed up for the Markha Valley trek. He asked her to accompany him but she refused, accusing him of wanting to take Akanksha on the trip. For a moment, he was stunned. Then, wearily, he suggested she check the airline passenger list. 'Well, you're clever. She may be meeting you there directly.'

'I wouldn't be asking you to come with me if I was meeting Akanksha,' he said.

Inwardly, he felt relieved at the idea of being alone.

He did not know why he had written that card to Akanksha. Maybe she had insidiously become the subtext of their lives, so that an actual acknowledgement of her existence seemed natural. Or had he written to her because he wished to continue their interrupted story? When he wrote out the card, it had seemed harmless enough. When Swati found it, it had become nothing short of a suicidal leap for their marriage.

The abbot's question about his real reason for coming to Ladakh gnawed at him. It was true that he wasn't here just to trek. Was it to think things through and decide whether he and Swati should part? Was he ready to live without her? No! Was he fleeing from her only to return to their dying relationship? He realised his feelings for Swati were far too complex to be resolved by a simple binary decision.

His last thought as his eyes closed in sleep was that he must get out of here by morning, no matter what. Outside, the breeze stilled, as though waiting for the river to find its shore.

Acceptance

9 August: Morning

Ajay woke to the simultaneous ringing of the temple gong and the deep bass notes of two trumpets from the roof, heralding the day. After a quick breakfast of tasteless barley gruel and a sour apple, he asked a monk if he could meet the abbot.

'Oh, yes. The abbot has been awake for a long time.'

Ajay was struck by the quiet of the room he was ushered into. A small image of the Buddha stood on a wooden table, exuding inwardness, with a single butter lamp burning beside it. Bookshelves, like ladders aspiring towards the ceiling, lined three sides of the room. A rolled-up mattress lay in one corner. The only incongruous item in the room was a delicately carved cherry-wood desk. The abbot sat on a rug in front of a pair of windows overlooking the distant ranges. Ajay was tentative, unsure of his ground in a room steeped in study and prayer.

The abbot looked up from his reading. Shorn of the cloak of the night, his eyes were arresting—deeply set, dark and

29

extraordinarily intense. The ageless, creaseless quality of the burnished face was enhanced by the shaven head and pronounced cheekbones. 'Did you sleep well?'

'It's very different from what I am used to.'

The abbot's eyes twinkled.

'Is there a route to the Markha Valley from here?' Ajay enquired.

'I am afraid there is none through the Hemis Sanctuary.'

Ajay's anxiety increased. 'How did this happen? How long will it be before I can get back?'

'I can't say. It depends on how quickly the army can clear the submerged roads and remove the debris. The mountain slopes surrounding Leh consist of loose sediments. The cloudburst soaked the rubble with huge volumes of water, and this slushy mass rapidly moved down to the river. They say it had a spread of over two kilometres and it travelled for nearly ten kilometres. Nature, when aroused, does not believe in half measures.'

'Even the cell phone is not working,' Ajay complained.

'Ah! Let down by the crown jewel of our civilizational effort!'

'You are not particularly concerned by all this?' Ajay asked annoyed.

'Not for the same reasons as you are,' the abbot replied swiftly. 'People are dead, homes have been destroyed, roads are gone, many are probably stranded without food, cattle may have drowned, a standing crop submerged. Oh, I am concerned.'

'But I can't just go on staying here.'

'You can, with my consent.' The abbot folded his arms across his chest, deliberately taking Ajay's statement at face value.

'Well, I don't mean that. I want to reach my trek site. That's what I am here for.'

The abbot looked at him quizzically, the question from the previous evening hanging between them.

'We think we choose our journeys, but some journeys choose us,' the abbot said gently.

'I chose this trip,' Ajay answered emphatically.

The abbot kept quiet. Ajay felt his irritation increase. Nothing was going as planned. Admitting helplessness, he asked, 'What should I do?'

'Remember the real reason why you came here. You could use the atmosphere of the monastery, its quiet, the restfulness.'

Unwilling to jettison his trek and stay on in the monastery, Ajay politely took leave of the abbot and went down to the road towards his car. Yeshe approached him in a flurry of agitation. 'I was looking for you. I need to leave immediately. More than fifty villages are affected by the floods; nearly two hundred people have died. News has come that ten bridges have been washed away, roughly a third of the roads have been damaged or are under heavy sludge. Luckily, my village and family are safe. But I have to go and help those who are stranded. I can ferry people from the affected areas and carry relief supplies.'

'But you can't leave me here in this wilderness.' Ajay looked shocked.

'Over five thousand tourists are stranded because the airport is damaged. You are all right here,' Yeshe pleaded. 'I have already requested the abbot to let you stay. Don't worry, I'll come back the minute the roads are cleared.'

Ajay stood rooted to the spot, watching as Yeshe reversed the car. Suddenly, he braked and came running back, a book in his hand. 'Please keep this with you. My last passenger forgot it. It will be safer with you than in the car.'

The taxi drove away, severing Ajay's last link to civilization.

He turned towards the monastery and surveyed it anew. With its air of regal autonomy, it gave the impression of a castle standing guard with the main building as the apex of its vigil. Compared to other monasteries he had visited, this one was rather small. The shining brass sheets of the roof glinted in the sun, and the spire pointed its determined finger towards the sky. The richly carved wooden cornices under the eaves looked like crocheted lace, offset by brick-red shades that hung over doors and windows painted a deep maroon. An interlaced triangle in gold was emblazoned above the main entrance of the monastery like an emblem.

He climbed the seventy-odd roughly hewn stone steps to the courtyard of the monastery. Out of breath, he sat down on the parapet facing the temple. On the far left, five monks were perambulating the forty-foot assembly of large, embossed, brass prayer wheels, turning them with one hand, holding a rosary in the other, intoning prayers. He looked up at the two storeys of the main temple. Limewashed stone walls rose to meet a wooden verandah that skirted the first floor.

He paced about restlessly, chafing at being marooned in this strange place and thinking that the abbot hadn't been much help.

He stopped near the eastern end of the courtyard, where his eyes were greeted by a riot of flowers. Pink hollyhocks strained tall against the drab walls; Himalayan blue poppies spilled over from below the flowerpots, providing a jaunty splash of colour. He moved closer and noticed half-barrels with trailing vines of tomatoes that were trained against the courtyard wall. A little ahead, tucked in an innocuous corner, was a small plastic greenhouse. An abundant variety of all kinds of seedlings and plants grew in pots on two parallel wooden benches—bouquets of purple irises in a barrel; cheerful lavender larkspurs; an eye-catching rose bush, the colour of sunset. A faint smell of wild mint and oregano filled the air. Ajay was spellbound by this bloom of life in an amphitheatre of stone and mountains. None of the monasteries he had visited had such a profusion of colour, and that too without fertile soil or water. The river ran far below in the valley. To hoist water up from it would be a near impossibility.

Walking back towards the courtyard, Ajay found a group of monks seated on the ground, engaged in what seemed like a robust discussion. One monk stood in front of the others, slapping the back of his right hand into the palm of his left every time he wished to emphasize a point. A moment later, a challenger rose to refute him, and ended by stomping his left foot heavily on the ground.

Ajay found a sun-splotched spot behind them and sat down. Immediately, one of them turned to him and asked, 'Tell me, where does happiness come from?'

Nonplussed, Ajay stared at him. No answer came instantly to mind.

Another monk answered for him. 'Happiness comes from getting what you want.'

Relieved at the onus shifting away from him, Ajay nodded.

'There will always be something you want which you can't afford. If you have lots of money you will be happy,' a chubby-faced monk said.

'Money buys happiness up to a point but it is short-lived,' retorted the first monk.

A fourth monk added, 'In fact, for some people, spending money on others gives greater happiness than spending it on themselves. *It is more blessed to give than to receive.*'

'You both are linking happiness to pleasure, to sensory delight,' said a rather serious-looking monk. 'As the Buddha said, pleasures are fleeting. Surely, happiness must come from elsewhere.'

'Like where?' Chubby-face challenged.

'From gratification. We may have to distinguish between pleasure and gratification. Pleasure makes us ask for more; gratification asks more of us. Pleasure is sensory delight, like a warm bed, good food, the sun on your back in the winter; gratification comes from activities that engage us fully, from accomplishments, from realizing goals.'

'That kind of happiness is also fleeting because, before long, you will ask yourself: what next?' another monk countered.

'Isn't good health central to being happy? What happens when I have a toothache?'

'But people can be happy and cheerful even in a morbid state of health. What makes *them* happy?' The serious one objected once again.

Out of the blue, a young novice meekly ventured, 'Our happiest moments are during sex.'

After a moment's stunned silence, the oldest of them thundered, 'How do you, a monastic trainee, know that?'

Ajay couldn't help smiling as the trapped red-faced novice stammered, 'I read it in a book. Not my…experience!'

'Where do you hide the books you read?' someone asked amidst a round of laughter.

Chubby-face tried once again. 'I would say happiness comes from living a good life, by cultivating goodness because goodness is its own reward.'

'Perhaps that is an oversimplification. People have struggled to define what is good. So, a life considered good two centuries ago may not give the same happiness as living by today's conception of a good life.'

'The problem is that we are equating happiness to an emotion, or an activity, or a state of mind. We don't need more possessions, more fame, a healthier body or a relationship to be happy.'

'I agree. As the Buddha taught, happiness can only be found within,' said a shy monk who had remained silent till now.

'Yes!' the serious and perhaps the oldest of the monks agreed unexpectedly. 'The road to happiness runs through calm inaction and desireless waiting.'

Ajay was amused by this novel recipe that valourised inaction. He had been taught to pull out his toolbox and fix anything that delayed progress.

'Suppose all your anxieties and worries are peeled off, and you become free from all expectations. Then what would your innate self be?' The serious one looked around at the other monks.

'Like a newborn baby?' Shy-face ventured.

'Precisely! Doesn't that prove that intrinsically we are happy? We merely layer it over with our anxieties and wants.' He looked at Ajay and pronounced, 'Sir, when you are not seeking it, *you* are happiness itself.'

'I beg your pardon, Sir,' Ajay said in the same refrain.

'It is not a question of seeking happiness. It is a question of uncovering happiness, by letting everything that is not you fall away. What remains is happiness.'

Intriguing, Ajay thought. I am happiness itself. I am its source, the light that makes the reflection dance. And I mistakenly believe that the reflection is the source of happiness.

'You seem familiar with the Bible. Are you?' Ajay asked the monks.

'Oh yes, the abbot wanted us to study other religions, and Western philosophy as well.'

'Why?'

'He says that knowledge of our own texts improves by seeing the interconnections with other schools of thought. And, as a bonus, we learn better English.'

What a mystifying place this was, Ajay thought, where irises grew in a greenhouse and you stumbled upon happiness in the courtyard!

As he left the debating monks and walked on, his path was crossed by a young monk who strode past him briskly. Ajay quickened his step, drew abreast and introduced himself. 'I am Ajay Kapur.'

'I am Tsering, and I am in charge of the weather!' The monk responded cheerfully. 'Every morning I record the maximum and minimum temperatures, rainfall and wind velocity.'

'What is the need for that?'

'Because, Sir, though we are monks, we still are not rid of the illusion that we need to eat.' His sonorous voice melted into an impish smile.

Ajay liked this monk's good-natured insouciance; at least he laced the drudgery of routine with humour and that too, within earshot of serious philosophical debate. 'I didn't mean to be rude. I only wondered because you could just as easily obtain the information from the local met office.'

'They can't give us information specific to this monastery. So, we have been collecting data for fifteen years.'

'And why is that necessary?'

'I told you, to grow food. You notice we grow small quantities of vegetables, in plastic tents, using controlled irrigation. How do you think the water gets up here? There is no internal supply. Usually, it has to be carried up. We are not rich enough to install a pump; also, the electricity is erratic. So, the abbot came up with different methods to pump water.' He tilted his head as though listening for a sound. 'Can you hear? Tung...tung...tung, like hammer on steel. That is the hydraulic ram. It pumps water from the spring below, just with the pressure of water falling from a height. The abbot had it installed many years ago.' Again the impish grin lit his face, 'The water to brush our teeth in the morning—you think it comes from the municipality?'

As they walked, they came upon a young monk planing wood. Tsering greeted him warmly. 'Cho-cho-la, this big engineer from Delhi wants to know what you are making.' Ajay was amused by the introduction. The carpenter-monk earnestly explained that he was fabricating the wooden frame of a wind-pump. Once finished, canvas would be stretched over it and it would be mounted on a steel shaft that ran on bearings. 'Windmill blades should be bigger but make small because only small wood available. Get past problem by making many blades. Very windy here but water down below. So put windmill near river,' he said haltingly.

'Since we have measured the wind velocity at many places here, the abbot calculated that a height of twenty-five feet from the ground was most suitable for the wind-pump. Now do you get the connection between weather conditions and food?' Tsering's smile broadened as he cocked a barely visible brow at Ajay. 'Our abbot isn't like Don Quixote tilting at windmills.'

Ajay was impressed. 'When driving up, I noticed a series of black-painted drums going up the hill. What are they?' he asked.

'That's our latest research project!' Tsering winked as he patted Ajay on the shoulder. 'Those 200-litre barrels are connected by airtight pipes. We are hoping to pump water by using the difference between day and night temperatures. Water in the barrels will expand and contract with the alternation of heat and cold, and this will act as a pump, raising water from one barrel to the next. If it works, we add more barrels to the chain and pump water for free, thanks to the weather-god! Our abbot is a genius; he has many ideas.'

'And he clearly has a very able research assistant!' Ajay said warmly.

Tsering smiled back at him. 'Okay. Researcher better go now and read the anemometer.'

Like bees, the people here were abuzz with ideas of all kinds. Ajay suspected this was not a typical monastery where scriptures were intoned and ritual and prayer filled the air. Through sheer innovation, the abbot had pushed back the limitations of a hostile environment to create not only viable living conditions but also a place of beauty. A lively sense of enquiry informed the place. It seemed as if once the 'whys' were asked, the 'how-tos' would flow naturally. If this was one man's vision, how had he accomplished it?

On his way back to the courtyard, Ajay bumped into the bespectacled Daropa, the monk he had met the evening before. In pidgin English, he said, 'No way out. Very bad flood. You stay here now?'

Obviously not everyone's English had benefitted from the debates!

'Your abbot has been good enough to allow me to.'

'Good man, good man,' Daropa intoned.

'You have been a monk long?'

'Since ten years old. Study and grow up here.'

'How long has your abbot been here?'

'More than fifteen years. Very intelligent man. Very knowledgeable.'

'How did he come to this monastery?'

'He student in Delhi University, get scholarship to Oxford,' Daropa said, clearly still in awe of his superior. 'He come back and become monk and learn Buddhist scriptures. Chosen to join Tibetan government in exile in Dharamsala. Then something happened. We don't know what. But he came here. Very unusual,' the monk said.

'Unusual?'

'Very broad-minded. Always give different view on things. He thinks.' In a comically intense gesture, he pointed a forefinger to his head. 'But more than anything else he has presence. What we Buddhists call "beingness".'

The sun was hot and Ajay sauntered indoors towards the main monastery. Just below the main steps leading to the temple was a small room. Ajay stepped in and stood still.

In the centre of the room, a monk was dancing, his flowing movements spare, formal and trancelike as he dipped and whirled, balancing first on one foot then on the other. Slowly he opened his arms and traced patterns in the air. His eyes were half-open but he seemed oblivious to everything. It appeared he was deep in contemplation while dancing, yet his body followed the soft rhythmic clang of the cymbals played by a fellow monk sitting in the far shadows of the room. In the pause between one strike of the cymbals and the next, the dancer stood still on one bare foot, the other held motionless at right angles to it. Suddenly, nothing moved; the notes of the cymbals faded into silence. The room seemed bereft of the dancer, music, all. Involuntarily Ajay's body relaxed. Then, gently, the cymbals struck, the dancer moved, and Ajay slowly let out a breath. Something powerful and intangible had been expressed by both the movement and its arrest. And, in the gap between the two, seemed the real dance.

Ajay sat down, filled with the spaciousness of the moment. Not even a full day here, and already this place was having a whimsical effect on him. His body, mind and heart seemed to be lifted in supplication to something beyond all three. Hanging atop a mountain, heaven seemed so near.

Akanksha

9 August: Late afternoon

Strange man this abbot, Ajay thought, sitting on the steps of the courtyard, watching the setting sun streak the clouds with fingers of gold and crimson. He was the heartbeat of this place. A man who observed more than he spoke and revealed less than he knew. A teacher who had made activity in the monastery meaningful, and its stillness vibrant.

As the day's brightness bled, and twilight fell like coal-dust on the barren landscape, he could not but help ask himself how he would fit in this monastery. Never had he entertained the possibility of living in one or being a part of its life. He was sure Akanksha would smile if she saw him now.

The few times Ajay and Akanksha had disagreed, it was to do with the suprapersonal. He had been taken aback by her resolute belief, her gentle mocking of a life without faith. It is better to believe in something that may not exist and be redeemed by it than to not believe and be condemned to the angst of meaninglessness, she would say.

More than the argument, it was Akanksha who had made him pause.

He had barely noticed her the first time they met in an old colonial Delhi bungalow, the headquarters of an aerated drinks company. In fact, he had paid scant attention to any of the three women in his batch of twenty management trainees. Until, one day, coming out of a seminar, he had overheard one of the girls saying to the others, 'Look at that beautiful bird on the tree!'

Ajay's eyes veered towards the striking bird with a long white tail, its head bobbing in sharp, quick movements.

'It's an Asian Paradise Flycatcher,' the bird-watcher explained. Her companions stared at her in amazement. So did Ajay.

One of them asked, 'How do you know?'

'I read a book and I have a pair of binoculars,' the girl said a little self-deprecatingly. 'It's been here for about a month and will be gone by April. Its plumage is at its best at this time.'

Ajay looked at her properly for the first time. In contrast to the rather dramatic-looking bird on the tree, nothing stood out about her—a round face, shoulder-length hair and an indifferent complexion. However, if you cared to look again, her eyes captured you—they had a dreamy softness to them. No wonder she looks out of the window more often than not, he thought somewhat dismissively then. But he did look at the bird again, and mentally lodged its name in his memory.

His next meeting with the bird-watcher lasted longer. They were to gauge the market receptivity of Quench, a drink recently launched by their company. Their brief was to interact with the small retailers on NH1 between Delhi and Ambala. Travelling by bus, questionnaires in hand, they had little to say to each other. She was an alien from Andhra; he was travelling down the road of his Punjabi origins with its earthy, somewhat crude male libidinal outflows. She spent her time looking out of the bus window; he was preoccupied with his dreams of drenching the world with Quench.

An hour outside Delhi, they stopped at the first dhaba that stocked Quench. The dhaba owner, a burly Sikh, was bent over a grease-darkened pan on an open fire. Ajay revelled in the familiar waft of onions sizzling in liberal ladlefuls of butter. He posed some routine questions to the owner: How much Quench did he sell? Which soft drink did people normally prefer? How did he try to promote Quench over other drinks? The dhaba owner latched onto the last question and said in earthy Punjabi, 'Wail kis nu hai?'

Akanksha looked at Ajay enquiringly and he translated for her benefit, 'Who has the time to promote anything?'

That elicited a bemused smile from her. 'And here we come with our management questions of channel efficiency, target profiles and velocity of inventory movement. What a mismatch of worlds.'

They made their way down the highway, sometimes hitching rides, sometimes walking. Once or twice, when Akanksha took the lead in asking the questions, she was met with furtive looks and guffawing from the hangers-on. Ajay could see that the petite young woman, her face lit with enthusiasm, was vulnerable to this kind of street sexuality, and a part of him resented the role of protector that had been thrust upon him.

Their brief included collecting payment from a defaulting dhaba located some distance off the main highway. The owner explained that often the Quench truck didn't come to his shop and hence his payments were irregular.

'How often do you get delivery? How many crates do you take at one time? How many bottles did you sell this month?' Ajay's rapid-fire questions to the man were met with silence.

Akanksha whispered to Ajay, 'I suspect he has a problem with selling, but is unwilling to lose the distributorship.' She turned to the owner and asked, 'Is it possible for us to see your stock?'

A quick look around the dimly lit shed showed that the unsold stock comprised largely of Diet Quench. Akanksha thought aloud, 'That is the problem. Slimness and fitness are city concepts. We are pushing this product on a highway with truck drivers, small-time manufacturers and farmers in tractors. These guys eat heartily and burn it up with hard work. It wouldn't occur to them to order a drink that cuts calories.' Ajay and Akanksha had set off as strangers, but they came out of that shed with a shared sense of camaraderie.

It was late by then, close to dinner time, and it didn't make sense to drive all the way back to Delhi. Ajay suggested they spend the night in Chandigarh, at a friend's place, and Akanksha agreed. His old-world courtesy and his protectiveness had put her at ease by then, and she felt perfectly safe sharing the house with two men, one of them a perfect stranger and the other only recently familiar. My mother would have a seizure if she knew, she smiled to herself, as she curled up in bed later.

Ajay, on his part, fell asleep with a mild sense of discomfort in his stomach. He woke in the middle of the night with a bout of nausea and rushed to the bathroom. When he emerged half an hour later, Akanksha was standing there with a glass of water in her hand.

'Sorry, did I disturb you?' he asked sheepishly.

'No,' she said calmly, handing him an antacid.

'How did you know?'

She didn't answer.

They walked out to the balcony to get some fresh air. In the quiet of the early morning, the gulmohar tree in full bloom stood vigil outside. They sat on the floor in harmony with the night and one another. Perhaps it takes only one small chink in the wall to let in the first sliver of light, to make patterns of cohesion on the floor of a relationship. Ajay knew that she was sitting up with him in case he felt sick again and needed help. At one point she dozed off next to him, but did not leave his side for the rest of that night.

After that field trip, they fell into an easy and comfortable friendship. She was perceptive, easy to converse with, a very good listener, but feisty when it came to defending her beliefs. Unlike other trainees, who were eager to make an impression, she never thrust herself forward, offered an opinion only when asked and always gave an intelligent account of herself. She introduced him to literature and Haiku; he offered her his zest for life by taking her on jaunts to Paranthewali Gali and Daulat ki Chaat at Nai Sadak.

Food was not their only journey of discovery into Delhi's past. They revisited old monuments, with him retracing the development of the keystone dome from the simple, flatter form built by the Slave dynasty to the aesthetic, bulbous double dome immortalized by the Mughals. He had a lively curiosity about almost everything, an engaging interest in people. He could as easily chat with a rickshaw-wallah as a restaurant manager, and ensure the best table by establishing some common linkage. Literally and symbolically, he was the first one to step through the door, and in doing so, he swept away her natural reticence, storming her diffidence with his innate self-confidence. For him, life was a vast canvas on which you had to throw all the paint you could, an adventurous trail where conquest was the stimulant. For her, it was a road where you paused, reflected and glanced back to see how far you had come. She was at ease with ambiguity and uncertainty; he always needed explanations and names for things. Her universe was imbued by the subtle, by providence and synchronicities. Each found the other's orientation alien to their nature but compensatory for the lack of it in their own. It was not long before they became inseparable, during work hours as well as after work, in the evenings. If you invited one, it was taken for granted the other was coming.

A bustle in the courtyard broke into his thoughts. In single file, ten monks, their hands folded inside their maroon robes, were walking towards the temple as quietly as the evening hour. Lost in his reverie, Ajay had failed to hear the gong for the evening prayer. He watched them disappear into the temple. So much was the past playing on him that Ajay's thoughts drifted back to Akanksha.

One night, they were out for dinner with a bunch of colleagues to celebrate the completion of the first phase of their training. Akanksha had slipped away to the washroom, leaving her cell phone in her purse. When it rang, Ajay opened the purse and answered without a second thought. He could see the others exchanging knowing looks as he spoke to Akanksha's mother and assured her that he would get her to call back. When Akanksha returned, she instantly sensed the shift in mood and looked enquiringly at Ajay, but he just shrugged and cracked a joke.

'Can't people accept that a man and a woman are capable of being just friends,' Ajay said, as he dropped her home that night. Akanksha merely smiled, but when Ajay opened the car door for her, she continued to sit, her fingers lacing and unlacing around her purse. They only stilled when he put his hand over hers to wish her goodnight.

Thinking back now, Ajay wondered what else he had ignored.

Who Are You?

9 August: Evening

The low, rumbling sounds from the temple subsided; the last strike of the gong brought the evening prayer to its conclusion. The monks walked out of the temple as quietly as they had entered. This time, Ajay followed them up the stairs to the small room adjacent to the abbot's quarters. He knew that after the evening service, the monks would meet here for an informal discussion with the abbot. Five of them were already seated on woollen mats. A beautiful handcrafted paper globe lampshade, with a single Tibetan letter inscribed on it, hung from the ceiling. Two low table lamps with cylindrical shades of white, rough cotton, a solitary iris painted on each, stood in opposite corners of the room. Facing the door sat the abbot, cross-legged. He smiled as Ajay entered.

Ajay took a woollen mat and sat down, shifting uneasily as he adjusted his bottom on the floor.

'Oh! You degenerate son of the ancient rishis, you have given up your birthright!' the abbot teased. 'You have even forgotten how to sit on the floor!'

Sheepishly, Ajay attempted once more to cross his legs. Just then a monk came in, bowed to the abbot, took a mat and sat down, effortlessly crossing his legs.

The abbot looked at Ajay, his eyes gleaming with interest. He seemed to be awaiting a question.

'Rather an unusual place you have here,' Ajay offered.

'Really?' the abbot asked, amused. 'And how would you know?'

'The few monasteries I have seen so far had no hydraulic rams or greenhouses, no monk extolling that I am happiness itself while another's movement erased the difference between dance and prayer.'

The abbot threw his head back and laughed a deep resounding laugh. Then he said softly, 'Touché! We may appear to be doing diverse things, yet all we are trying to do is live in the service of love.'

'You mean, by helping others?' Ajay said.

'That may be part of it. But first, you have to look at yourself, towards yourself, into yourself. Strengthen what is within. Otherwise, you will end up thinking of love as the possession of an object, a bargain, something the other needs to do to fulfill you.'

'Isn't that natural to love?'

'Most people see the problem of love primarily as that of being loved, rather than that of loving. Does love really depend on finding the right person?' When Ajay remained silent, the abbot continued, 'There is a difference between "instinctive" love and "conscious" love. Instinctive love relies on affinities, attractions and repulsions. It is rooted in chemistry. You get turned on and off involuntarily, blindly. Conscious love asks you to develop the capacity to love. It demands discipline, choice and constant watchfulness. It's a state of being where the separation between "you" and "I" disappears.'

Ajay thought for a moment, then said, 'This distinction may hold for ordinary people, but how is love relevant for a monk like you?'

'Conscious love makes you put the other first, and drop your narcissism…'

'And for a monk?' Ajay cut in.

'It should make him get out of the way. He must let go of personal desires, wants and fears. We try to live not by my will but "Thy will".' The abbot grew pensive. 'It is only then that we may discover that love is not a result but the very foundation of being. That is what the monks you saw today were attempting. Debate, dance and even routine activity become an invocation to something beyond their little selves.'

'Perhaps they can do this because they live isolated lives. Most of us share our world with others.'

'All of us live in an external world. But is that the actual world we live in? You will have to concede that our real world is that of feelings and ideas, of attractions, values, motives and aspirations, a mental world altogether. Our problems are created not by other people but by *our* desires and fears, by *our* memories and expectations, by the mind. It is the mind that becomes the impediment to loving. And it is the mind that doesn't allow the monk to get past his little self. Both the monk and the ordinary person need to get past the mind.'

'What does it mean to go past the mind?'

'Like you go past the body,' the abbot said enigmatically.

'Do I?'

'You pay a lot of attention to food, but once eaten, do you closely follow the process of its digestion? Your body deals with it automatically. That is how the mind should work, without capturing all your attention. Observe your own mental activity and you will find that the greater part of your life is spent in worrying.'

A brief silence fell upon them, as though the conversation had plateaued. Then the abbot changed gears and brought it back to the starting point. 'Think about it in another way. What most of us attempt through love is to overcome our aloneness. And we do this by submerging the lonely "I" within the "we"; by becoming the same as everybody else. Here the attempt is in a different direction. We aim for oneness, not sameness. Oneness is the essence of love.' The abbot looked steadily at him.

Did he mean, perhaps, that at the pinnacle of intimacy the distance between lovers is erased? Ajay couldn't ask—it would be too personal. Instead, he asked, 'How did you learn all this?'

The abbot closed his eyes. The silence stretched. After a few seconds, he said, 'I surrendered to love instead of demanding it. It didn't change the world, only gave me new eyes to see it.' The power in the abbot's eyes was compelling. Yet, for a fleeting second, was there a shadow of pain in them?

A movement near the door splintered the moment, and the focus of attention dispersed. A tall woman entered the room. She had short hair and eyes that held a hint of aloofness. Something about her was familiar. For a moment, Ajay felt reassured that he was not the only one marooned in this way-out place.

'Ah! Come in,' said the abbot smiling gently at her. He turned to Ajay. 'This is Anna. She teaches Comparative Religion at Harvard.'

Anna gave Ajay a brief, unsmiling look. 'And this is Ajay, caught and lost in the floods.' The abbot waved a hand towards Ajay.

'We met at Spituk. You were talking to a monk with a thigh bone in his hand, remember?'

'Perhaps.' Anna gave Ajay the briefest of looks. Ajay frowned. Another link to civilization receded. Anna took a mat, fluidly crossed her legs in a semi-lotus position and sat near the abbot.

'How was your day?' the abbot enquired.

'Pretty bad, all around. Most of the village has been evacuated. Those left behind were without food. What we took with us was barely enough. The water is contaminated, and I suspect typhoid may soon be rampant. I shudder to think what is happening in areas where help hasn't reached.'

'Why haven't our monks returned?'

'They stayed back as they were constructing a makeshift shelter.'

Suddenly the lights went out. Darkness plunged them all into anonymity. No one stirred. Ajay shifted, uncomfortable in the darkness to which the others in the room seemed to have easily submitted. The abbot seemed without form or outline. Just the sense of a presence, both distinct from and one with the darkness.

'Were there any signs?'

'There were!' Anna said softly. 'The monk at Spituk spoke of a dream in which his teacher told him: That which quenches but also drowns...'

'It was a warning about the coming floods.' The abbot's voice pierced the dark.

'What's the use of being warned when it cannot be prevented?'

The darkness seemed to have sharpened Ajay's senses. He sensed a personal regret underlying her words.

'An augury is not meant to prevent what it foretells; it only prepares you for what is to follow.'

The ensuing silence gave no answer. 'Sometimes I wonder what it's all about,' Anna said, her voice brooding.

'It's about accepting. Letting go of the scars.'

Feeling like an intruder in what seemed to be a private conversation, and piqued by the woman's indifference, Ajay ventured, 'Anna, what drew you to Buddhism?'

The pause between his question and her response was unduly long. Then she said coldly, 'That's a rather personal question.'

'Did you manage to get to Thangse,' the abbot intervened smoothly.

'I did. They said the abbot was out. Last time, he was not well. Next time, I am sure he will be in retreat.'

Ajay noted that her speech was halting and hesitant even when she was annoyed.

'He is avoiding you, knowing what you are after.'

'That convinces me he is hiding something.'

Ajay wanted to know what they were talking about, but feared her perfunctory dismissal. However, something compelled him to say, 'A long time ago, I heard of a manuscript hidden in a Ladakhi monastery that spoke of Jesus coming to India.'

At that moment, the lights came on, and he found Anna and the abbot looking at each other with a stunned expression.

For the first time Anna addressed him directly. 'How could you have known?' She shook her head in bewilderment, 'It's a one-in-a-million chance that you could have guessed what we were discussing!'

A young monk entered, prostrated before the abbot and whispered something to him. The abbot rose abruptly, but before leaving, he said to Ajay, 'Anna knows all about Jesus's visit to Ladakh. You can discuss it with her.'

Ajay didn't miss the familiarity: the abbot had presumed she would be ready to talk, and he hadn't requested her willingness. Her eyes betrayed her struggle to overcome her reticence. Finally, she asked him what he knew about the Jesus story.

'Next to nothing. A friend narrated it to us with great aplomb at a party. Everyone had pooh-poohed it, saying it was typical to try and find an Indian connection for everything and teased my friend saying, "Next, you are going to tell us that Shakespeare was born in Kashmir and his actual name was Sheikh Peroo!"'

A fleeting smile touched Anna's face and her taut features mellowed.

'Perhaps that was unfair.'

'Really?'

'All the four Gospels are silent about Jesus's life from the age of thirteen to twenty-nine. In Luke's Gospel, on one page, a twelve-year-old Jesus is listening to teachers in the temple at Jerusalem, and on the next, he is being baptised at age thirty at the River Jordan by John the Baptist.' She paused and added, 'Where was he for those eighteen years?' It was a question she seemed to have asked herself more than once. 'Luke also tells us that he had grown in stature and wisdom in the meanwhile. Who taught him; what did he learn? It's not impossible that Jesus visited India during the silent period. After all, when he was born, the three wise Magi had visited him from the East.' Eyes twinkling, she asked, 'Were they from India?' She paused, and then said, 'Most importantly, a hundred years ago, a manuscript dating from the first century AD was discovered in the Hemis monastery, which gave details of the missing years. It says he came to India with merchants, following the Silk Route; then he travelled through Rajasthan to Puri, and then to Benares and Nepal. Before he was thirty, he returned to Judea via Ladakh, where he was known as Issa.'

Anna's eyes had come alive, her speech gathering tempo. Gone was the aloofness. 'And why would Jesus send St. Thomas to India after the Crucifixion, if he did not know the importance of India? Thomas preached the Gospel here for twenty years, and died here. Where Jesus was in the missing years is only one aspect of the many links that suggest he lived in India. So what is the truth? You can decide.'

'Is that what you were discussing with the lama at Spituk?'

'Oh no. That was about my research project.'

'Which is?'

'The meditational practices among the various Tibetan Buddhist sects in Ladakh.'

'Wow! Why should their practices differ when these monasteries are so close to each other?'

'Because each monastery is part of a different lineage.' Anna thought a little and then explained, 'Like Hindus have different gotras.' The last word was pronounced in a distinctly American accent.

They sat in silence; the conversation had gone way beyond his reach. He puzzled over the gotras, and then he remembered a fracas last year on TV about honour killings and out-of-gotra marriages. Not that he knew his gotra, or even what a gotra signified. It felt so far removed from his world. After much thought, he said, 'I suppose the end goal of all these meditational techniques must be the same: to live a healthy and peaceful life.'

'I wish it was as straightforward as that. There are two schools: one sees meditation as a method to gain happiness; the other believes it is an enquiry.'

'Into what?'

'Into who you are.'

He chuckled. Was that also in question now!

Notovitch

10 August: Morning

Ajay was sitting in the courtyard soaking in the morning sun, when he saw Anna walking from the courtyard to the back of the monastery, where she seemed to disappear. Curious, he followed her, and came upon an open verandah leading into a room at the back. A faded mural of a mandala adorned the left wall of the verandah and, on the right, was painted the Wheel of Life in a tired blue, seeming weary of its gyrations in the endless cycles of creation.

Anna must have come here, Ajay thought as he walked to the back and stepped through a low door and found himself in a room full of square wooden pigeon-holes skirted in gold. They were crammed with bound manuscripts, tied with yellow silk. Every wall seemed busy with these little windows. For a library, the space was dimly lit. A single light hung over a dark wooden table, where Tsering and Anna sat studying a manuscript. It looked like bound strips of dried bark on which the Tibetan script had been painstakingly inscribed. Tsering rose and bowed his head towards Ajay, his cherubic face lit with a smile. Anna frowned slightly at the intrusion.

'I'm sorry. I did not mean to disturb you,' Ajay mumbled apologetically. 'Are you looking for something on meditational practices?'

Before she could reply, Tsering's mischievous voice piped in, 'No, she is hunting for Notovitch!'

'Who is he?' Ajay asked.

'A Russian journalist. While travelling in Ladakh in 1887, he stumbled upon a Tibetan manuscript. I mentioned it yesterday,' Anna replied without looking up from the manuscript.

'Yes, I remember. But why are you searching for Jesus in India? Just because the Gospels are silent about the missing years doesn't mean Jesus left Galilee. Couldn't he have been working as a carpenter in or near Nazareth?'

'But then how would the boy have grown in stature and wisdom, as is said? Nazareth was a tiny Jewish village that subsisted on the meagre produce from the land. To the Romans, the villagers were "tektons", illiterate peasants. They didn't even have a synagogue.' Her eyes rested on Ajay, but he wasn't sure she actually saw him.

'After his return to Israel, even people from Nazareth didn't recognize him. Luke's Gospel tells us that they asked, "Isn't this Joseph's son?", and in Mark, they questioned, "How did he come by all this? Is this the carpenter, the son of Mary?" Had he been living in Galilee all along, they wouldn't have found his speech unfamiliar. They didn't recognize him because of his long absence.'

'Okay, you may have a point, but couldn't he have been somewhere else in Israel?'

'He could have practised with the Essenes and Therapeutae communities. Even his contemplative withdrawal into the desert for forty days takes place after his baptism, and not before. And anyway, much of all this is highly conjectural,' Anna said.

'But you think the discovery of this manuscript makes India a possibility,' Ajay persisted.

'The text is not conclusive evidence, but for the moment, it's all we have to go on. Besides, had he stayed in Galilee or anywhere in Judea, he would have been married at thirteen, as was the custom. Maybe he left home because his parents were pressing him to do so.'

'So who is this Notovitch and why do you need to hunt for him?'

Anna pushed the manuscript away reluctantly, as if she had no option but to complete the story, now that he was hooked to it. 'It is a long story, full of mystery and intrigue. About a hundred years ago, Notovitch was stranded in Ladakh, just as you are now!' So, she was capable of getting personal! Ajay felt his face go warm. Maybe he was wrong in presuming she was all reserve and ice. Perhaps she was just quiet and self-contained.

'He broke his leg in a fall from a horse and was taken to the Hemis monastery to recuperate. There, a monk, like my friend here,' Anna pointed towards Tsering, 'showed him a very unusual text yellowed with age. It was about Saint Issa, his birth in far away Israel and his journey to India at the age of fourteen, and how here, he studied the Vedas from Brahmins in Puri and Benares. But then, he displeased them by beginning to educate the Sudras in the scriptures. After six years, he had to flee to Nepal because of a plot to harm him. He lived there for another six years, learning the Pali sutras. Notovitch's Issa opposes the abuses of the caste system in India, just as Jesus of Nazareth would later challenge the priestly class in Jerusalem. Sounds like the same man, doesn't he?'

Anna's hands lingered on the bark-like surface of the manuscript as if she loved the feel of it. 'Back in Europe, Notovitch informed Church dignitaries about his astounding discovery. Most of them advised him not to publish it, warning him that he'd make a lot of enemies. A cardinal even offered to buy his notes.'

'Which just shows that it was important enough to need suppression,' Ajay interjected, completely caught up in the story.

'Precisely! It would undermine the word of the Church, but perhaps it skipped their attention that Notovitch's text had shortcomings. For example, the Tibetan script only came into being around the sixth century, so what does that say about the authenticity of the account, and the claim of it having been recorded in the first century? Yet, the vigorous denial of the text makes me suspect it is true.'

'Couldn't he have contacted some scholars?'

'Western scholars are unwilling to believe that Jesus learned from Hindu and Buddhist sages. Even Max Mueller, the great Orientalist, called Notovitch a fraud without investigating his claims. He declared that Notovitch had never been to India, let alone found a manuscript!'

'If I were a Christian, I too would side with two millennia of Church belief and not the lone voice of some unknown Russian traveller.'

'I wouldn't blame you for that, but there is more to the story! Notovitch was not the only person to have seen the manuscript. Swami Abhedanand, from the Ramakrishna Mission, who visited Hemis in 1922, had found a text that exactly matched Notovitch's account. Soon after, the Russian painter, Roerich, also saw the manuscript. There were still others who claimed to have seen the manuscript.'

'So how come you haven't found the manuscript?'

'Because it just disappeared. No one, even from the Tibetan side, is prepared to talk about it anymore,' Anna said rubbing her shoulder as though trying to knead out a pain.

'Not even the abbot?'

He was surprised at her silence.

'And Acha-la wants that I find the manuscript. What would happen to me then? I would have my throat cut!' Tsering dramatically ran a finger across his throat. 'Too dangerous. Better hidden.'

'Why are you hunting for it in a library? They wouldn't hide it here, would they?' Ajay gestured at the little wooden holes stuffed with texts.

'I am hoping to find some reference, some hint in other texts.'

'But, Acha-la, there is no reference. I have been reading these texts since I was a little boy. I promise you there is no reference,' Tsering pleaded.

'You came here only three years ago, Tsering,' Anna said sternly.

'I don't mind. I'll gladly help. I'll go through all the texts in the library. Soon I'll be a scholar too,' Tsering said, smiling broadly at his own joke.

Gathering the leaves of the manuscript, Tsering placed a wooden cover on either side of it, and tied it with the yellow cloth. 'I'll get another one for you to reject,' he announced, disappearing into the darkness at the back of the room.

'What is your interest in this manuscript?' Ajay asked.

'I have a debt to pay,' Anna said, her face suddenly shuttered. She knotted her fingers behind her neck and stretched before rubbing her left shoulder.

Tsering returned with another manuscript in hand, and soon he and Anna forgot about Ajay's presence as they spread it out on the table. He had no choice but to leave.

Ajay wandered into the courtyard, puzzling over the debt Anna had spoken of. Clearly it was something she seemed hard pressed to repay. To her teacher, perhaps? His attention was caught by a group of children in maroon robes, heads shaved, sitting at the sunny end of the courtyard and learning to chant the liturgy from a monk. So young to give up the world. Sheltered and shuttered, would they ever walk the marketplace of opportunity, choosing from its wares? Would they taste the liberating freedom of striding unhindered towards their goal? Giving up what they would never taste seemed as sad as never being allowed to dream.

The abbot was talking to a group of people displaced by the floods, who had taken shelter in a nearby village. The previous day, he and some other monks had gone to the village, taking with them the monastery's meagre food supplies. The monks had helped dig pit latrines while the abbot had attended to injuries, improvising splints, applying a mixture of herbs on bruises and wounds, trying to heal by touch and words. Like another man who may have come here over two millennia ago?

Once the abbot was alone, Ajay went up and asked him about Notovitch and the manuscript.

'The original was recorded in Pali in the first century and was kept in Lhasa. Many hundreds of years later, some monks translated it into Tibetan and brought it here. At least, that's the story,' the abbot said.

'Why do you call it a story?'

'The book begins by relating what merchants from Israel said about the life of Moses. Then we are told Jesus spent six years in Puri and Benares, and the next six in Nepal before returning to the West. The manuscript is mainly about his teachings and contains only the bare details of his years in India. It is more hagiographical than historical. Also, nowhere does Notovitch's text say that Jesus lived in Hemis.'

Pressed for more details, the abbot withdrew. 'Can't say. The beginning and the end don't add up.' Hastily he added, 'Though I have not seen it.'

'But, Sir, many people have!' Ajay persisted.

'In any case, I understand the original is no longer to be found in the Potala Palace. It has disappeared.'

'How come everything keeps disappearing?'

'That you'll have to ask the Chinese! Besides, Ladakhis are not interested in whether Jesus lived here or not. Ask any of them if they have heard of Issa.' He pointed to the displaced people talking to the monks at the far end of the courtyard. Clearly, he had no desire to pursue the subject.

Ajay decided to go out of the monastery for a walk. He wanted time to think. So many things did not add up. If the abbot had doubts about the veracity of the manuscript, why had he asked Anna with such interest last night whether she had made any headway at Thangse? His familiarity with the details of the contents was proof enough that his interest in the manuscript went beyond a cursory reading of it. Ajay had the distinct impression that he was deliberately downplaying it, as though he could not afford to do otherwise. Had the Tibetans washed their hands off the subject? But that couldn't include the abbot.

He wondered then if the drama was being played out on a larger stage. The Chinese? The Church? But then, why had Anna made it her own personal crusade? To the extent that her shoulders seemed sore with its burden. A burden of obligation or of love? And, he asked himself, whose untold story was it that drew him more—Notovitch or Anna's?

An Old Diary Leaf

10 August: Late afternoon

Ajay went down to the river, securing footholds on the loosely strewn stones all the way down to the bank. The mountains glinted mica in the sun, wrapped in a shawl of shingle and stone that draped down to the riverbed. Reaching the water, he sat at the edge of the river, picked up a flat stone and sent it skimming over the water. It bounced on the surface thrice, creating a dance of ripples before disappearing. He continued throwing stones, but each of them sank after a single plop. Weary with his failures, and spying a bridle path in the mountain ahead, he started to climb uphill.

Ajay climbed for over an hour, the nearest he thought he would get to trekking on this trip. Then, he found a shaded spot and sat down, immersed in the silence. Idly, he wondered about the absence of any traditional wheeled transport in the region. He couldn't say that the locals didn't know about the wheel; after all, the prayer wheel was in common use. Perhaps, in this terrain, he thought, it was more practical to use pack animals to transport loads rather than push a cart up a steep and stony path or struggle to restrain it on its descent.

After resting awhile, Ajay decided to return to the monastery. Very soon, though, he realized he had lost his bearings and had no idea how to get back to the road. An hour-and-a-half later, walking and worry became simultaneous. Then, finally, he saw a figure in the distance. His steps quickened. Much to his relief and surprise, it was Anna, with a backpack slung over her shoulders.

Ajay caught up with her, a little out of breath. 'Am I glad to see you! I think I'm lost.'

'That's the path you need to take.' She pointed to a dirt track just ahead of them, 'It will take us to the opposite side of the bank.' He noted her use of the inclusive 'us' instead of 'you'.

She took the lead and he followed. After a while he asked, 'Where are you coming from?'

'Oh, I had gone to see a hermit who lives in the caves further up this stream.'

'You keep unusual company.'

She did not respond, visibly focused on climbing. Twenty minutes later, they came upon a rope bridge, and then they were on the main road.

Ajay turned to Anna and said, 'Thank you. I may not have been able to make it on my own. You are clearly very familiar with this area.'

Looking down at the gushing river, Anna said sombrely, 'This land does not allow for familiarity, only a humble obeisance to its grandeur.'

'Yes, it's a place that shakes up your senses, isn't it? And doesn't take long to penetrate deeper.'

Anna gave him a considering look, as though she found his unexpected remark worthy of attention. Then she smiled and tilted her head in acknowledgement.

'I see you in the monastery, but where do you live?' Ajay inquired.

'Just outside the monastery. As you climb the hill, there are a few huts. I live in one of them.'

'Was it a difficult life to adopt?'

'Well, the discomfort is in your face. I am still not used to the food, or the fact that often I have to carry water to my cottage. Despite boiling, it still upsets my stomach. Neither is the pit latrine my idea of sanitation, nor the flickering lights in the evening. Or walking into a cold room, fetching wood for a fire, crouching near it for warmth.' She smiled wryly and peered at the mountains through narrowed eyes. 'But I have found something else here. You can be content in simplicity, feel freer with less, sense the quiet without the chatter of thoughts.' She rubbed her shoulder as she spoke.

'May I carry that for you?' Ajay offered, pointing to the bag on her back.

'Thanks, it's okay. I'm going to rest under those boulders. Carry on down the road, it will take you to the monastery.' The impersonal tone was back.

Ajay ignored it, and together, they walked towards a huge bank of rocks perched at an escarpment, as if defying gravity. Anna gratefully shrugged off her haversack and sank into the shade. Ajay lowered himself on a boulder. Flustered by their sudden appearance, a bird took off, flying languidly over the river. A comfortable silence followed, merging into the late afternoon haze, spreading over the sun-dappled poplar trees and the distant mustard fields, whose aroma hung heavy in the warm air. Ajay looked at Anna from the periphery of his eye. She was supine, her eyelids closed. In repose she seemed unselfconscious, as though she were alone. She had an air of composure, as restful as the shade, as impersonal as the sun. He found her quietly beautiful. It was a beauty that did not announce itself, but when you turned to look, you looked again. It touched him lightly with the fingertips of longing. When was it that he had last noticed a woman in this way?

Anna opened her eyes and caught Ajay staring at her. With a slight air of bashfulness, he said, 'You looked so peaceful.' Her expression softened. At that moment, something in the air changed between them. Shedding her reserve for a moment, she said, 'What do you do? I enjoyed your questions this morning, the way you came up with anomalies in what I was suggesting. Do you write software?'

'No, I am an engineer. I am into manufacturing, which requires that I constantly enquire: "Why this way? Can it be done differently?" It's an approach that has helped me greatly.' Ajay restrained his desire to go on talking about himself, not sure if she'd be interested.

'Do you have a family business?'

'Oh! No, no. I worked my way up the corporate ladder, thanks to a few serendipitous breaks.'

'Like what?'

'The factory owner was deeply in the red and forced to make a distress sale. If the financials improved, it would fetch him a better price. With his back against the wall, he asked me, a mid-level manager, to run the place. The odds were stacked against me but I accepted the challenge. After all, I was staring at unemployment. I don't know why but the union leader, who had been difficult till then, decided to cooperate and help me improve the out-turn of the plant.'

'Hmm. Curious.' Anna's words echoed his own thoughts. Sometimes, in hindsight, we not only translate images into thoughts but give them life anew.

'The owner received a better price, and I was appointed the general manager by the MNC that bought the unit. But my big-big break came two years later. Profitability was not increasing; the company's marginal growth was merely keeping pace with inflation. My boss called me and confronted me with the stagnation in real terms. Perhaps he was toying with the idea of a foreigner replacing me. I don't know what came over me but I said to him, we are like Alice, having to keep running just to stay in place. He looked at me, surprised and rather taken with the analogy. Perhaps he had been reading *Alice in Wonderland* to his granddaughter, or he had lately realized the intransigence of Indian trade unions and that a foreigner may not grasp the nuances of labour relations in India. Whatever it was, he kept faith with me, giving me a free hand to increase profitability without compromising on quality.'

Thrust centre stage, with the spotlight firmly focused on him, Ajay did not disappoint. Very quickly, the trajectory of the company changed. The Indian arm was now a cash cow, while the other multinationals were bleeding. Soon, managers from other countries were sent to see how the Indians did it. By the time he turned forty, he was the CEO of the Indian arm, with rumours of a seat on the board in London. As he came to the end of his account, Ajay realized that he had not given any credit to Swati for his success. Why was he not being transparent with Anna?

As they began to walk, Ajay thought how Swati's magnetic charm, her engaging smile, her easy-going manner could draw out anyone and put people at ease. The Chairman, on his visits to India, preferred to stay with them rather than at a hotel. He said he felt as relaxed as he did in his daughter's home.

But Swati was much more than a foil to his curious, questioning ways; the friendly face of the executive who needs to take tough decisions. Her contribution was not easy to articulate. He had grown up in middle-class governmental Delhi with his parents' aspirations stretching merely to changing an old car for a new one. Swati, on the other hand, had always been comfortable with affluence. Wordlessly she had conveyed her self-belief to Ajay. She had given him the courage to think big. Sometimes someone else has to dream for you because it falls outside your band of dreaming.

'Your wife did not accompany you?' Anna asked, looking at him restlessly rotating his wedding ring with his thumb and forefinger.

He did not answer. She did not press. They walked in silence until they reached the monastery. Her last question had created a gaping void that no conversation could fill. Anna went up the hill to her cottage and he to his room.

Ajay sat on his bed, letting the quiet of the hour seep into his breath, his thoughts. Just two days ago, his driver had left him marooned in a monastery in the middle of nowhere. But this nowhere had a strange coherence to it. Activity became meaningful here, not because of gain or profit, but because it was an aim in itself. You did not pluck a flower to possess it; instead, you watered the plant so that it could express its own innate purpose. Forty-eight hours ago, he would not have believed that he would be even remotely interested in whether two thousand years ago a carpenter's son had travelled to India, and today he had actively tried to engage with its truth. He smiled, thinking of how Anna seemed to become a different person when she talked of the unknown story, the manuscript, the man.

Why had he left Anna's last question unanswered? Had Swati been here, would she have viewed his growing friendship with Anna with the same conflicted gaze that she had viewed Akanksha with? Would she have accused him now as she had done with Akanksha, bringing their marriage to the edge? Who would have ever thought that a chance meeting could precipitate such a stalemate in their lives?

After a gap of many years, Swati and he had accidentally met Akanksha at a common friend's house. Akanksha's eyes danced with delight as they rested on him. Ajay was so surprised to see her that all he did was to stand in front of her, unable even to muster the automatic response of a conventional greeting as she rose to meet him. A spontaneous moment when they could have hugged each other passed, as Ajay hesitated a wee bit too long. A lukewarm handshake, a stilted smile on his side and a bewildered question in her eyes before he moved a little too quickly to greet the next guest. Later, Ajay found his gaze drawn to her across the room, where she stood listening to someone speak, her hand running through her thick, short hair, a characteristic expression of quiet concentration on her face. Her cheekbones seemed more prominent, he thought, as he looked at her more carefully, as though the years had chiselled away the rounded folds of youth, sharpening and defining the face and shadowing the eyes with a kind of watchful gravity. Aware of his scrutiny, Akanksha turned and looked at Ajay across the room. He smiled, his eyes asking her forgiveness, which she readily gave with a tilt of her head.

He was almost halfway across the room when Swati came up and linked arms with him. He sat quietly next to his wife as she bombarded Akanksha with questions to fill the intervening years: Where were you? When did you get married? Why were we not invited? How come we never met sooner? Swati's impatient, livewire queries were answered by a self-contained Akanksha. 'Nikhil and I got married quickly because he was going on an assignment to South Africa.'

'We must have Nikhil and you over for dinner,' Swati said, glancing sideways at Ajay, who was looking at Akanksha. It was the oddest of glances between two people, acknowledging the affections of the past, but reluctant to grant it any legitimacy in the present. 'Sure,' replied Ajay automatically. Akanksha turned her face away to put her glass on the side table. Ajay suspected it was a ruse to hide her disappointment.

Somehow, he had failed her again. He could feel Swati watching him keenly and tried to keep his face impassive. He wondered if, without knowing it, he had already betrayed something. Why did he find it so hard to take his eyes off Akanksha's face? Was it the need to get in touch with his feelings, as if she were the mirror that could both reflect and contain him? In her gaze, he saw more of himself than he ever had.

Abruptly Swati rose. 'Come on, Ajay. Let's not monopolize Akanksha. I think we should circulate.' Ajay did not move. Swati left, her back stiff with disapproval.

'It's been a long time, Akanksha. One day you were there and the next day you disappeared.'

'I needed to disappear.'

'Why?'

'That's my secret,' Akanksha said gently. 'Maybe I should let it remain a mystery for you to puzzle over.'

There was a pause before Ajay asked, 'And what have these years been like for you?'

'Often bumpy, seldom dull, with shelters of satisfaction dotting the way.'

'Bumpy and satisfying?'

'Bumpy because a dearly held dream died; satisfying when I could step beyond that dream.'

Almost against his will, Ajay asked, 'What was that dream?'

She laughed. 'Oh, that the next wave would lift treasures from the bottom of the sea to the shore.'

'Dreams of youth,' Ajay said, his smile indulgent.

'More like dreams of hope. They seldom die with youth, only change their appearance when reality intrudes.'

Ajay deflected the thought. 'I often wondered how you were.'

'So did I. Yet, in the house of memory, sometimes the shape of rooms grows vague.'

'But some memories bear only your name.' Ajay was taken aback at the intensity of his own statement.

'Do they?'

'Weren't we two people caught in a single dream?'

'What happened then?' Akanksha looked at him searchingly.

'I chose to live in another dream.'

'And has it been worthwhile?'

'In parts. But that doesn't mean I forgot the other dream. In some inexplicable way, it endures in its own space.'

Akanksha smiled. 'Sometimes, I feel we are too ordinary, too flawed to contain something extraordinary when it happens to us.' Her words were a nuanced, many-layered utterance. They fell silent, as they used to often do a long time ago, when words were merely a prelude to togetherness. When Ajay looked up, he found Swati watching them from across the room with tightened lips.

Later, in their bedroom, Swati sat in front of the mahogany dressing table, unclasping her necklace. Ajay looked at her through the oval mirror and spotted a pulse beating in her temple. He switched on the airconditioner, and the curtains rustled in the draft. As he passed her, she pinned him in the mirror with her eyes and asked, 'What were you and Akanksha talking about?'

Ajay hesitated. How was he to replay a conversation that was more poignant in its undertones than in words? 'Oh, just the usual, where she had been, what she was doing… Her husband is an engineer in an oil company.'

'Did she tell you why she didn't keep in touch?'

'She was rather quiet about that.'

'Does she have kids?'

'I don't know,' Ajay shrugged.

'Is she working?'

'We never got around to that.'

'So what did you talk about?' Swati smiled encouragingly as she swivelled the dressing stool around.

Ajay grew silent, unsure of what to say. In retrospect, he realized that Akanksha and he had exchanged none of the mundane details of their lives. Their meeting had seemed a moment out of time. The intervening years had blurred as they found themselves in a sanctuary they had once known.

Swati waited. The unanswered question hung in the air, and the longer Ajay took to answer, the more annoyed she seemed to grow. As though wondering how many more layers of concealment were being added to the actual exchange between them.

'Is there something you don't want to tell me, Ajay?'

'There are some conversations that don't make good reportage,' Ajay said noncommittally.

'Or you can't tell me because the exchange was loaded?' Swati took off her silver sandals and flung them in a corner.

'Loaded?' Ajay mumbled as he pulled the kurta down over his head.

'You were behaving oddly.'

'Was I?' Ajay tensed as he climbed into bed.

'When you first saw her you looked stunned. You couldn't even greet her properly. Later, when I left you two alone, the world faded for both of you. All very intense and cosy.'

'Come on, Swati. The last person I had expected to see at the party was Akanksha, so I was taken aback. And there is nothing intimate about catching up on news.'

'That's not what your body language said.'

'Body language?'

'The kind where words make love.'

'That's rubbish! We never had that kind of relationship, so how can it erupt in body language?'

'Are you actually unaware of what is happening inside you or are you pretending to be ignorant?' Swati was visibly annoyed. Ajay found himself bristling at the options she had outlined.

'You are making a big deal out of nothing! I meet an old friend after fifteen years, and because I chat with her for ten minutes, you begin to imagine I am having an affair with her. For god's sake, be sensible.'

Swati walked away into the bathroom. When she emerged, she said, 'Ajay, do you know that while you and Akanksha were talking, I deliberately passed by you. But you were oblivious to everything except one another. You were talking about dreams—letting go of one and being caught in another.'

Had his absorption been so complete that he had not even noticed her? Swati's hesitant question broke into his thoughts. 'You are not having regrets, are you?' She waited for a moment before switching off the lights, letting the ensuing darkness echo the question.

Naively, Ajay had thought the argument would blow over by the morrow. To some extent, he was right. Swati did not mention it the next morning or in the course of the next few days. But it never disappeared. It merely revisited them in another way.

Now, sloughing off his thoughts, Ajay rose and moved fitfully around his monastic room. He opened his suitcase, arranged his clothes, dusted his shoes. He hunted for his torch, took out his notebook and pen, rearranging his room, his life. He pulled out his haversack from under the bed and emptied it, looking for the Swiss army knife he had brought for the trek. The black book that Yeshe had given him fell open and a photograph flew from its pages onto the dusty floor. Perhaps it might give a clue to the owner of the book, he thought, as he picked the photograph from the floor and dusted it off.

It was a diary entry. Why would anyone photograph their own diary? It must be someone else's diary. He read the contents cursorily. The writing was decidedly old-fashioned, with well-looped letters. It was a bit difficult to read the tightly packed neat lines in the dim light of the room. He shone the torch on it and soon figured out that the name Notovitch appeared again and again on the page. He rubbed his eyes and read it carefully. Good heavens! It was the record of a meeting with Notovitch, a man he had heard of only this morning. How very strange! Could he be the same man whom Anna was interested in?

Ajay sat down on the bed, his head spinning. Who did this belong to? Why had it landed with him? And today? Had he seen it even the day before, it would have meant nothing. He lay back listening to the sound of the cold desert wind and thinking that something in this place was drawing him from the circumference to its centre.

Rigzin

10 August: Night

The abbot wrenched his eyes open through layers of sleep. It was the same dream. He lay still, counting his heartbeats, consciously slowing them down. He squinted at the small clock on his bedside table. It was 2 a.m. How little is the difference between a dream and waking. Each state so real while it lasts, each so symbolic in expressing something other than that which is seen. He felt the coldness in his feet but refrained from reaching for a sheet to warm them. The chill came from elsewhere, from a memory imprinted on his body and marked in his psyche. The dream had expressed it anew.

It was, when he thought about it, a study in contrasts. The womb of darkness lit by white snow everywhere. A six-year-old boy, his feet numb and blue with the cold. One hand shaded his eyes from the strong ultraviolet reflection that threatened snow blindness; the other hand was persistently pulled by a man in a fur cap who whispered sibilantly, 'Faster, faster, we have to hide.' Tears flowed down his cheeks, and terror filled his little heart as he sank into the snow. The man released his hand and ran ahead. Inch by inch, the snow sucked the little boy into its cold whiteness as his hands tried desperately to claw a way out. The horror of being sucked into the snow was equal to the fear of gunshots that were drawing closer.

What, he wondered, had provoked this dream tonight? For the last five years, it had not recurred. Perhaps memory, painful and frozen, had been lit by the flint of a conversation yesterday. Or was it the sight of the children who had taken shelter from the floods in the monastery? Homeless, bewildered, hungry. Like he once was.

The previous afternoon, the families who had lost their homes in the flood, sat on rush mats in an orderly line in the courtyard, waiting to be served rice and dal. Every bowl in the monastery had been commissioned into use for the thirty-odd people. The monks carried the food in aluminium buckets. Ajay had begun serving from the far right side of the line, followed by the abbot, who put a few dried apricots in each child's hand.

After the meal was over, Ajay had noticed that a girl around four years old had wandered away. She was crying and rubbing her eyes with tiny fists, her short hair fringing her forehead. He picked her up and brought her back. As the abbot watched, the little girl stretched out her arms to her mother. Momentarily, the abbot felt a tug at his heart.

Ajay had turned to the abbot and said, 'She reminds me of my daughter. I miss her so much. One whimsical act of nature and so many lives change. This little girl,' Ajay pointed to the child now nestled in her mother's arms, 'will she ever be the same again after the destruction of her home?'

'She has her parents. That's all she needs to call home,' the abbot replied.

'Home is more than your parents.'

'Is it? In fact, it is nothing but your parents. It is merely an extension of the sense of belonging that comes from being with them.'

'You had to leave your homeland too?' Ajay asked.

'Early in life, I had to learn to survive in an alien land, amidst conflicting experiences. My blood used to boil at the brutalization of our people by the Chinese. They stripped us of dignity; they ransacked our monasteries to destroy our identity; they urinated on our sacred objects.' The abbot's eyes flashed as he spoke.

'Will you ever be able to come to terms with that?'

'I used to toss in bed all night, on many nights. Then, one day, I realized that while I writhed in anguish, the Chinese official at whom my anger was directed was probably watching TV with his wife and children, unconcerned and unaffected.'

They had been walking together in the courtyard. The abbot stopped and continued, 'I have learned an odd thing about anger. It is usually born from humiliation and sustained by the desire to scorch the transgressor. But anger rarely harms the other. It harms only oneself.'

'Isn't personal anger very different from the collective anguish caused by the fate of a nation?'

'Not personal?' the abbot shot back. 'To be separated from your mother at the age of six, never to see her again—is that not personal? To be forever distant from your parents, who live only a few hundred miles away, is not personal?'

There was a moment's pause, then Ajay said, 'I am sorry, I did not mean to suggest…' His voice trailed away.

The abbot shook his head as if to shake off a mood. Tentatively, Ajay asked, 'Where are your parents?'

'In Kham, Tibet, or so I believe,' the abbot said flatly.

'What happened?'

The abbot lay in bed with eyes that were reluctant to open to the past, and were never permitted to be shut from it either. The camera of memory opened its store of pictures and presented two contrary images: one was of a six-year-old, happy and cocooned in his parents' care and love; the other was of a sudden and incomprehensible parting from them under a deceitful darkness. Taken away by a man with a fur cap. A journey of terror and abandonment, where he walked and, at times, was carried piggyback. Other people joined them—three monks, two boys and a girl, a kindly older woman and another man who seldom spoke. Exhausted, lonely and hungry, he often huddled next to the kindly woman. But she did not smell and feel like his mother. And, most of all, she did not have his mother's smile, which lit up her eyes when they rested on him.

They walked through the night, their progression measured by slow, beleaguered steps. Conversation had long retreated into silence, everyone mindful only of their own laboured breathing. They crossed boulder-strewn terrain, swollen rivers and thickets of trees, making frequent about-turns as they journeyed on in unguided terrain. Danger lurked everywhere. Chinese guards were on the prowl. If caught, they would be sent to hard labour camps. Anyone could be an informant and, therefore, they could not trust anyone, not even a Tibetan. Like a deer at a creek that raises its head after every sip, they constantly feared for their survival. The Himalayan passes were their only gateway to freedom.

The abbot got up, slung the loose end of his maroon robe over his shoulder, and walked towards the balcony. A new moon barely illumined the inky sky, the stars carelessly strewn like broken pieces of glass. The constellations looked like smashed mirrors stricken with longing for their lost wholeness. Or was it he who was in search of his own reflection in the events of the past?

He knew that last night's dream had been born from that journey when they tramped through ankle-deep snow, without proper shoes or warm clothing or even sunglasses to protect them from the glare. It took him back to the many nights he had slept on what seemed the very roof of the Himalayas.

The freezing air had shrouded his body, his breath turning to ice on his coat collar. The howling wind hit the lonely rocks that towered above them, and he had felt every atom of air turn into cold blades peeling off his soft skin. His fingertips felt as though thousands of little pins were stabbing him all at once, as sharp-edged, cold and piercing as the stars in the sky. Slowly, the cold turned to pain and pain to numbness. Perhaps his body was turning into a star.

The only warmth came from his first tears, silently shed. The man with the fur cap consoled him by promising, 'Tomorrow we will be in India.' But that he said every night, like a prayer that found no answering voice.

That child looked for his mother when they reached India, awaited her in the Tibetan Children's Village (TCV) in Dharamsala. He searched for her in the face of the housemother who oversaw forty other children. He became one of a number, fed, clothed and pushed ahead in the assembly line of children. Seldom did a personal touch or a look from any of the adults single him out with the warmth of a special connection.

That child learned the difference between pain and suffering then. Pain you could bear because it often had to do with the body. But suffering was anchored in the mind, often a result of being denied what you cherished. As he ate food he had never eaten before, sat next to children unknown to him in an alien place, he would look at the far mountains and wonder which one contained his home. At night, he would instinctively move a little closer to the child next to him for warmth, a need that went beyond the body. He would concentrate his thoughts on the faces of his parents and brothers, and soundlessly repeat their names. He would pore over every picture of his homeland to revivify its contours in his mind. Gradually, he found the familiar outlines blurring and those of the adopted land replacing them.

A strange inner bewilderment became the backdrop to his being. Snow and the crossing became a symbol of many things—of being alone and defenceless; of pain buried and preserved. Snow was also a reminder of kindness from the fur-capped man who had broken his own sunglasses into two so that the little boy could have one half of it.

Turning away from the balcony, the abbot sat cross-legged on the still-warm mattress. Resting his head against the wall, he closed his eyes. It occurred to him then that the dream was not merely a replay of a journey in the past. Its sheer repetition was alerting him to something he had missed all along. Maybe there was a hint in the surge of feelings it evoked in him when he saw the little girl reaching out to her mother. She had smiled at Ajay only after she was within the safety of her mother's arms. Does a ruptured sense of belonging leave a gaping hole in the psyche, where dreams swirl with memories? Can pain from what happened long ago ever be healed? Only a question answers a question.

Friendship

Ajay had never felt so imprisoned by time, so excited at being the bearer of significant tidings. It was only 7 a.m. He knew Anna came to the library by 9 a.m. Two hours more. He paced the courtyard, certain that she would be as enthusiastic about his discovery. Would it provide a clue that she could use in her hunt?

Anna strode in at 8.30 a.m., carrying her laptop. He approached her eagerly, opened the diary in his hand and showed her the page. Her eyes narrowed as she tried to read the cramped writing. She followed the text with her forefinger, muttering, 'Not clear,' and went over the lines again. Then, she shook her head and mumbled, 'Unlikely.' She seemed to take forever to finish reading it, Ajay thought. Finally, she looked up and burst forth, 'This is incredible! I can't believe it. This is a photocopy from the diary of Dr Karl Marx of the Ladane Charitable Dispensary. He was the director of the hospital in Leh and had treated Notovitch's toothache.'

Lost in excitement, she looked at the page again. 'Where is the date…the date?' Her finger reached the top left corner of the page. 'Aha! 5 November 1887. Fits!' she said, her hand running through her hair in short, quick movements. 'How the hell did you get this?' she asked, staring at Ajay in disbelief.

He revelled in her attention. 'Interesting, isn't it? Another person searching for the same thing as you!'

She moved towards the library. 'You realize this diary entry is precious because it confirms Notovitch's presence in Leh.' She scrutinized the rest of the diary leaf minutely.

'What is the big deal about Notovitch's toothache?'

'You remember what I said about Max Mueller discrediting Notovitch? He had contacted a British colonial officer to verify if Notovitch had been to Ladakh. The officer told him there was no trace of Notovitch's presence in any document, anywhere in Ladakh, thereby confirming that Notovitch was a fraud. That is why this diary noting about an ordinary toothache is so important. It makes Notovitch's visit authentic. He was in Leh,' she declared triumphantly.

'All this while, I wanted to see Dr. Marx's diary, but that too had disappeared. The Leh hospital said it had been with them for some time before it was "stolen". Familiar story! Luckily, before it was stolen, a professor from Srinagar photographed the diary. And this is a copy of that photograph.' She looked at him, eyes shining, 'Ajay, I hope you realize you are a part of history. At least, for me!'

Ajay smiled broadly before responding, 'You mean, if Notovitch was in Leh, he could have visited Hemis. And he *could* have discovered the manuscript, which, in turn, implies that Jesus could have come to India.'

'Conditional logic. But logic all the same.'

They both laughed.

'Anna,' he asked, 'Why is this so important to you?'

She looked reflectively out of the window. 'There is a big gap between the Jesus of history and the Christ of the Christians. Very little is known about the historical Jesus, the Nazarene. I am trying to discover the Jesus that was, not what I am told he was.'

'Who was he?'

Anna smiled. 'That is one of the most difficult questions in history. Also, the most personal.'

She silently looked down at her hands, now lying quietly folded on the table. When she looked up, her eyes were far away. 'For me, he is a more compelling figure because he struggled as a seeker before becoming divine. He wasn't just the son of God who came down perfect. He becomes more real because he withdrew into the desert and meditated for forty days, struggling with his everyday self. It gives me the courage to follow suit. Otherwise he remains antiseptic, too far out of my reach.'

'So, your hunt is not really for Notovitch and his toothache.'

She laughed delightedly as she opened her laptop and said, 'At least we have proved one thing. His dental problems were real!'

Later that afternoon, Ajay waited for Anna to emerge from the library. Their morning conversation lingered in his mind. How effortlessly her reasoning and passion had raised the bar, transforming information to personal aspiration. She was not just a research scholar. Rather, the Jesus story was a search for the grounds of her faith. For him, this searching was alien as he had never felt any particular need for anchorage to his own religious roots, and he was convinced he was none the worse for it. But there are those who feel this need, he reasoned, who yearn to see the ocean floor beneath the tides. Was Anna leading a life of religious devotion beneath the scholarly one? That would explain the reason for her being in a monastery. She wasn't here because she was trapped by the floods, like him. She had chosen this life. Was she married? Why had he not asked her earlier? She wore no rings; she dressed simply, lived in very basic conditions and did not seek out company. Something in her eyes intrigued him. They were alive with intelligence, shadowed by sorrow. Earlier, in the library, he'd had a strong urge to tenderly cup his hands over hers and tell her to let go, that she was safe.

He knew that once she left the library, she would go for a walk. He waited in the courtyard for her, amused at his patience, startled at his own sense of anticipation. Of late, he mused, I keep imagining ways to be with her. And when I am with her, I want to prolong the moment.

Half an hour later, he looked up to see Anna standing near the limewashed wall in front of the monastery, with a single hollyhock standing tall behind her, as if propping up her hidden frailty. Hands on hips, with her face turned towards the greenhouse, she seemed to be debating which way to go down—from the back of the monastery or the front. Her thoughts still seemed to rest in the place she had emerged from, the sunlight an odd intrusion.

Then, she turned her head slowly and looked at him. He had the distinct feeling that she was not surprised to see him there.

'Any luck?'

She smiled wistfully. 'Not a hint so far. In the last month, I must have gone through at least thirty manuscripts here and in other monasteries.' She rubbed her eyes, visibly tired of hunting down ancient secrets.

By an unspoken mutual consent, they began walking across the courtyard. Anna stopped near the raised cemented platform with a flagpole in its centre. She squinted at the distant mountains now under the cover of billowing cottony clouds. 'Hour by hour, the mountains shed their clothes to wear new ones, depending on the shifting light and shade,' she said.

Had they glanced up, they would have seen the abbot looking down from his window. What he saw made him shake his head slightly; maybe there was even a hint of a smile. He watched Ajay held captive to Anna's presence, and she, her head slanted sideways, smiling, acknowledging the invisible skeins of his interest. They moved across the courtyard, Ajay instinctively matching his steps to Anna's. A presentiment of the future made the abbot shiver. Or had something more personal been evoked? He looked down at his robe, as though to remind himself of something, and then at Anna and Ajay, who were fast disappearing down the steps of the monastery. Sometimes, in an odd reversal of time, the outcome of a journey is visible in its origins. The abbot bent his head in deference to the moment of foreknowledge before turning away from the window.

Unaware of the prescient gaze that had swept over them, Anna and Ajay continued their walk, taking a new path up the mountains. A shallow rivulet below wandered aimlessly, as though lost far away from home. Ajay looked at her sideways and asked, 'What brought you to India in the first place?'

She thought for a moment, 'I have often wondered about that. If I am honest, I don't really know. Perhaps many things. I had an unusual childhood with a mother who seemed to hold a dual citizenship to this reality and some other, sometimes coalescing the past and the future in the present. It was very unsettling for the family, particularly my father, who used to be pretty shaken by her hunches. She told him once that a university colleague, whom he was collaborating with, would deceive him. My father brushed her warning aside. Later, it turned out that this man had published parts of my father's research without acknowledging it. I grew up believing in her, even though she lived by no comfortable stereotypes.

'When I was in my teens, my mother confided something to me. She told me that at the moment of conceiving each of her three children, she knew exactly what kind of soul was hovering around ready to reserve its space in her womb. "And the three of you have turned out exactly that way," she told me.'

'What did she say about you?' Ajay asked.

Anna smiled almost bashfully. 'She said I was very diffident to take birth. I hovered near her a shy, gentle, wistful creature. But then, I decided to take the plunge because I had unfinished business to attend to. Perhaps that is the reason for my coming to India.'

They walked on in a connected silence, with the smell of wood smoke from a shepherd's fire wafting around them and mingling with the scent of branching streams and fallen, bruised leaves. A birdsong of haunting beauty echoed in the expanding vistas of the rugged mountains.

Anna turned towards him as if about to say something, then changed her mind.

'You were going to say...'

'Well, you may find it hard to believe,' Anna said hesitantly.

'Try me.'

'My mother said there was a fourth pregnancy, but she refused it. She told the hovering soul, "You won't be happy here." She miscarried two days later.'

An incredulous Ajay halted mid-step, almost bumping into Anna. 'Did your mother believe in reincarnation?'

'You mean, was that my India connection? Maybe. Who knows? All I know is that I got a scholarship to Harvard and, without knowing why, I signed up in my undergrad days for a course in Hinduism. Later, I wondered what made me do it. I mean, there I was, confronted by a disorienting array of 33,000 gods and goddesses with the most irrational behaviour and deeply suspect morality!'

Ajay laughed. 'And what happened then?'

As an undergraduate, she was often in the Oriental section of the library, trying to understand Hindu iconography. One day, her friend Lisa and she were puzzling over a book of erotic sculptures from Khajuraho. Anna suggested that the erotic carvings, interspersed with those of everyday activities, were perhaps indicative of sex as a normal human function. Lisa wondered whether, given the abundance of the carvings, it might have been a protest against some puritanical and repressive view of sex in that period. Their subdued tones gradually rose as they exclaimed over some new figure or frieze they had discovered.

A bearded man of about thirty was sitting next to them. He came over and, peering through his glasses, said, 'These carvings really draw one to the "why" of their creation, don't they? Look,' he said, pointing at the carvings on the outer walls of the temples. 'They are arranged in three distinct bands. I wonder if the erotic ones follow a pattern. You can see there is no erotica inside the temples, it is only on the walls outside.'

He was right. His simple observation caught their interest. Anna remembered being struck by his lean, almost ascetically gaunt appearance. An exquisite alertness coursed through her as she watched his long, aesthetic fingers placed on the open book, and looked up into his animated eyes, glowing with interest.

'Surely the intention was to convey something about sexuality that is not obvious,' he said.

'What?' Lisa asked.

He stroked his beard and said earnestly, 'We are apt to read these sculptures as though sexuality is just another instinct, at par with hunger, fear, survival or play, because that is currently *our* dominant belief. Perhaps the builders of these temples didn't treat sexuality as only a biological urge.'

'But what else is it? After all, we share it with other animals,' Anna said.

'There is a difference. Animals have sex only in the mating season. For humans, sexuality is never in the background. We constantly confront each other with signals of sexual attractiveness and preparedness. For us, sex is perhaps more than what it is for our mammalian cousins!' He smiled.

'What do you think is the "more" that they are trying to depict?' Lisa asked.

'It's interesting that the sexual panels are always located near carvings of divine figures. While women adorning themselves, mundane scenes of musicians, potters, farmers and so on, are always at some distance. Does this juxtaposition suggest a connection between sexuality and the sacred? You would notice that the erotic figures are invariably in standing poses. Are they intended to merge with the rising surge of the temple? A gesture representing a reaching out to the transcendent?'

Anna looked at Ajay and said, 'When I asked him if he was a scholar of Hinduism, he laughed. "No, I am not into Hinduism. I am a Buddhist scholar teaching Tibetan Buddhism," he said.

'Soon after that, I dropped Hindu philosophy and went on to do my post-graduation in Tibetan Buddhism. Now you know how I chose India.'

'The bearded man was your husband?' Ajay ventured.

'Yes,' said Anna with a long drawn-out sigh, her lips pursed together.

'Where is he?'

'John died five years ago.'

Ajay let out his breath slowly and looked at her. She seemed wrapped in the silence of the dead. He knew the sharing had ended. John's death had intervened. Some untold story hung in the air.

Bidding him a short goodbye, Anna set out for her hut, the falling dusk swiftly swallowing her figure.

The Two Closed Doors

11 August: Night

The abbot woke again in the middle of the night. It was not the same dream but another image, one that had been with him since his childhood, an image that churned his mind even more than the dream of sinking into the snow.

An empty corridor with doors at either end. Both doors are closed. He does not know what lies behind them.

In his dream, he would wait for something to happen, someone to emerge, but no one ever did. Nothing stirred behind the doors or in the corridor. He would startle awake, sweating as though from a night terror. Tonight, too, his forehead was moist. The previous night's dream may have been triggered by his conversation with Ajay. But this one? Its recurrence had ravaged him in his early days here, causing him to get out of bed and pace the terrace restlessly, late into the night. Was its return, tonight, a reminder of the road scorched by love and the inevitability of loss?

He had carried the burden of personal loss to this monastery, to this stone-and-boulder wilderness, haunted by that last look in her eyes. Initially, this place was a refuge from his pain, and then it became his meditation, his pilgrimage from wound to worship.

His mind went back to the time when he had first dreamt of the closed doors and his gradual struggle over three decades to understand what they alluded to. The passage of years had reduced the frequency of the dream, and its meaning had changed in his imagination, becoming more nuanced, the doors evolving from a barrier to an entrance.

It had occurred in his first year in Dharamsala, when he would awake to the nearly audible thump of his heartbeats. Slowly, he would venture to look around the dormitory with its white, painted beds and young sleeping occupants, some a little better known than others. But even that familiarity could not lull him back to sleep. Initially, he had wondered whether he was unused to the heat and if the sweating had roused him from sleep. Soon he realized that it woke him even in the dead of winter.

It was not long before young Rigzin became aware that many boys in his dormitory suffered from disturbed sleep. The boy who slept closest to the door often moaned plaintively. Down the corridor, someone tossed and thrashed, another grunted and sometimes shouted, presumably at a dream figure. One boy was prone to sleepwalk.

Sometimes, a few boys confessed to nightmares and described them to the others. He didn't even have the comfort of calling his dream a nightmare. There was nothing frightening about the two closed doors. They never held any sense of threat or harm. Then why did they frighten him so much?

When he was eleven, he confided about the dream to his favourite teacher, Urgyen-la. This teacher had won his trust because he often related stories from the Jataka, just like Rigzin's father used to. Urgyen-la always paused dramatically when he was about to relate a dream in the tale, and Rigzin would know a turning point was about to unfold.

After one such story session, Rigzin asked his teacher, 'Is there something wrong with me?'

Reassuringly his teacher said, 'I don't think so. But why do you ask?'

When Rigzin told him about the recurrent image, his teacher said matter-of-factly, 'It is quite normal to have bad dreams.' Gently, he questioned the frightened boy, 'Did your house have a corridor like in your dream?'

'I don't remember, but there were many doors.'

'Tell me something about those doors.'

After some hesitation, Rigzin ventured, 'Father would often remind us to bolt the front door after dark, and I would be afraid to go without Mother.'

Ah! The tragedy and bravery of childhood, Urgyen-la thought. In fact, we are all bound together by a common loss we cannot afford to remember, but are condemned never to forget. He whispered under his breath, 'What are the closed doors hiding? What is it that frightens yet beckons you to find out?'

That was the first clue.

Another year elapsed and he realized that the corridor dream came mostly after the dream of sinking in the snow. Sometimes a day or two later. As if the two dreams were connected. Was there a link between the two doors and his journey through the snow? He asked Urgyen-la, 'Could one of them be the front door of my home?'

'Possibly, but why is it shut?'

'The front door is my last memory of home, my parents, my brothers, my life. It shut me out from my family.'

Some memories cannot be confronted directly, Urgyen-la realized. He skirted the issue and told Rigzin of his own arduous journey from home. He spoke of his trials, his wife's death in childbirth, and of his parents who were too frail to hazard the journey but constantly urged him to go. He often thought about them, he said, living with the knowledge that he had left behind all he had.

One day, Rigzin heard the housemother sing an old Tibetan folk song, and the tune reminded him of something similar his mother used to sing to him. Memory surged through him, at first in broken images, then like a leaf wafting down from a high branch.

It was that fateful night. The fur-capped man arrived. After a brief, hurried prayer in front of the family deity, Rigzin's father gave the man a cloth pouch with money. He then turned to Rigzin and commanded him to go with the stranger. Rigzin obeyed without understanding. But his six-year-old mind did register that he was being taken away, and it was being done stealthily under the cover of darkness. His father had wrapped a warm coat around his shoulders. Never before had he done that, for only his mother worried about his clothes. He desperately wanted his mother to say it was all right for him to go, but she was nowhere to be seen. He thought she would emerge from her room and the sombre evening would end. But she didn't. Where was she? Why did she not come out of her room? His father held him close to him awhile, but he broke free and ran and stood outside the closed door of his mother's room, calling out to her. Silence followed. Nothing stirred behind the door. Why was she punishing him by not coming out? He had not been naughty that day. He stood there, tears streaming down his cheeks, his little hands banging the door like a bird with a broken wing, flapping in fright.

The man with the fur cap picked him up and propelled him through the front door even as he continued to gaze at the closed door where he thought his mother was. Then the front door closed, and he heard it being bolted for the night. By then, his mother's door and the front door had coalesced into one image: a closed door. That was his last memory.

Rigzin's earliest memory was of soothing sounds as his mother urged him to eat the aromatic broth of meat and vegetables she had set before him in a bowl. Brushing back a recalcitrant strand of jet-black hair from her face, ladle in hand, a slight smile on her lips, eyes alight from the fire, she had looked at him with that brief and special look of tenderness bestowed on the favourite child. He had felt physically enveloped by her. Everything had blurred in that moment: his two brothers sitting next to him, his father with calloused hands and feet stretched out towards the fire, the little room sooty with smoke, the cold, dry winter wind outside.

Even as a young twelve-year-old, he had sensed the dream image was not drawing him back to these memories. Something else, something more immediately personal, lay hidden behind those doors.

Lying at night in the dormitory, Urgyen-la's earlier question came to his mind, 'Who is behind those closed doors? If you knock, who will come out?'

No one, his heart cried in desolation. No one, whispered the fall of his tears.

Often, as he lay awake, he wondered if that was what the dream was about. One door stood for exile from home and the other from his mother. Long, long ago this door had not been opened. And if he did manage to open it now, what would he find? A mother whom he could not recognize? An explanation from her that would come too late?

When Rigzin was thirteen years old, a refugee from Tibet had given him a letter. It wasn't signed, or even addressed to him. Anyone could have written it, and it could have been for anyone, except there was a brief reference to the front door.

Dear Son,

How are you? We are all doing well. We had a good crop of potatoes, the cows give good milk, and with a little money we bought a new kettle. Your brothers are growing well, they are learning Chinese.

We all remember you. I am happy your cousins are looking after you. When the mountains turn green, I know you are growing as tall and straight as the trees that grow on them.

Your father is well and repairing the front door.

Yours as always.

The unsigned paper blew a storm wind in him. His heart knew it was from her. After seven long years, the first communication turned out to be more disturbing than comforting.

It was strange that the closed door of his nightmare was being repaired. Who was doing it—his father? Or his mother, by writing the letter? Could it ever be repaired? Why had she not spoken of her love for him, of how much she missed him and how she never stopped looking towards the front door in case he came through it? *We all remember you.* An impersonal collective remembering of a past connection. That was all! Even the bit about the cattle, kettle and potatoes made him feel his family was all right without him. It would have been better if it were someone else's letter given to him by mistake. Surely his mother knew the extent of his longing for her. In all these years, he had been sustained by the belief that the longing was not his alone but hers in equal measure, if not more. But this letter revealed nothing from her side. He wished he could ride on a draught of wind to his mother and ask her: Why? Why? Why?

Urgyen-la tried to explain to him that it was an act of love. Sending him away was a gift, not a punishment. Despairing of the Chinese, they must have used all their savings to arrange for the crossing. But that did not assuage Rigzin's torment. All he knew was that his mother had not opened that door when he stood outside it, weeping. Was her refusal to open it an indication of her preference for his brothers, and was that why he had to be sent away? If only one of them had to go, why was he, the youngest, sent away? Did she not know of the snow-bound mountainous terrain with its treacherous passes that could have killed him?

At a preconscious level, the two closed doors began a debate within him. Was it better to live near your mother, grow up playing with your brothers in your homeland, surviving on barely sustainable produce that was liable to be confiscated by the Chinese? Or was it better to live in sterile freedom, exiled from home, never to know the sap of nurturance from one's family that translates into one's faith in life? At the age of six or seven, your feet totter, as both parents have let go of your hands far too soon, and tragically, no one comes forward to fill the empty space on either side of you. Long before you can walk, you are forced to run towards a survival that in itself seems meaningless.

Unwittingly, the letter had conferred fresh meaning upon the two closed doors. One door became imbued with the enchantment of her maternal presence as he imagined her coming out of the door to sweep him up in her arms in a burst of joy. She seemed to be everywhere; all of a sudden, he would be arrested by a song, a tune she had sung to him a long time ago. At night, he saw her face in the moon, watching over him, and he believed the winds carried her fragrance to him. The other door, through which she never came out, permeated his being with a quiet despair rather than overt anger. He did not blame her, only himself for not being good enough to draw her out one last time.

He finally wrote to her six months later:

Dear Amala,

When I think of you, I think of home. There were so many things I wanted to do with you. I wanted to hear fairy stories from you, and be soothed when I tossed and turned at night. I wanted you to scold me when I was naughty, and cheer with joy when my essay won a prize in school.

Sometimes when I cried and tears ran down my face, I imagined that each one turned into your face. I had wanted to write to you several times. I had imagined your joy in receiving my letter, your going to my father, then to my brothers, weeping and laughing together as you said, 'My son has written to me.'

I did not write to you fearing my letter may be confiscated by the Red Army as it was from India. They would make your life worse than hell. Accuse you of sending your child to the enemy, branding you a traitor. No one would ever know where you vanished and I would lose you forever.

I keep missing you and pray that one day we meet. These days, you often come to me in my dreams at dawn.

Your loving son always,
Rigzin

PS: You never told me it was such a long journey. And why did you never say goodbye?

He did not send the letter but kept it under his pillow until it grew parched and brown with age. It was his sacrifice, to protect her, in case the letter was intercepted. In doing so, he sacrificed his right to tell her of his longing for her. Gradually, through his sacrifice, he understood hers and the gift of freedom she had offered him at the cost of an irrevocable separation, a death that was all the more poignant because they were both alive to feel it. How do you repay a debt except by understanding that a loved one has offered you a tremendous opportunity, denying a vital part of herself in doing so?

It would be many years before Rigzin realized that what had actually happened in the past was less important than what he *believed* had happened. The historical events of his early life were one thing; how he remembered them was another matter altogether.

As he grew older, the dream's frequency diminished, but the image never completely left him. He was certain it had layers of meaning. Over time, he understood some of them but, with each unveiling, a new puzzlement would surface, such that its mystery remained undiminished. The two closed doors morphed into a theme that repeated itself, like a signature song sung in different tunes at various stages of his life.

Perhaps this was also how he embarked on a lifelong striving to produce harmony between the two doors; between fact and fantasy; loss and love; nurturance and abandonment. He learned to sit in the middle of the metaphorical corridor, looking from one door to the other, as if at the contrariness of life, in which any one point of view automatically generates its opposite. Little did he realize that he had begun the journey to distinguish between shadow and substance.

Eventually, Rigzin was awarded a full scholarship to St. Stephen's College in Delhi University for a graduation course in Economics. He revelled in his newly discovered independence, and regularly wrote to his teacher.

Dear Urgyen-la,

I am sorry for not writing earlier, but the last few weeks have been a vortex of seminars and tutorials that sucked me in, and time collapsed! Then, two days before the final exams, I received a jolt when a policeman came to the hostel enquiring why I had not renewed my residence permit. The comfort zone I had created for myself was ripped away.

I had believed I was the same as all my classmates. We ate the same food, listened to the same Bollywood songs, smoked in the back lawns discussing Salman Rushdie, the economy and the latest offering of motorcycles in the market. The bonhomie felt real.

Why am I, then, the only one who has to go and get his residence permit extended every year by the passport authorities? Not even the students from the North-East, who share my features, need to. It seems my 'now' can never be distant from my 'long-ago'.

Urgyen-la, do I belong 'there' or 'here'? The truth of my everyday life is that I am not 'there' and neither am I allowed to belong 'here'.

What kind of freedom have my parents gifted me?

With reverence and regard,
Rigzin

He did not have to wait long for the reply.

Rigzin, my dear,

Imagine that your father is dying and he holds your hand and whispers that he departs satisfied that you have been given the opportunity for a better life. Rigzin, how would you respond to him?

Unlike students of free nations, we have extra responsibilities that are sometimes burdensome. Are these the closed doors again? This time, bringing a sense of isolation from your classmates? Perhaps you need to see your alienation differently, as you had done in TCV. In time, you may learn to value the very qualities that exile

demands—uncertainty and a divided identity. These
may become the means for you to find your life's direction.
    You have never been a 'normal' student, but one who
has had to fight for his freedom. It is up to you how you
define freedom, as also where the fight lies.

With affection and blessings,
Urgyen

After his graduation, Rigzin joined a commercial
organization and threw himself into work. It was almost a
year before he met his teacher and told him enthusiastically
about his projects.

'I'm very glad for you, Rigzin,' Urgyen-la said. 'I hope,
finally, you are happy?'

Rigzin fell into a troubled silence. When he spoke,
it was once more about his old angst. 'Sir, I'm financially
independent but the feeling of alienation still hounds me.
People see me only as a Tibetan exile. What real choice can
I exercise?'

'I promise you, a door will open. When and how, I can't
say. The two doors no longer belong to your father's house;
they now represent exile and opportunity, alienation and
assimilation. They pertain to the fate of our community.'

'Is our defiant hope merely a refusal to accept the actual
situation of Tibet? Perhaps the doors to Tibet are closed to us
forever,' Rigzin said.

'I too fear that. Yet, after years of oppression, the spirit of
our people remains intact. We have never won and yet we
have never accepted defeat. Meanwhile, I want to draw your

attention to the compound wall in TCV, and what it said in bold letters: Come to learn. Go out to serve.'

It wasn't long before Rigzin, willingly taking a hit in salary, began working for an agency facilitating educational opportunities in foreign universities. In the evenings, he volunteered to work for a charitable organization raising funds for Tibetan children. It brought him closer to the lives of children who had escaped from Tibet.

One day, he was filling in the form for an eight-year-old who had reached India after thirty-four days of a gruelling journey from Tibet. Sunburnt and snow-blistered, dehydrated, hungry, eyes watering, he was like a little soldier standing to attention in the imperceptible pause between a battle just fought and another yet to begin. Rigzin held the boy's hand and then embraced his stiff body. Gently, he whispered soothing words in the boy's ears, letting the heat of his own body and heart reach the slender frame in his arms. He rested his head on the top of the boy's head. In that moment, he was finally kind to himself. Somewhere, long awaited, he heard the soft murmur of a familiar voice behind the closed doors.

Two years later, as Rigzin stood in the muted midnight hour at the Delhi airport, on his way to Oxford, he wondered at the serendipity of his being offered a foreign scholarship. After meeting him at a conference in Delhi on the Tibetan plight, a professor from the School of Oriental and African Studies had quietly moved things to facilitate this opportunity.

An exultation filled him when he arrived at Oxford University, with its stone buildings covered with ivy, with its sights, sounds and smells of privilege. Within a week of his being there, it happened that a student wanted to discuss the *Tibetan Book of the Dead* with him, while another wanted to show him some obscure Tibetan text, which her father had purchased from a Tibetan monk. Mutual respect, he thought, marks our camaraderie, and with that, he began to feel his cultural wounds healing.

Six months later, he was sitting in the Bodleian Library with the hush of the evening hour upon him. He put down his book and smiled as he felt the moment of solitude deepen, become full. It struck him that had he remained in Tibet with his family, he would have grown up huddled in dark classrooms, repeating memorized texts and reading poetry in praise of Chairman Mao, too indoctrinated with lies to be capable of making any choice. He would have been an exile in his own country.

He realized his journey from home had not only forced him to cross geographical borders but also transcend mental confines. Most people experience one family, one home and one culture; he realized he was lucky to have been exposed to three. Wasn't this what his mother had hoped for him? The two doors, about which he continued to dream, now stood in contemplation over how the past might be redeemed and transformed by the present.

One day, when introduced to some new students, one of them—a Chinese national, asked him, 'Are you Indian?'

'I was born in Tibet but raised in India,' Rigzin replied.

The Chinese student smiled and said, 'Then you are Chinese, because Tibet is a part of China.'

An unspeakable anger flashed through him. But he kept an even tone as he replied, 'Well, I am more Indian than Chinese, but more Tibetan than Indian.'

'What does your passport say?'

Rigzin needed no further reminder. The calm was broken once again. No document proved his Tibetan identity because no country accepts Tibet as a separate nation. He was a part of what he abhorred.

Two events helped change his worldview. First came Tiananmen Square, changing the nature of the enemy for Rigzin. Powerful Chinese had mercilessly massacred defenceless Chinese. A firm distinction between the 'state' and the 'people' was now evident to him. The Chinese *state* had invaded Tibet, desecrated their culture and brutally repressed its people. Not all Chinese were the enemy. It also struck him that though his people had lost their country, and many were in exile, most of them did not feel bitterness or anger. Longing, yes; searing rage, no. Was this because his culture had some powerful tools to cope with suffering?

The second event gradually built intensity within him. One day, he stood on a stone bridge over a stream, admiring the weeping willows dipping their feathery fingers in the coolness of the water. He went and sat at the edge of the water, and watched his reflection. It occurred to him that no person or event had betrayed him; his expectations had. Events, in themselves, are neutral, he thought. When expectations are attached to them, they become pleasant or painful.

Was that why the dream of the two closed doors was empty of emotion? When he was a child, on awakening, his expectations imbued the dream with fright because he had expected nurturance. As he grew older, his expectations changed, and the two closed doors became a gift from his parents.

It occurred to him that since his expectations changed from year to year, sometimes even from day to day, who was the Rigzin who was sometimes happy and at other times sad, who grew or who stagnated?

He reasoned further, that there must be 'something' within him that did not change, that remained steady, and in relation to which the other aspects of him keep changing. Events and experiences are merely the stammering articulations of that intangible 'something', he reflected.

Late one afternoon, Rigzin stood in the British Museum, in front of the life-sized statue of the Lohan, an Arhat. It was discovered in the caves near Beijing in 1912. A strip of sunlight fell from the window and criss-crossed the floor as he looked at the man sitting cross-legged, with a noble head and a powerful face. There was a pensive contraction of the brows, the lips set in a faint smile, as if in triumph over the ordinary struggle. He could not meet the half-open eyes, for they seemed to look past and beyond him. He felt a strange power in his solar plexus. For a long while, he stood there transfixed by the thought that if such a state could shine through a statue, it had to be real. What one man could attain, it was possible for another to follow suit.

Silently, Rigzin sought the Lohan's permission to follow in his footsteps. For a flicker of a second, he felt the Lohan looked directly at him, the shaven head bathed in an odd radiance of assent. Or had the angle of the light changed just then? Wordlessly, the Lohan asked Rigzin to locate the source of a joy that is beyond the crucifixions of ambiguity, the darkening stains of conflict, the capriciousness of change. As if in confirmation, Rigzin's heart and mind became empty in a timeless moment of deep, soul-quenching silence. Only a luminescence remained, complete in itself. How long he remained in that state, he didn't know.

Find a path to return to that distilled moment, and between the searching and the finding, I will walk alongside you all the way, the Lohan seemed to say.

Rigzin knew the Lohan would keep his promise. Momentarily, the two closed doors had opened, not to let him in, but to go through.

The abbot resisted the urge to look at his watch. One cannot measure memory by time. From where I had stood, all roads led away from you, and yet they all converged towards you. Did the dream return tonight because I was reminded of something long forgotten? Anna's eyes echo the ache of irrevocable separations. And the look in Ajay's eyes, as they rested on Anna this afternoon, had the same ineffable feeling I had when I was with you. Perhaps we forget something, not because it is unimportant, but because it is too important.

Rozabal

12 August

Anna was a widow! The thought hammered at him as he mulched the newly planted pots in the greenhouse. He felt an odd sense of protectiveness towards her, overlaid with a mild discomfiture, knowing that his feelings were permitted entry, now that he knew her husband was dead. It was five years since his death, a long enough period for her to have recovered from the grief. No bereavement can be unending. Then what was she sorrowing about? Did she regret marrying him; was she grieving for the squandered years? He shook his head. That couldn't be. Her eyes turned as opaque as a river pebble and her voice sounded bewildered when she spoke of him, as though he were still real, his death unreal.

Ajay rested his chin on the shovel for a moment. Why did she inundate his thoughts? Was her past intersecting his in an odd confluence that could create a new story between them? In the process, would the past merely repeat itself or be redeemed?

Ajay's reverie was broken by the sound of Anna's voice. 'There are some cave paintings nearby, which I want to photograph. Would you like to come?'

This was certainly a first, she inviting him! Where was the shield of solitariness today?

They took the path up to the mountains, skirting the river. A chorten with a tapering spire glinting white in the brilliant sunlight was followed by a mani wall. In keeping with Buddhist tradition, Anna scrupulously kept both of them to her right. Ajay wanted to ask if John had taught her these little customs, but refrained. Instead, he asked if the diary leaf had yielded any more clues about the Notovitch manuscript.

'You realize, this discovery is not conclusive proof. It only introduces the idea of Jesus coming to India. There are other aspects that are perhaps more persuasive.'

'Oh, really?'

'Yes. You see, though Jesus was crucified, he may not have died on the Cross. One of the theories is that he was taken off and smuggled out of Jerusalem; some say to Devon, others to France. But both these places were within the footprint of the Roman Empire, and he wouldn't have been safe there. Notovitch makes India a strong possibility. If Jesus was here in his youth, he may have wanted to return.' The expectant look was back in her eyes.

'Give me a break, Anna! First, Jesus came to India in his youth. Now he did not die on the Cross! You don't expect me to buy that,' Ajay said incredulously.

'You think it can't be true?' She reacted sharply, her chin jutting out stubbornly.

They walked in silence for over an hour until they reached the caves, gouged into the mountain with huge boulders guarding the mouth. Carved on the walls were simple line etchings of ibexes, goats, and hunters with bows and arrows. Anna outlined the figures with her index finger, as if seeking a connection to the inscribed antiquity. 'These etchings could date back to the Neolithic Age,' she said, as she lifted her camera and began to take pictures.

Ajay shook his head in amazement. 'Is there anything you are not researching? Do you do anything for fun?'

'This is fun. These paintings, their origins, are relatively unknown. The only documented ones in this region are at Biamah. We don't know if these are ancient or recent copies.'

Ajay watched silently as she moved from painting to painting, taking close-ups and carefully angled shots. Then, unable to help himself, he blurted, 'Tell me, was your interest in the Jesus manuscript sparked by your husband?'

'Yes. It was his idea.' Anna lowered the camera and looked straight into Ajay's eyes.

'How did he get interested in the subject?' Ajay struggled to keep his tone impersonal.

Anna put her camera away and sat down on a boulder. 'It began when he was still in his teens. He was shocked to find discrepancies in the Bible, especially among the four Gospels. The three Synoptic ones—Matthew, Mark and Luke— disagree with each other, and with the Gospel of John. For example, in the latter, the ministry of Jesus was mainly in Judea, while in the others, it was in Galilee. Then there is disagreement over who carried the Cross. The Synoptic ones say it was Simon, while in John it was Jesus himself.'

'Doesn't that raise questions about the authenticity of the Gospels?'

'Not really. Jesus may have carried the Cross part of the way and then Simon may have helped. John's Gospel mentions only the former while the Synoptic ones describe Simon carrying the Cross. So, neither of them is wrong.'

She shook her head, as though in an effort to return to the present. 'The priests must have addressed John's early doubts. However, Notovitch's claim intrigued him. John argued that the Gospels were compiled more than forty years after the Crucifixion; their historical accuracy may not be reliable. So he decided to ascertain the truth for himself.'

'Even if there are discrepancies, it seems an improbable hypothesis. Difficult to believe.' Ajay sat down opposite her.

She nodded her head enthusiastically and said, 'Exactly! That's what I told John. Why did he believe Jesus lived through the Crucifixion much less that he came to India?'

'What did he say?'

Anna's eyes sparkled. 'He believed Jesus's death was as much a mystery as his early life. There are enough clues that made him believe that he was taken off the Cross when he was unconscious and then secretly healed.'

'Isn't death by crucifixion instantaneous?'

'Usually, it would take anywhere between two to five days. But if the full body weight was suspended solely at the wrists, death would occur within five to six hours; the shoulder muscles would go into spasm and gradually suffocate the crucified person. To prevent such an "easy" death, a small wooden crosspiece, a suppedaneum, was often fixed to the vertical post of the cross, on which the victim might prop himself and relieve the stress on the shoulders. However, if they wanted to hasten death, the legs would be broken.

'Some Gospels report that Jesus was nailed on the Cross at noon, and all of them state that he gave up the spirit at around 3 p.m. Death in three hours! Even Pilate was surprised by such a quick death. He sent for the leading centurion to confirm if Jesus was actually dead before he allowed his body to be taken off the Cross. Doesn't that make you wonder?'

'But, Anna, you just said if the legs are broken, it hastens death.'

'The soldiers, at the behest of Pilate, broke the legs of the other two men crucified along with him but Jesus was spared as they believed he was already dead. Jesus was as strongly built as the other two. Yet he died much earlier, while the others needed their legs to be broken! Inexplicable, isn't it?'

'Wasn't he weakened by the lashing he had received prior to the crucifixion?' Ajay asked.

'As per Jewish law, everyone who was crucified received thirty-nine lashes. Jesus was treated no differently. If the scourging had weakened him severely, would he have been able to carry the heavy patibulum, the crossbeam, on his shoulders to Golgotha? On the other hand, if Simon had carried it part of the way, he would have been less exhausted than the other two. Yet, he died very quickly. One of the soldiers had pierced Jesus's side with a spear, causing a sudden spurt of blood. If he was already dead, his heart would have stopped pumping. So what brought about this flow of blood?'

'Didn't that alert the soldiers to the fact that he wasn't dead?'

'That is the strange part. These same soldiers who had mocked Jesus now sympathetically offered him a sponge soaked in wine vinegar. Perhaps this bitter drink made him unconscious and led them to believe he had died. The Gospels are silent about the reason for this change of mood in the soldiers. Was it because of Joseph of Arimathea? A wealthy and influential man, he had asked Pilate for the body, and the centurion had willingly confirmed the rapid death. It is believed that he had been heavily bribed.'

Anna wrapped her arms around her knees and propped her chin on them, staring into the far distance. The boulder they were sitting on was still warm from the sun. 'Besides,' she rose as she said, 'why did Pilate allow the body to be taken down? According to Roman custom, the body was left to hang limp for days, a prey to ravenous birds, as a deterrent against sedition.'

'Are you suggesting that Joseph of Arimathea had anticipated all this? What was he trying to achieve?' Ajay felt that Anna's arguments made sense but a niggling doubt persisted: what was she trying to achieve? Her review of the Gospels was not evidence enough to rewrite history. Perhaps, concealed behind the search for clues to the missing years was her own untold story.

Anna nodded. 'I suppose he was trying to save Jesus.'

'Where was the medical help that could have saved him? Surely word would have reached Pilate if he had received medical attention.'

'Joseph of Arimathea, with the help of Nicodemus, had moved him to a newly prepared tomb near Golgotha. John's Gospel tells us that Nicodemus brought 75 pounds of healing herbs—aloe and myrrh, and applied them on Jesus's body, wrapping it in strips of linen.'

'The herbs may have been part of the Jewish burial custom,' countered Ajay. 'Why read a mystery story into it?'

She stopped mid-stride and turned to face him. 'Because, my dear Ajay, Jewish custom prescribes that the body should be washed and oiled, the hair cut and tidied, the body dressed and the face covered with a cloth. The use of herbs is mentioned nowhere. Aloe, in antiquity, was used for healing wounds and inflammations; myrrh, a gum resin, served as a disinfectant.'

Ajay watched her as she gazed at the mountains, his heart oddly attuned to this unusual woman with her extraordinary interests.

'May I also point out, that in John's Gospel, there is no mention of the body being washed. Instead, it says the women came to the tomb early on Sunday to oil Jesus's body. So, till then the body hadn't even been anointed with oil. Whatever Joseph and Nicodemus did with the herbs, it certainly had nothing to do with Jewish burial custom.' Anna's voice trailed away into silence.

She was two millennia away. Or was she remembering John?

After a long pause, Anna said reflectively, 'Individually, these facts may not raise any doubts. But on the whole, there are too many unanswered questions, and one is forced to ask if there could be another story, different from what we've heard these last two thousand years.' Returning to the Gospels, she said, 'The mystery doesn't end with the healing herbs and the lack of ritual oiling prior to burial. When the women came on Sunday, they found the tomb empty. The large stone guarding the entrance had been removed.'

'Jesus had resurrected!' Ajay stated the obvious.

'Yes. But to roll the stone back? The mystery of the Resurrection would have been greatly enhanced if they had found the stone still covering the entrance and the tomb empty.'

'Simple. The open entrance meant the resurrected Jesus had moved the stone to walk out of the sepulchre.'

'You, a Hindu, believe that!' thundered Anna. 'What resurrects: the spirit or the mortal body? Even if we believe it is the body, why couldn't it leave the tomb with the stone in place? Later on, when the resurrected Lord appeared to the Apostles, he walked through closed doors without opening them. If he did it then, why not that Sunday morning?'

'But you are denying the Resurrection! And, instead, suggesting that his disappearance from the tomb meant that he had recovered and was taken elsewhere to heal?' Ajay could hear the agitation in his own voice.

'What else? The empty tomb has a far simpler explanation than the Resurrection. They let him recuperate the whole of the Sabbath as no one would stir out, but he couldn't be left there for fear of the Jewish Council discovering he was alive. So they had to move him before anyone came on Sunday. Don't forget his body would have been unusually heavy with 75 pounds of herbs and the linen binding. If he had to be moved from the tomb, the stone would have to be removed.'

Ajay sat in silence, mulling it over.

'Okay. How would the subsequent events sound if we assume he was indeed revived?' There was an odd catch in Anna's voice as she tripped over the last word. 'Jesus demonstrating the earthly nature of his body to his followers by allowing them to touch him, his eating food with them and then telling them plainly that he was no ghost. Even showing the marks of his wounds and asking Thomas to touch them makes more sense if he had revived and his wounds had healed. The Resurrection can easily be understood as the resuscitation.' Anna's usually measured tones were fast and tripping, as if matching the rapidity of her thoughts.

It dawned on Ajay that she was telling two stories at the same time. The outer story involved the objective world of documents and proofs of the historical Jesus, and the private, inner narrative was one of loyalty to the hidden world of her desires. Those desires impelled her to defy Jesus's death, interpreting 'resurrection' to mean his revival. Ajay had often heard his bereaved relatives say that they dreamt of their loved ones being alive again. Was Jesus's revival her disguised alive-again dream for John? Were these two narratives—of scholarship and her love for a particular scholar, powering each other?

Anna stood there looking expectantly at Ajay. He pulled himself out of his thoughts and asked, 'Isn't Christian dogma uniquely centred on the Resurrection?'

'Perhaps that is why this thesis cannot be considered,' Anna said wistfully. It was the wistfulness of an opportunity lost.

Ajay was quiet. Centuries of history couldn't be overthrown by a single contrarian view. 'All this is circumstantial evidence. Is there no tangible proof?'

'For that matter, there is not a single piece of scientific evidence that a historical figure named Jesus existed in the real world. Our belief is based on the account given in the Gospels. And what do they tell us? There was virgin conception, he raises the dead back to life, miraculously feeds five thousand people with a single loaf of bread and, after his crucifixion, he bodily resurrects and then ascends to Heaven. This is closer to mythology than science. Just because people have believed for two thousand years that he died on the Cross doesn't necessarily mean it's the truth!'

'Still, to discard an age-old belief for another hypothesis, a tangible argument must be given.'

Anna thought for a moment, then said, 'The Turin Shroud. A linen cloth long enough to be a burial shroud, and which is kept in the royal chapel of the Cathedral of Saint John the Baptist, in Turin. It comes close to what you are looking for. Imprinted on it is the image of Jesus. One half carries the impression of his back, and the other half, of the front of his body.'

'Why would you say the Shroud belonged to Jesus?'

'It clearly shows the imprint of someone who was crucified, the bleeding feet and hands. I know that could apply to anyone, but this cloth is bloodstained at the side where he was lanced and at the forehead, where the crown of thorns had dug into his flesh. Perhaps it is Christianity's most important relic. It miraculously preserves its most significant moment for posterity.' Her voice was low, almost venerable.

'But other victims could have bled from the side and the forehead?'

'No injury to the thighs or calves is visible, since his legs were not broken. Then, in 1898, when the Shroud was photographed for the first time, the negatives showed the real face of Jesus. The divided beard and the central parting of the hair indicate he was from Palestine and a member of the Nazarene community. A dozen or more different and unmistakable features can be seen on the face, that are also found in the Byzantine portraits of Jesus. All this cannot be a coincidence.'

Anna continued, 'Electron microscope investigations of the fibres of the Shroud revealed that the image was not painted on to the linen. It had become visible because the blood had darkened some fibres. In contrast, others appeared in a lighter shade. So, we have a three-dimensional life-sized image. Through this, his height was estimated to be five-feet-eleven and his weight eighty kilos.'

'And how does the Shroud prove that he didn't die on the Cross?'

'Because two separate bouts of bleeding are encrusted on it. One lot is the caked blood that must have flowed when he was nailed and alive. A second trail of blood, which must have flowed much later, is visible on the Shroud in many areas, especially at the back of his head. When alive and on the Cross, Jesus's head had slumped forward, and any fresh blood would have trickled downwards and not to the back of his head. However, when he was laid horizontally in the tomb, any fresh bleeding, arising from the removal of the superficially embedded thorns in the skin of the head, would have trickled to the back of his head and marked the linen.'

'That is incontestable.'

'But if he was already dead then, what caused this second bout of bleeding?' The question hung in the air between them for a moment before she continued, 'Blood is pumped to the capillary vessels just under the surface of the skin only when the circulatory system is functioning. There is no way any fresh blood can emerge from a wound after death, as any residual intra-vascular blood immediately clots. But the back of the head clearly shows many large-sized blood trails streaming in all directions. This, and similar evidence from other wounds, leads one to ask whether he did indeed die on the Cross.'

'How does the Church view the authenticity of the Shroud?'

'They neither endorse it, nor deny it, though Pope John Paul II reputedly called the Shroud "a mirror of the Gospel". What I've given you is a brief and rather simple account of the analysis that the Shroud has undergone. Perhaps it is the most researched object in the history of the world!'

The silence was like a shawl wrapped around them. Anna's mind lingered with the story she had just read into the Gospels; his with what had been left unsaid. In reversing Christian history, was she in some inexplicable way inverting her personal one too?

'If Jesus had lived in India for a long time, there must be some proof of it. I am not going to quote the Indian scriptures and literature that refer to his presence here, because you will wash it away as oral tradition. There is more solid evidence, a testimony in stone that has survived the millennia,' Anna said earnestly.

Ajay looked at her, surprised. 'Really!'

'I am talking about the grave in Rozabal, in Srinagar, and the plaster cast of feet with holes, as if nails had been driven into them.'

'Come on. Anyone could have done that knowing about the Crucifixion.'

'Except, in this case, the holes are not in the centre of the feet. They correspond exactly to the place where the spike was driven into Jesus's feet placed one atop the other, the left over the right.'

'And the holes match those on the Turin Shroud?'

'Yes, sir!' Anna's voice rose three notches as she delivered the clinching proof. 'In fact, there are two tombstones at Rozabal; the smaller one is of a fifteenth-century Islamic saint, and the larger one is of Yuz Asaf.'

Ajay interrupted, 'So why should we believe that Jesus was buried there?'

'Both tombstones are aligned north–south, following the Islamic tradition. But, as we know from other tombs in India, the actual grave is located in a burial chamber below, and the sarcophagus of Yuz Asaf is aligned east–west, in accordance with Jewish custom! Clearly, Yuz Asaf was not a Muslim saint. Also, documentary evidence exists that a building had already been constructed over the crypt by 112 AD.'

'Okay, that is centuries before the Prophet. Granted Yuz Asaf was Jewish. That still doesn't mean he was Jesus,' Ajay argued.

'John's research led to evidence of a charismatic preacher by the name of Yuz Asaf, who arrived in Kashmir from Israel, sixteen years after Jesus's crucifixion,' Anna said slowly.

'Hang on! So Jesus was crucified and possibly revived. Years later, Yuz Asaf appeared in Kashmir. The two events may have nothing to do with each other,' Ajay protested.

Her faintly intoxicating fragrance and the warmth of her breath lay heavy in the air as Anna leaned forward, and continued eagerly, 'That's precisely what I said to John. But then he told me that in Parthia, olden-day Persia, Jesus was known as Yuz Asaf. Yuz means "leader" and the healed lepers were called Asaf —"the purified". So Yuz Asaf means "leader of the healed". Various manuscripts confirm that Yuz Asaf and Jesus were one and the same man.' She fell silent and he could tell that each time she said those words, they moved her.

'In 1989, a request was made to the Kashmir administration to open the sarcophagus of Yuz Asaf and examine its contents. On the evening before work could commence, violence erupted in the old town of Srinagar. Nothing more can be done in that direction. We will have to wait until peace returns to the valley.'

Anna's words seemed to merge with the silence of the centuries.

After a pause, she said, 'Look, it isn't as if I don't have reservations about all this. That's why I keep searching. Suppose, just suppose, we come across an ancient manuscript that tells of Jesus visiting India. It would be a personal confirmation that John was right in his belief. It would terminate my search. I would have discharged my debt. I cannot rest until then.'

She pressed her fingers into her shoulder muscles, as he had watched her do many times, and winced with the pain. Her shoulders ached most, Ajay thought, when she spoke of John and her debt to him. She stretched her neck backwards and pushed her shoulders out, as though following an exercise regimen.

Ajay sat watching her, threading together the strands of their conversation. She couldn't *rest* because it was John's interest she was carrying forward. She was keeping him alive by keeping his research alive. If she could establish that Jesus had come to India, it would vindicate John. Central to her interest in Buddhism and Jesus, Ajay realized, was the figure of her dead husband. Notovitch neatly connected the two together—that Jesus had lived in India, and that Buddhism had influenced his teachings.

Her research of the Christ story formed a Mobius strip, which had only one surface, one boundary. Cut the strip and you got two interlocked circles: one circle was the historicity of Jesus and the other revealed her deep desire for John. And, within those two circles, she spiralled backward and forward, with the result that there was no closure to her loss, only an unspeakable longing. Why, he wondered, was the debt she spoke of so painful and its discharge so difficult?

If you scratched the surface, each anomaly in the Jesus story could become a metaphor for John's death and perhaps her debt. The sum of her argument was that Jesus's death was mysterious. Was John's too? That Jesus could not have died so quickly on the Cross perhaps meant the reverse. Had John died unexpectedly? Jesus was revived by healing herbs; why couldn't John be revived by modern medicine?

Was there something mysterious about John's death, so that her shoulders ached even if she mentioned it? She had buried John but not her pain. Maybe her debt to him was connected to his death. Ajay wondered whether it was her love for John or its absence that was creating the compulsion.

Deadlock

13 August

The pealing of temple bells and the dying notes of the gong echoed in the early morning stillness. The sounds wove themselves into his dream of Swati persistently calling his name. Hurriedly Ajay swung his legs off the bed, and groped for his phone, worried that all his attempts to call Swati had failed. He switched on his cell phone. No signal. Perhaps he could catch the network in the village. Cool air greeted him as he reached the courtyard. He hurried down the steps to the road and checked his mobile again. Still nothing. It was a good twenty-minute walk to the three shops that constituted civilization. None of them were open. Ajay enquired of a lone Ladakhi man walking past if the signal in the phone booth had been restored. The shake of the man's head could have meant anything, from incomprehension to the absence of a phone connection anywhere.

He walked ahead, pondering the situation. He had been desperate to get away from Swati and the detritus of their marriage, only to find himself becoming embroiled in thoughts of her. Would that wretched birthday card to Akanksha continue to sit between them, translating all his truths into lies for her? His feet ached by the time he reached another hamlet and checked with the lone phone booth there, only to be greeted again with a shake of heads. No connection, no signal. An apt metaphor for his relationship with Swati, he thought wryly, as he headed back to the monastery, the scattered autumnal leaves on the side of the road a stark reminder of approaching winter.

How ironical, he thought. The abbot talks of the mind being an impediment to loving, of giving in love, while the reality of my marriage is so far removed from that.

On reaching the monastery he went straight to the abbot's room.

'You are troubled,' the abbot said without raising his eyes.

'How did you know?' Ajay asked, startled.

The abbot looked up. 'Your thoughts entered before you.'

Silence stretched between them; Ajay kept standing, restlessly shifting his weight from one leg to the other.

'I feel dissatisfied...stuck! I am left with the feeling that the most important years of my life are behind me. And I ask myself: What has it all amounted to?'

'Has something specific brought this on?' the abbot inquired.

There was an infinitesimal pause before Ajay said, 'Probably. My wife and I...something is not right between us.' He faltered and then went on, 'No communication and much resentment. The spark is gone, and even the ashes are cold now.'

'They wouldn't have gone cold if the fire had been stoked.'

Thrown off balance by the abbot's comment, Ajay's restlessness stilled. Was there a subtle admonition in the abbot's words? Ajay picked up a mat and sat down next to the abbot, and, in a stream of words, poured out the entire story.

'Swati keeps accusing me of being in love with Akanksha, despite my assuring her time and again that I am not. She is convinced I am refusing to accept the truth. She has pushed our marriage to the edge with all her drama and unnecessary intensity, forcing me to dialogue with her delusions, reversing the order of who the real victim is.' Ajay pulled himself short. 'I don't know why I am telling you all this. Of what interest could it be to you?'

'If your nose is clean, then why are you flustered by her accusations?' asked the abbot.

'Don't you understand, it's not me but she who is upset!'

'Are you aware that your breathing is short and fast, and your voice is raised? That usually happens when people are angry.'

'I am sorry, but I am at my wit's end. I have never touched Akanksha. How am I unfaithful?' Ajay pushed his hands deep into his pockets.

'What does she say?'

'Swati says unfaithfulness begins in one's thoughts and it's only a matter of time before they will translate into action. I am being condemned for a crime I have yet to commit,' Ajay said, his voice rising in indignation.

'Aren't you equating love with sensuality? Does lack of sexual attraction mean absence of love?' The abbot chuckled and added, 'Sometimes there can be sexuality but no love.'

'I have never felt attracted to Akanksha in that way.'

'Sometimes we love without being aware of it.' Seeing Ajay's disbelieving look, the abbot said, 'Does an infant know that it loves its mother? Yet, that is the most profound form of love we experience. Before I was taken away from my home, was I consciously aware that I was deeply attached to my mother?'

'Swati is certainly not implying that I love Akanksha like a child loves its mother,' Ajay retorted. 'To add grist to her mill, we met an old acquaintance at a movie theatre one day, from our management trainee days. Swati had gone off to buy popcorn and returned exactly at the moment when he was asking me about Akanksha. In fact, he was asking when we had got married.'

'What did you say?' the abbot asked.

'You can imagine, all hell broke loose as soon as we were alone. A mere acquaintance had confirmed what I had dismissed as her overactive imagination. She capped it all by saying anyone could see the way feelings were flowing between Akanksha and me when we first met again, at the party.' Ajay rubbed his chin in a self-calming gesture.

'After that, she became the third in our marriage. My denial and Swati's affirmation kept her alive long after she had gone from our lives. Akanksha was just a friend to me, no doubt my best friend.'

'You may think you are friends but subconsciously there may be other forces at work. As Freud famously said, we are not masters of our own house.' The abbot changed tack. 'If the whole fault lies with your wife, then it would need to be asked, why she is doing this? Is she against you?'

'Not at all! It's just that she is pinning on Akanksha all the unresolved problems between us. Then she won't have to face her own problems,' Ajay said.

'Agreed. But you said *our* problems. Did you contribute to those problems?' The abbot looked piercingly at Ajay.

'In this instance, the blame is hers.' Ajay paused, shaking his head and frowning. 'Akanksha was never the real issue between us. She only triggered our fault lines. Much before her brief re-entry, our marriage had its irritants, kept at bay by our mutually cordoned-off roles. That reduced friction but also prevented any real intimacy.'

'When did it start?' the abbot asked.

'I think it began after Neha's birth, five years into our marriage. I was mesmerized by our little daughter. When she wrapped her soft, boneless fingers around my little finger, I became her slave for life.' Ajay's brow cleared, his eyes lit up.

The abbot smiled at Ajay's transformed face.

'One day, we were at the doctor's, arguing over the cure for diaper rash and Neha's persistent cough, when the doctor looked at me and said: As a rule, the mother is always right. From then onwards, Swati took almost all the decisions regarding Neha. I became the parent who played with her briefly before she was whisked away by the ayah or her mother. Swati complained that I never helped and I felt she never let me.'

With regret in his voice he said, 'Neha also became the excuse for us to never confront our issues. Everything became: not now; not in front of the baby.' Ajay's voice mimicked a hissed whisper. 'How can you speak to me like that when I have not slept a wink in a week? You do nothing but find fault.' His voice rose in pitch to match the grievance.

Suddenly the abbot clapped his hands. The loud, sharp sound startled Ajay.

'Both hands were needed to make that sound.'

For a moment Ajay was stumped. Not a thought, not a stir of a response came to his mind.

'You are suggesting that Swati revels in her neurosis and you are a helpless bystander, passively involved in a marriage over which you have no control. When a conflict arose, you contributed nothing to it and were merely its victim. That cannot be the truth.'

The abbot looked at Ajay assessingly. 'You don't appear to be the sort who can be easily walked over. You are in this situation because you want to be in it. Rather than blame her, identify what you are doing to keep the situation alive. Change that and things will change.'

Ajay felt like he was being shown a mirror, one in which a rather unflattering reflection looked back at him. The two men sat quietly, lost in thought. The abbot broke the silence. 'What happens to two porcupines on a cold winter night?'

Ajay waited for him to continue without attempting a response.

'They huddle together to keep warm, but then their quills poke and they withdraw from each other. That is what happens to most couples. We are always aware of the other's quills poking us, but seldom of our own.

'If she has come to the marriage with baggage, so have you. You feel she created a "third" in the marriage—Akanksha— to displace her own problems. By the same token it can be asked: what is the "third" you created to displace your own shortcomings?' He smiled to soften the directness of his query. 'Maybe, all Swati is looking for is the lost love between you and her, pleading for it to be rekindled. Please accept, that like you, she too is suffering. In fact, her accusations may in reality be a cry for help.'

Ajay had expected sympathy, some consolation. Instead, he had been put in the hot seat. He hesitated for a moment, trying to read the abbot's expression, amazed that a celibate monk could discuss his marital imbroglio with the ease of a seasoned counsellor.

After a while he asked, 'Which part of me do you think is keeping the situation alive?'

'I am not a magician,' the abbot said. 'But yes, something did occur to me. Why didn't you immediately post the birthday card to Akanksha? By leaving it in your bedside drawer, did you want Swati to find it? Was it a means to tell her about your feelings for Akanksha? Or was it to convey your hurt about other things? And, if so, why was Akanksha the medium through which you sought to convey your feelings of hurt to Swati?'

Each question jolted him. Did I unconsciously leave the card there for Swati to see? I couldn't have done it to convey my feelings for Akanksha. There had been too much upheaval already about it. A thought flashed past, taking him by surprise. Perhaps his hurt predated the Akanksha episode. But then, did he feel like a victim too? Perhaps Swati was not the only one who was being neurotic. As the abbot had asked: why had he used Akanksha to convey his hurt to Swati?

Ajay rested his head against the wall, confused.

The abbot's eyes remained alert as he watched Ajay. Was a long shut window edging open?

Finally, Ajay turned to the abbot. 'I don't know why I did that. Maybe I was desperate. Maybe I feared my own feeling of deadness. Maybe I dimly realized that I could see Swati only through the lens of my hurt. I see now that it had nothing to do with Swati's accusations about Akanksha.

The seeds lay in the earlier part of our marriage. And yet, I still regard my hurt as a reaction to Swati and not as my contribution to the mess.'

The abbot sighed. 'Isn't it strange? When you first met your wife, she was a stranger. When you married her, she became a part of you. When she questioned you, she became your enemy. Can't you see it is your perception of her that has changed from love to antagonism? She has probably remained the same person. So, there must be something within you that is causing the changed perception.'

To Ajay's fanciful gaze, it seemed as though the abbot's eyes flashed black lightning that penetrated his mind and reached the very depths of it. He looked away, disconcerted, and then took his leave. When he looked back at the door, the abbot was sitting with his eyes shut, rosary in hand.

Honeymoon

14 August

'Did you know that Akanksha and Swati were best friends?' Ajay declared urgently to the abbot as soon as he entered his room early in the morning. His voice was excited, as though a very important clue had been withheld, one that could alter the abbot's opinion of the situation. 'It was *Akanksha* who introduced me to Swati.'

The abbot looked surprised.

'We had gone to Mumbai for an assignment, and Akanksha was keen that I meet her childhood friend over dinner.'

Uncharacteristically, the abbot interrupted Ajay. 'Why?'

'I don't know. All I remember is that I had ordered fish in tomato and basil sauce. Swati had looked at me and said, "How strange, that's my favourite too. I'll have the same." She shut the menu and smiled broadly at me. And I was hooked.'

'How did Akanksha respond?'

'Very strangely, as a matter of fact. She looked at Swati and exclaimed, "But you can't marry him!" It was so completely out of context that Swati and I looked at each other, wondering what had come over her.'

'Interesting, very interesting!'

Ajay rocked back on his heels in defence. 'If I had loved Akanksha, what would have prevented me from marrying her? I fell in love. Where is the complication?'

'None,' the abbot said with a touch of amusement. 'Agreed, it was love at first sight. But does that mean you forgot Akanksha?'

'No. She was still my *best* friend.'

'Of course! I wouldn't be surprised if your best friend had invited Swati to dinner so she could approve of you. Maybe Akanksha's remark was meant to warn Swati: he's mine, so keep off!'

Ajay took a deep breath and said, 'I thought it was more than evident that I had eyes only for Swati?'

'That didn't mean Akanksha was left behind. She was the pair of spectacles through which you viewed Swati. The "third"…'

Ajay frowned.

'Akanksha may have moulded your image of how your wife should behave—appreciative without expressing her own preferences; always sensitive to your needs. Perhaps Swati's accusations are not about sexual infidelity but emotional infidelity.'

Ajay grew thoughtful. The abbot was not defending Swati, but he was questioning Ajay's static understanding of the situation.

'Can't you see, all three of you were powerfully connected? But none of you could afford to acknowledge the extent of it, and therefore had to part ways. Just as inevitably, it came back into your lives.'

'I am sorry, what was that?' Ajay said.

'The shadow of the road not taken.'

There was a pregnant pause. Then the abbot said, 'Isn't it curious? The whole thing surfaced at that party where the three of you accidentally met.'

'No, it was later. A slip of the tongue became the flashpoint. I don't know what came over me!'

Ajay sighed with relief at being able to talk about the contentious incident. 'We were with our friends Mohit and Rachna. After dinner, a message beeped on my cell phone. I was reading it as I turned towards Swati and said: "Akanksha, pour me a glass of water please".'

'What happened then?'

'I think Rachna poured the water for me. Nobody spoke. I was absentminded enough to think the evening had wound to a close, and asked Swati if we should go?

'I can still remember the way she got up and said, "I hope you know which woman you are going home with?" Her voice was strained.'

The abbot nodded.

'Later, I pleaded that it was just a slip of the tongue. A switch in names is hardly an eruption of obscured passion, the smell of infidelity or some deadly denial. Just a simple processing error of the brain that happens all the time to practically everyone.

'But she wouldn't relent. I remember exactly what she said. "It matters very much when the slip occurs. You did it in a conversation about making choices."'

'Choices?' the abbot enquired.

'Oh! I didn't tell you. We had gone to see *The Merchant of Venice* earlier that evening and it had evoked many memories of our schooldays. Swati told us that her English teacher, an Irish nun, had told them: "Think like Bassanio. Open the least favourable and find the most valuable." That's how the discussion on choices had taken off. Mohit said one chooses what one desires. I had protested, saying we may be unaware of what we desire.'

'You said that!' The abbot quickly seized the connection. 'Yet, you disagreed when I suggested it the other day?'

Yes, Ajay wondered, why had he resisted?

'I told Mohit that I had been unaware of how much poetry interested me until I picked up a book of poems and read it. That pleased Swati immensely. I held her hand and quoted Bassanio: "Madam, you have bereft me of all words, only my blood speaks to you in my veins." The evening was humming. It was then that I committed the self-sabotage.'

'Did you ask yourself why?' the abbot said.

'Our relationship skidded downhill after that. I can't take it back. I don't know what came over me, why that slip occurred,' Ajay said, lost in regret.

'Don't you, even by now?' the abbot retorted.

The mirror was foggy. Superimposed on his reflection was Swati's, making unclear whose awkward edges were actually showing.

'Help me,' Ajay appealed to the abbot.

'Akanksha remained your invisible companion. For you, she represented intimacy, fusion, a sense of completeness. She was an ineffable feeling, your expectation from love.' The abbot then presented the simplest way to resolve the problem. 'Let go of those expectations and the "third" disappears!'

15 August

An unexpected mood of restfulness came upon him. The burden of not knowing had lifted a little. There was a light switch somewhere in the dark room. All he had to do was grope his way towards it, and maybe, the complexities of his story would come to light.

The seeds of what happened later lay in that first meeting with Swati. His entry altered the equation that existed between the two friends. By choosing Swati, he had turned it volatile. Swati and Akanksha were unlike one another. Akanksha grew upon you unnoticed; Swati, you could not help but notice. Akanksha entered the room quietly, spoke softly and dressed conservatively. She openly admired Swati's quick wit, her ability to hold people's attention, the bold splash of colours in her clothes and in her paintings. It was as if Swati was Akanksha's unexpressed and unlived self.

Ironically, Swati secretly admired Akanksha for being far more observant, for her self-containment, in which she sensed wisdom. Despite that, a hierarchy existed between the two friends. Swati was the leader, and held all the privileges of that role. Maybe his instant attraction to her only confirmed Akanksha's worst fear—Swati, by right, would take the first pick. No wonder she had protested: "But you can't marry him!"

In this unravelling of the skeins of the past, something forgotten stirred in Ajay—the memory of their honeymoon in Mauritius.

They had just finished enjoying a barbecue dinner on the beach, the dark blue sea indistinguishable from the night sky above them. Swati's shining hair framed her oval face, her eyes danced as they rested on him. When she smiled at him, her heart in her eyes, a glow spread from the soles of his feet to his legs, became a roaring fire, engulfed his torso and spiralled up to his head. In that instant, he felt his body and everything else vanish—Swati, the sand, the sea, the sky. He did not know how long he stayed in that state.

From afar, Swati's voice drifted to him. 'Where have you gone?'

Slowly, he became aware of his body again, his hand on the table, the sea singing its way to the shore, and the breeze a balm of benediction.

He focused on Swati's face as she said, 'You looked so happy, almost exultant. What were you thinking?'

'Of you, and being one with you.'

She looked startled, then said softly, 'How beautiful, Ajay.'

'I was transported. Like I had left myself behind.' He spoke tentatively, unsure of how to capture the essence of the experience. 'Something soaked in joy filled me.'

'Honeymoon highs,' Swati teased.

It was as perfect a moment as any mortal could wish for. He closed his eyes and wished for it to last forever.

Surprisingly, from the cold ashes of their relationship had arisen, phoenix-like, this warm, glowing ember. Ajay's respect for the abbot grew. He was not alluding to a fabled story when he had asked him to look within. He had succeeded in reminding him of something experienced a long time ago, an epiphany where neither he nor she had existed, only the music of an undying bliss. Was he truly awake then, or now?

When listening to a symphony on a disc, if there is a scratch near the end that makes a screeching sound, it tends to ruin the whole experience. The fact that it ended imperfectly does not mean all of it was bad. Similarly, Ajay asked himself: why was he dwelling on his relationship with Swati by the screeches of the recent past? Did the greater part of their life count for nothing? If he were to look back, his feelings for Swati had remained unchanged, even long after their courtship and wedding. Often, his eyes would be drawn to her in a room full of people. He enjoyed listening to her relate a story, her turn of phrase, her great knack for mimicry, her unerring sense of picking the comical. Swati had brought a passionate nature and a loyal commitment to their marriage. She had supported him in his choices, whether it was a change of jobs, moving to a new city or adapting to the demands of his career. She fought fiercely for those she loved, devoted herself to them. When her sister's child, Atul, was diagnosed as autistic, she had applied herself to try and comprehend his world.

She loved Neha with all the gratitude of a parent who had not been tested as her sister was. She taught Neha how to give to Atul, and to do so without expectations. When Neha wanted a puppy, they went to a kennel and brought home an old, lame Alsatian abandoned by his owner. Mother and daughter had stood in front of him, and Swati had spontaneously called out, 'Frodo! Want to come home with us?' The dog did not respond. But when they opened the car door, he jumped into the back seat without any prompting. Ajay remembered how surprised he had been to see Swati drive into the house with a new passenger sitting upright and staring ahead calmly. He was not sure what had moved him more—Frodo owning them, or Swati's empathy.

Inseparable from that empathetic and devoted Swati was the other side to her, which was demanding, possessive and deeply emotional. When hurt, she shouted, slammed doors or subjected him to evenings of frosty silences.

Would this impasse with Swati end if he could reconnect to the state he had felt on their honeymoon? How could that moment have vanished so completely, thwarted by unmet expectations, where words became wounds leading to festering sores? Time had cleaved a wide chasm between this remembering and the forgetting, with no bridge to navigate the distance. Why is one unable to see the disarray in one's life until the fault lines give way, Ajay asked himself helplessly.

Had he been endlessly ingenious in devising ways not to accept the problem? He found himself sitting opposite the abbot, his normal machinery of denial in abeyance.

'When you are in love, your feelings flow naturally. So to say, the veils of self-centredness are to some extent lifted. You didn't only rekindle the memory of an event on your honeymoon; it was also a reminder of how you viewed Swati then? Can you tell me what you felt for her?'

'Not only me, but both of us saw each other through blissful eyes.'

'You were given a glimpse of what love is. It happened spontaneously.' There was a flash of sadness in the abbot's eyes. 'This spontaneous state, however, seldom lasts very long. The veils fall again. Most people then blame the other person for not being what he or she seemed to be. Or they blame themselves for having succumbed to an illusion inspired by sexual desire.'

Ajay looked curiously at the monk. How did he know all this?

'What do you think I am? Only a monk? I am also a man,' the abbot laughed at what he saw on Ajay's face.

By now, Ajay thought, I should be used to the man's ability to pick up the unspoken, but it still unnerves me and leaves me uncomfortable at being so transparent. Yet, it broke a barrier within him and he confessed, 'Maybe I do not know what love is besides the flush of sexual desire.'

'*You* did not fall in love; through Swati, you felt the presence of love itself. Lovers do not seek pleasure; they seek the loss of the self in each other. Isn't that what you experienced spontaneously in Mauritius?'

'Can it be recaptured?' Ajay asked quietly.

'Yes! Even in the experience of ordinary sex, there is always an element of self-transcendence. But, to be able to do that, you must remember you are not the husband or the wife; you are the love between the two,' the abbot remarked as he got up to open the window.

Ajay closed his eyes and leaned back against the wall. A breeze blew in from the window, the paper lamp hanging from the ceiling swayed and spread the muted light in spiral pathways across the floor.

Ajay opened his eyes and looked at the dim silhouette of the man outlined against the window frame in the lengthening evening shadows. Who was this unknown man who seemed so familiar, who seemed to have bent down to gather the spilled sadness of his broken dreams, and offered him slivers of hope, his words glimmering like a talisman in the darkness?

'At the moment, your love is an instinctive love. For now, she is merely an object that either fulfils or frustrates you. Can you look through the person to the presence of love itself? To that which unites you both?'

'Well, Swati and I...' Ajay fumbled, unable to answer the question.

'You can only know real love by getting yourself out of the picture.'

Ajay looked quizzically at him.

'It means looking at one's hurts, anger, resentments as symptoms of an inability to face one's own weaknesses. Real love is based on conscious choices.'

'Does such love exist?'

The abbot's face softened, his eyes shone like embers glowing in the fireplace of faith or experience, Ajay could not tell which. They were lit by a power that spoke more than words ever could. Then the abbot looked straight at him and said, 'I am not asking you to believe in me. Turn back if you want to. Do what you must, but don't stand irresolute.'

Ajay lowered his eyes in confusion and the last words he heard, before he returned to his room, were, 'It's always the mind that gets in the way. Stop the mind. Silence your thoughts and then you will look through your eyes with the light of love.'

Ambivalence

Out of sheer curiosity, Ajay tried stopping his thoughts. Sitting cross-legged on the floor, he closed his eyes. A strand of hair fell on his forehead and triggered a chain of thoughts. I need a haircut… Sylvie is a neat hairdresser… The mirrors in his salon seduce you to look at yourself… How strange there are no mirrors in the monastery… How does the abbot shave without a mirror… Tibetans have much less hair… Would Swati have talked to the abbot about her side of the story… How would she have reacted if the abbot had told her she was an equal contributor… Anna is often in the abbot's room… How come he knows so much about marriage… about love?

A muscle in his leg went into a spasm and Ajay's eyes flew open. He shook his head and got up. Bloody hell, not a pause between one thought and the next.

What a pointless exercise, he thought as he wandered into the courtyard, and then decided to go down towards the river where Anna and he usually went for their afternoon walk. Is it possible to locate a quiet place within a person that wakes to no anguish? A grove of poplar trees gently swayed in the cool and crisp air, the sun drizzling them with a soft glow. He found a shaded spot and reclined against a tree. When he opened his eyes, Anna was standing beside him.

'Deep in thought. What were you thinking?' she asked.

'How to stop thinking!' Ajay quipped. 'Tell me, what's the big deal about stopping thoughts?'

She smiled, 'For a brief moment, you are powerful enough to stop the world.'

'Isn't the ability to think important?'

'No one is suggesting you stop thinking. In fact, the mind should be used when needed, and then withdrawn back into stillness, like a pencil on a spring returns to its original position.'

'And what happens when you can stop thoughts?' Ajay asked.

'The quiet mind is like being in love, without any person to love.'

Ajay sat silently chewing on the analogy. It was provocative; it was personal. Was she conveying something to him?

'Why did the abbot ask you to quieten your thoughts? Are you getting interested in the meditational practices in Tibetan monasteries!' she teased.

After a while he confessed, 'My tidy, picture-book life is not all intact.'

'Whose is?' she said, with an odd mingling of vulnerability and empathy in her voice.

He told her his story. Then, he mentioned how the abbot was nudging him to see his contribution to the impasse in his marriage.

'Have you been able to get in touch with Swati?'

'No. I've tried several times.'

'Poor Swati. I imagine once it hit her that Akanksha was in love with you, it must have been difficult for Swati to come to terms with marrying her best friend's man? Maybe a part of her inverted the guilt into believing Akanksha was stealing her husband,' Anna said.

'I never thought of that!' A startled Ajay said.

Good lord, yes! Guilt could very well be the ghost that haunted her, he thought. With her accusations, she pushed him back to Akanksha and, at the same time, she didn't want to let him go. She oscillated between the satisfaction of returning what she had stolen and her anxiety at losing him. What a goddamn tangle!

'I wish I could tell her that I can see my side of the story better now,' Ajay sighed. 'The abbot suggested that I may have conflicting feelings for both of them.'

'You know, Ajay, for a long time I believed you either love a person or you don't. Now I realize that is a piece of fiction. One both loves and is confused about the same person. Are you not able to understand Swati better once you accept that she might have ambivalent feelings for you that both draw her to you and also make her back off? To question whether she loves you or doesn't would be simplistic.'

He felt relieved that she had expressed a simple truth shorn of any disguise. Also, by stepping beyond accusations and infidelity, she had given a wide-angled view.

They climbed down a steep pathway and came to a bridge. The banks of the river were strewn with huge boulders acting like ineffectual checks in the purposeful haste of the flowing water. Together, they watched the play of light streaming through the trees onto the water. Anna's voice broke into his thoughts. 'There must be something else. Guilt alone does not explain the situation.'

He looked at her quizzically.

'What was your mother like?' Anna asked unexpectedly.

'What? What does she have to do with anything?'

Anna laughed. 'Sorry. That wasn't well put. What I meant to ask was about Swati's relationship with your mother.'

'My mother was very fond of her. It's her own father that confuses Swati. She idealizes him, but feels she gets only the crumbs of his affection. Her elder sister is his favourite,' Ajay said flatly.

'But of course!' Anna muttered something under her breath that Ajay didn't quite catch. 'Why didn't it strike me?'

'Uh?'

'The feelings she has about her father got transferred onto you. For Swati, you are the father who never gives enough, who prefers the other: Akanksha.'

'Come on, Anna. Surely she knows I am not her father.'

'When under stress, we tend to carry over emotions we had felt for our parents. Everyone does. I do. You do. So must she. Have you ever asked her father how Swati combatted stress as a child?'

Anna is one hell of a smart woman, Ajay thought. She is distracting me by letting Swati shoulder part of the blame.

'You appreciate that I know Swati only through your eyes. I may have picked up your unintentional bias,' Anna said, as if answering him.

They left the bridge to return to the monastery. Her hand brushed against his. Was that accidental, he wondered. Of late, she had seemed less distant. He picked up a smooth white pebble and placed it in her hand.

She looked at it lying on her open palm and closed her fingers over it. A wistful look flitted across her face. A breeze blew unobstructed between them.

He wanted to tell her of Swati's chilling rejection in the bedroom before he had left. More than anything, that had diminished him. 'Anna,' he said, and then broke off, stopped short by an innate hesitancy to share such an intimate detail. 'Did you and John holiday often?'

'Oh yes, we drove around the country, stopping often at farmhouses or little places that caught our fancy. John would seek out like-minded people.'

He looked up to find her face flushed and watching him intently. 'Swati and I had some great holidays… She loves to paint. I told you that.'

It occurred to him then that they were talking of their spouses as if to stem something that was coming into being between them. She wore no ring on her finger, though he had noticed that the skin was a shade fairer where once she had. For a long time, the finger must have felt naked.

Ajay touched her arm. He felt her warmth, or was it his own reflected back to him?

'It's getting cold. We are losing light rapidly. We better walk faster,' Anna said abruptly.

Anna's change of mood was a salutary reminder that either he had overstepped his bounds or she was skittish and scared. The mountains were a muted monochromatic brown in the dusky afterglow of the setting sun. Mirroring her mood. He smiled. Now I have begun giving a colour to her.

Silence had descended on the monastery; it was the 'quiet hour'. Ajay stretched his legs on the bed, his back propped on a pillow upright against the wall. He closed his eyes, evened his breathing and attempted to turn off the flow of images and thoughts from the mental projector. He was assailed by memories of his mother, most of them sights and smells. Strange. He had seldom thought of her since her death four years ago.

He was seated at the dining table with his two older brothers in their childhood home. His mother stood close by his side, smelling of garlic. The folds of her fleshy upper arm brushed his cheek as she put an extra dollop of meat curry—still his favourite dish—into his plate. Her affection was directly proportional to the amount of food she ladled into your plate. Why was he thinking of her? Was he pining for her food rather than be subjected to yet another supper of barley porridge?

His mother's large presence had filled their lives; her voice used to be everywhere: reprimanding the servant, haggling with the vegetable vendor, or trilling with laughter on the telephone. Always, Mother's friends and relatives filled the house. Father, as usual, sat in a corner of the living room, quietly reading the newspaper, relentlessly interrupted by her when he spoke and ignored when he did not.

His mind was all over the place. He had to stop it. He had to slow down the breathing. And his mind wandered again... I don't recall how old I was when I first realized that her affection and ministrations were devouring in nature, rather than an expression of maternal selflessness. She was controlling, always wanting her way. How I feared I would become like Father. How often I prayed that once, just once, my father would stand up to her, tell her to shut up or ignore her when she asked him to do something just when we were beginning a game of chess.

Are Mother's memories invading me because of Anna's question about her? Perhaps I am not accepting something by being critical of my mother. What frustrations had she hid behind her domineering ways? How come she permitted no dreams for herself, but dreamt through me? Whose dream has my success been fulfilling—my own or my mother's?

Maybe something in me longed to make up for the deficit life had dealt her. Alongside, without being conscious of it, had another part of me decided not to let anyone swamp me, as Father had been by Mother? Maybe from then onwards I developed crisp boundaries. Was that the reason for my not being able to flow towards Akanksha? Or as Anna might ask, is that why I felt injured and shut Swati out after Neha's birth?

Ajay shook his head ruefully. He could not believe that a difficult and demanding woman, dead and gone, was still the prism through which he viewed his relationships. Maybe Anna was right. We love and hate the same person.

The gong sounded, announcing supper.

Lhapa

18 August: Morning

An unexpected crisis hit the monastery. Nawang, a thirty-year-old monk with doe-eyes, was writhing with pain on the floor, clutching his left abdomen.

'Seems like a kidney stone. Horrid things! Probably eight on the Richter scale of pain to make Nawang groan like this,' the abbot muttered, looking worried. Nawang closed his eyes tightly as a fresh spasm of pain twisted his small frame and a single involuntary tear slipped past his clenched eyelids. Ajay rushed to his room for a painkiller. Half an hour later, Nawang was no better.

'We can't even get him to a hospital with the roads blocked,' Anna said.

One of the monks coughed. The abbot turned to him and he said something in Tibetan. The abbot nodded his head and said to Anna, 'A lhapa has come from the upper Changpa reaches, and he is in the village below for a short time. Our only option is to take Nawang to him.'

'But he needs a doctor,' Ajay protested.

'A lhapa is another kind of doctor. He is a shaman, a healer.' The abbot rose and gave rapid instructions to two of the monks.

Within minutes, a stretcher was improvised, and four monks carried Nawang on it. The abbot nodded his consent to Ajay and Anna to accompany the monks. Tsering led the party, walking ahead briskly as a self-appointed guide. The four men cautiously climbed down the monastery steps, careful not to jerk Nawang. 'Take your attention away from the pain,' Tsering advised Nawang. 'Focus on a blank white screen. Once attention is withdrawn, the pain becomes more bearable.' Nawang closed his eyes, and for a few moments, his body did relax.

'Practise with pain, practise without pain, but practise all the time,' Anna murmured with respect. The teaching seemed like a living being walking alongside them in every situation.

'Only a lithotripsy can remove kidney stones,' Ajay whispered sceptically to Anna. 'What can a lhapa do in a situation like this?'

'Oh Ajay! The shamanistic conception of disease is a different belief system. Like the allopath, the shaman also attributes disease to specific causes, but their attribution appears very strange to us. They believe demons and evil spirits enter human bodies, bringing illness. Or objects are magically intruded into the victims, causing disease. Just as we are convinced germs cause them, they believe black magic is the source,' Anna explained.

'Unbelievable. What's the proof?'

'I may develop an infection from a cut with a rusty knife. They ask what made the knife slip. An evil thought or a curse might have caused it to slip. They look for causes that made the knife slip while we attribute cause to what happens after the knife cut the skin.'

Ajay shrugged. 'Ok, you can't argue about someone's belief. But even if we grant this bizarre cause, how is the disease cured?'

'A lhapa mediates between this world and that of the gods. With the help of drumming or chanting, he enters a trance. I suppose you could say the lhapa vacates the body for the god called Lha to enter. This is a signal moment in the healing séance. The god then diagnoses and heals the sick person, or prophecies future happenings. After the god departs, the lhapa returns to his normal state, with no memory of what has taken place.'

Ajay said, 'If you were ill, where would you go?'

'You are being unfair. I would go to a modern hospital. But there are no doctors or hospitals in these remote areas. These people are poor. What are they to do? Resign themselves to their pain and not do anything because there is no lithotripsy available? Their forms of healing are different, but they may cure as well as antibiotics and surgery do. Have you ever asked yourself what people did before modern medicine, which is only two or three hundred years old? Did they just die? Surely, what is more important is whether a cure is found and not how rational the theory appears to us.'

Anna's remark hung in the air as they followed the river down to the village. Apple, apricot and walnut trees irregularly dotted the landscape. Cattle grazed on the edge of the fields, amidst the singing of a few village women working the land. The four stretcher-bearers kept up a steady trot, thanks to their Ladakhi lungs and their ascetic discipline.

Good-humouredly, they teased Nawang, telling him that one day, he would have to carry all four of them together as repayment of his karmic debt! Nawang's effort to smile turned into a grimace of pain, which was met with another story by the monk in the front, while another hummed along, as though to put music to the story.

On arrival, the little group was led to a flat piece of land where the lhapa's large black tent was pitched. Tsering went inside and soon motioned the others to enter. A few other people were already seated inside the tent.

Loosely woven, the hand-knotted yak-skin tent stood on a strange complication of sticks and strings, like a giant spider standing motionless on its long, lanky legs. A surprising amount of light streamed in from the pinhole gaps in the roof and focused on the centre of the tent, where a kettle hissed on a stove lit by firewood. Near the stove sat the shaman, his skin like tanned leather, his forehead creased and furrowed with deeply carved lines. A lean, rough face, with deep-set eyes and high cheekbones, was framed by dark, matted shoulder-length hair tied in a pigtail. There seemed little difference between the man and the mountains he roamed.

Perhaps garnered from the same mountains were two beautiful shining turquoise rings that adorned his dark-brown hands; matching earrings were secured with a thread through his earlobes. On a stone stand near the shaman was a small altar with a faded picture of the Dalai Lama and two butter lamps beside it. Piled up around the edge of the tent were saddlery, rolled-up bedding, a tin trunk, prayer wheels, bags of barley, two battered jerry cans and a large black cauldron for cooking.

The lhapa glanced at the sick man and then nodded to the five monks, who stood in a semicircle with folded hands and bent heads. Tsering stepped forward and, looking towards Nawang, requested healing. Ajay sat down next to Anna, facing the lhapa.

The lhapa began preparing the altar in a leisurely fashion. He placed seven bowls of offerings on it, gently murmuring a monotonous chant as he proceeded. Amidst the chatter of the assembled people, Anna explained to Ajay that of the seven bowls, one symbolized the holy mountain, another, the holy lake, and one of them the heart of the shaman. He was invoking their blessing in the healing as a preparation for the god to enter.

The lhapa lit the butter lamps at the altar and, immediately, the chatter subsided, an atmosphere of formality now pervading the tent. Removing his threadbare coat and, still squatting, the lhapa dressed for the occasion by tying a red cloth around his head and draping a golden-coloured wrap around his shoulders. Meanwhile, his assistant, a young boy of about fifteen, prepared the incense bowl at the altar, and soon, a thick haze of incense filled the tent. Anna coughed. Ajay's eyes stung. The shaman picked up his damaru and began drumming. The droning singsong gradually turned into clear singing.

After half an hour, the lhapa's body began to tremble, his eyes focused upwards as though welcoming an honoured guest. He reached for his magnificent maroon, orange and black headdress from which hung a chaos of innumerable shaggy braids, and donned it. The drumming and chanting resumed more vigorously.

Anna whispered, 'He is preparing for Lha to enter.' Her breath smelt of wood and smoke.

The lhapa's singing picked up tempo, the damaru became more frantic, and soon his head began to shake from side to side. His body trembled, his eyes began to roll back, he seemed awestruck. Some time elapsed as the tension in the room mounted. Then abruptly, he began to sing in a very different voice. Suddenly, Ajay heard a quiet whistling sound. Tsering whispered to Ajay, 'Shaman gone. Lha presides.'

The shaman seemed to doze off as his head drooped. Then all of a sudden he jumped to his feet and leapt across the room to stand over Nawang, who was trembling from a combination of fear and pain. The lhapa felt Nawang's pulse. In a quick and dramatic gesture, he lifted Nawang's robe right up to his stomach, placed his mouth directly on the skin on the lower left side and sucked. Nawang let out a yelp. Like a tiger that has his teeth in his prey, the shaman did not release his hold on Nawang. Nawang tried to sit up but collapsed; and a coin-sized area of his abdomen turned blue. A few agonizing moments later, the shaman growled and spat out into a tin bowl two small stones, the size of lentil grains, along with a mouthful of thick, dark, foul-smelling fluid. Then he collapsed on the floor, his head slumped to one side in exhaustion.

Nawang's body quietened and he lay back. A few moments passed in silence. Then slowly he rose and tentatively began to walk. With an incredulous expression of relief, he turned to Tsering and said, 'Pain gone. I walk!'

Ajay turned to Anna in disbelief. 'Maybe the lhapa already had the stones in his mouth, and he merely spat them out as a theatrical gesture.'

'The lhapa never claimed they were kidney stones. The black seeds are the magical "dirt" that caused the pain. Their removal made the pain disappear,' Anna replied.

'But then how did he locate the "dirt" so accurately? He knew where to suck and didn't hesitate at all,' Ajay persisted.

'You mean, how could he have done it without a CT scan? Why can't you accept that the lhapa doesn't subscribe to the "germ" theory; he believes diseases have magical causes,' Anna whispered.

Tsering turned to them. 'Nawang is walking without pain, no? That's more important than why and how?' he said.

Ajay glanced at Anna. She was taking notes. She is either photographing or making notes, Ajay thought. Why does she have to record every experience instead of just living it? Nawang prostrated before the lhapa, gratitude seeping through the entire length of his supine body. Ajay kept shaking his head, but he looked at the lhapa anew. The strangeness of it all made him a bit dizzy. His measurable and quantifiable universe had been challenged by the intangible and the unseen, which now displayed a compelling power in its ability to show results.

The drumming started again, building to a familiar tempo. The lhapa was once again the god. He looked at Anna and said to Tsering, who translated, 'Milk-white woman needs healing!'

Anna's head jerked up from her field notes, startled. All eyes were on her, including the lhapa's. The drums scaled down their tempo, waiting, urging…

'Don't need healing. I just came to watch,' Anna said firmly.

The lhapa shook his head as though he understood Anna's words. 'He says you carry too much sorrow. Has to be released. Not yours to hold anymore,' Tsering said, looking puzzled.

Anna's face grew pale. 'I am not sure what he is talking about,' she whispered fiercely.

'He says he can tell you what happened and how to let go,' Tsering said tentatively.

Silence filled the room. The drumming resumed and reached a crescendo. Anna's expression was wary, almost scared. 'What can he tell me that I don't already know,' she said, looking down at her tightly clasped hands.

'If you are not ready, he will let it be, not insist,' Tsering said gently.

'It's all right, I'll do it. It may help me gather some practical material,' Anna said, shrugging her shoulders nonchalantly. Her defences were back, her eyes impersonal again.

As Anna lay on the ground, straight and tense, the lhapa took out his rosary and, with eyes closed, slowly began to turn the beads. The room turned quiet. A prickle of apprehension passed down Ajay's spine. The last of the incense on the altar had burnt down. The rosary had slipped out of the lhapa's hand and he seemed to have gone into a light trance. Even the distant singing of the women had stopped; the breeze stilled, as though holding its breath for the drama to unfold. Through half-closed eyes, the lhapa said very softly and unexpectedly, 'Carmen suicide kara.' There was a pause, and this time, Tsering needed to translate. 'Pain stored in body… locked in shoulders…lot of pain.'

The lhapa picked up his drum and held it above Anna's shoulders, then moved it above her neck, her head, her temples, pausing each time and blowing on the drum skin, making an impressively long, deep and arresting vibratory note that resounded in the tent.

'Lha breathes healing force into her,' Tsering murmured to Ajay.

The lhapa placed his hands a few inches above her body and made two complete passes over it from head to toe. 'Many knots in shoulders. Accident cause. I see Death. One dead. Another one in coma saved.' He paused again, looking startled, as though seeing an image above Anna's head. He stopped drumming. 'Carmen suicide kara. Carmen kaun hai?'

He took a black scarf and gently touched each side of her shoulder with it, and then began to pray. From the corner of Anna's eyes, tears rolled down, carving pathways of silent desolation across her face. What is memory but salt to a wound that has never healed? Ajay looked away from Anna, confounded at her tears, which seemed to affirm the significance of the lhapa's cryptic words. Tsering began to chant in a low voice, thanking the gods.

The lhapa had withdrawn after his final question to the supine Anna. The god had left and the shaman was back in the present, without any memory of what had transpired. There was no point in plying him with questions. They made the customary offering and emerged from the tent.

Ajay walked alongside Anna, who kept shaking her head in disbelief as if both the memory that had been invoked and the pain were too great, either to hold or to release. She kept whispering through her tears, 'It's all true. Didn't see the car coming until it was too late. Too late for too many things,' she mourned. Ajay felt a lump in his throat.

They walked back silently to the monastery, with Anna keeping to herself. Privacy and sadness are old companions, Ajay thought. Anna had been claimed by her past, but had she ever been free of it?

Accident

Two weeks ago, he had lived in another world, in an ordinary, predictable world, Ajay thought, as he trekked back to the monastery. What he had witnessed today was not something he could believe in. Yet, his rational belief had been shaken when he saw the writhing monk get up and walk away pain free. No diagnosis, no puncture, not a drop of blood. Just two kidney stones. What was this strange overlapping of matter and spirit? Here gods were the doctors who diagnosed, and faith was the cure.

Stranger still was the ability of the lhapa to voluntarily vacate his body for a disembodied entity to occupy. And bizarrely, this act of self-effacement was intended to serve other people. The feeling of having slipped through time and fallen through a rabbit hole was complete when the realm of the unseen extended its domain beyond material objects to bygone events as well. The lhapa, or the disembodied entity, seemed to know Anna's past. Where had this information been accessed from? Not from the deeper recesses of Anna's

161

mind. It had been retrieved from her body, as though grief is housed not only in memory but in the shoulders that had given it lodging. The lhapa had knocked on that door and something had answered. Uncharacteristically, it had spoken in an odd mix of Hindi and English. But who was it that spoke? Not the lhapa, for he only knew Ladakhi.

Ajay shook his head. However much he was willing to expand his beliefs, he could not account for it all. Yet, how much could he disregard? Reality was a cured monk striding briskly ahead and a shattered woman trailing behind.

The abbot was in the courtyard when Ajay arrived. Nawang, Tsering and the other monks had already retired to their quarters after meeting him.

'Ah ha! I was waiting for you. A magical universe indeed. One can only be grateful that it is so,' said a beaming abbot. 'However, despite the unusual cure, I sensed a sadness hanging over the group. What else happened there?'

Just then, the setting sun slipped out from the cloudscape, bathing them in its lowering light. Sorting his disarrayed thoughts, Ajay replied, 'It was extraordinary, the whole thing. At the end of Nawang's treatment, the lhapa singled out Anna and told her she needed healing. He said she was harbouring a secret sorrow. Something about an accident in which someone had died, and how she had stored the grief in her shoulders. Do you know who died?'

'John, but she has never wanted to talk about it.'

'Oh, my god! But why? Does she hold herself responsible for his death?' Ajay asked.

'Because I have every reason to.' Anna's voice was quiet, and sad.

Ajay swung around to see her standing just behind him. The abbot's gaze enveloped her in warmth and empathy as he said, 'There is tea in my room. Why not come up?'

'Genuine or yak butter tea?' Ajay tried to lighten the sombre mood.

'The genuine stuff. The kind you can risk.'

As he followed Anna up the stairs, Ajay realized his presumption in including himself in what could be a private counsel between the abbot and Anna. Anna did not resist his coming though and, oddly enough, the abbot seemed to want him there.

The light filtering in from the window drew cryptic patterns on the floor of the room. Ajay took two mats and placed them on either side of the abbot.

In a tone that had the softness of snowfall, the abbot asked, 'What happened?'

Haltingly, and with difficulty, Anna ventured into the past, piercing the barricades she had erected around her pain. 'After John's return from India, we were going to meet some friends in Pennsylvania. John said he'd drive, but I said I would because I wanted him to talk about his trip. The road was empty, and he began relating all the minutiae of his visit to Ladakh.

'I am not entirely sure about the exact sequence of events. I think I had turned to look at John, or maybe it was becoming dark and the road was wet. Suddenly a truck came out of nowhere, straight at us. I swerved, but it still hit us head-on. I don't remember any more.

'I awoke in hospital with a bandaged head, a couple of broken ribs and a dislocated shoulder. I remember calling out for John. The nurses hurried in and out but no one would tell me where he was. They kept hushing me and pumping me with sedatives. Through a haze of sleep, I knew something was horribly wrong.

'Much later, a senior doctor told me the details. With great difficulty, John had hailed a car and brought me to the hospital. Once I was on a gurney, he collapsed in the reception area and died of internal haemorrhaging. Apparently, he kept going till I was in safe hands.' Anna stood up unsteadily and moved towards the window, where she stood mutely staring outside. Eventually, she turned around, her face pale, and said in a barely audible whisper, 'I took his life while he saved mine. What a love story.

'It took me months to recover. The pain in the shoulder never fully healed. The lhapa was right. "One dead. Another one in coma saved". Maybe I carry a burden that can never be shed,' she said closing her eyes. The grief in her voice ricocheted in the room.

What a millstone she carried around her neck, trapped in the purgatory of the guilt and pain of killing the man she loved, thought Ajay. Would there ever be a thaw in her winter of grief?

'It's a sorrow no human being should have to carry,' the abbot said softly. 'It must have changed you in many ways.'

'I suppose so. John used to tease me, calling me his bubbling brook. He said he loved my effervescence, what he called my quick and joyous response to life. Now my speech has become hesitant,' she said, looking at Ajay.

The abbot sat watching them, quiet in body and steady of gaze, his presence radiating understanding and compassion. Ajay realized that the abbot had risen above his loss and transmuted his pain to become the man he was today. He felt the utter triviality of his own so-called anguish. It was non-existent compared to what the other two in the room had experienced. They had suffered. He was merely confused.

'But how could the lhapa have known about the accident?' Anna asked.

'And even more bizarre was his statement: "Carmen suicide kara",' Ajay added.

'I have no idea what that meant.' Anna shook her head.

'We can try and decode it like a dream. By itself, the sentence doesn't mean anything. So can we treat it as a metaphor for something else? Maybe Carmen holds the key,' the abbot reflected. 'What does it signify? Carmen is a name. Were you talking about Carmen while driving?'

Anna's response was immediate. 'No. I still remember the conversation between us even though it was five years ago. Just ten minutes before the accident, as I swerved to overtake a jeep, John had laughed and said, "Death rides on our shoulders", and his foot had slammed down on imaginary brakes. He said, "If I die, I will haunt Ladakh till I find out for sure whether Jesus went there or not." I made light of his remark. "Wouldn't it be simpler if you found that out before you died?" I asked him.

'In hindsight, the conversation was bizarre. However flippantly we spoke of death, subconsciously perhaps we were acknowledging its lengthening shadow over us.'

'Did you or John know someone called Carmen?' the abbot enquired.

'No.'

'Did either of you ever see the opera *Carmen*? If I remember right, it was by a French composer.'

'I haven't, and if John did, he never mentioned it.'

'Prior to the conversation about death, were you talking about something that rhymed with Carmen?' asked the abbot, intent on decoding the symbolism of the phrase.

'Nope.'

'Was it a carmine-coloured car? You know, the rich purplish-red colour?'

Anna nodded her head vigorously. 'Yes, it was. That's absolutely correct. Was that what the lhapa was alluding to? The colour of the car?'

'But who committed suicide? The carmine car?' Ajay asked.

'Could the lhapa have meant "car mein suicide kara"? The suicide took place in the car. Or maybe "car man suicide kara". Meaning the man in the car committed suicide,' the abbot said slowly, as though fitting together the pieces of a jigsaw puzzle.

'It was an accident, not suicide,' Anna reacted sharply, sitting up ramrod straight.

'Sometimes accidents are not merely accidents but represent an opting out from life. An unconscious suicide,' the abbot spoke tentatively, as if feeling his way.

'That's nonsense. An accident is something unexpected and unplanned, while suicide is a wilful act,' Anna said, tension coiled in her voice.

'Sometimes we generate circumstances we are not conscious of. Don't we fall ill because unconsciously we want a break from a trying situation, or wish to escape an irksome responsibility? The illness allows us to rest, which otherwise may not be permissible. Similarly, can death become a way out?' The abbot paused. Ajay felt the tension in his stomach at the abbot's dogged pursuit of this line of thought despite Anna's obvious distress.

'I remember reading about a curious case—the collapse of a bridge in which nine people died. None of them knew each other. They were together only coincidentally when the bridge collapsed. Yet, a journalist who traced their past found that each of them had reached a dead end in their life. Was their death an accident? Were there forces that moved them towards that bridge as a way out of their stalemate? It raises questions about how often we are controlled by forces that we are unaware of. Anyway, finally it's just one explanation,' said the abbot, shrugging the thought away.

Ajay saw Anna clenching her fingers and knew that she was layering her defences all over again. If John and Anna had been happy together, why would John have felt the need to opt out?

'What is the yardstick for judging a dead end? So many dead ends are actually challenges we can use to open new doors. A failed relationship, a loss of money or an illness may seem temporary dead ends, which people struggle with and often do overcome. So, a dead end is only a subjective interpretation,' Anna said emphatically.

'And what is death?' asked the abbot. 'Is it merely about the heart stopping and the brain shutting down? I see it as a point when a person feels he or she has reached a dead end. In youth, the world brims over with endless possibilities that are waiting to be explored. With time, that infinite promise recedes until it becomes an illusion. Life becomes a routine from which there seems no escape. Then the feeling creeps upon you that you can no longer paint on the canvas of possibility, and before long you realize a fresh canvas is needed. That, to me, is death, a way out.'

'What about when a one-month-old child dies? Does it also feel it can do no more, when its life has not even begun?'

'I can only think of that as a false start. You abort the journey because you feel it does not lead to your destination,' the abbot said promptly and then added, 'No, that doesn't work either. I don't know the answer to that one. What I am suggesting is that such choices are not decided by the surface mind but come from the deeper layers of the psyche.'

'I can't imagine anyone wanting to die. Irrespective of how defeated I may feel, I have never felt that I cannot do anymore,' Ajay said with the zest of the forties still upon him.

'I agree. The conscious part does not want to die. The deeper part may know when to let go,' the abbot said.

An elegiac silence hovered in the air as though the very contemplation of death had turned it into a person, the fourth in the room, whom the other three were dialoguing with.

'Do you think John had reached some dead end in his life, which he could not surmount,' out of the blue, the abbot asked.

'That's ridiculous,' Anna retorted. 'The lhapa does not have to be right about everything.'

'No... Yes...' said the abbot hesitatingly. 'His last question—Car mein kaun hai—shows he didn't know who was sitting in the car. But if the accident was a suicide, the fault was not yours.'

'I was driving.'

'And the bridge collapsed. Who brought that about?' the abbot asked.

'Why should he have?' Anna's voice echoed forlornly in the room.

'There is always a reason or purpose for an event.'

'John loved life too much to do that,' Anna said vehemently.

Was there a suggestion of doubt in her voice, Ajay wondered.

'Do you think my blaming myself for killing him is in any way better than blaming him for opting out and abandoning me? You are not giving me an option worth choosing,' she said angrily. A second later she got up and left.

The abbot turned to Ajay. 'The wound is the place where the light enters you, so said Rumi. Our greatest lessons come from our greatest pain.'

John

18 August: Evening

Anna raced down the steps from the abbot's room, her agitation directing her to the room below the temple where she held her weekly class. She hoped its sheer emptiness would calm her.

Five years of marriage, and five years post John's death, she was convinced that she was the person who had known him best. She couldn't believe he had wanted out. All of a sudden she felt unsure. Could she have missed the clues? Had John reached an insurmountable dead end? Was his 'suicide' a way of confronting the terror of death as a measure of his preparedness? The line from Nietzsche came to mind: The final reward of the dead is to die no more.

Torn between disbelief and belief, she sat down in the centre of the room. She had ascribed John's death to a single cause: herself. How many times had she prayed for forgiveness? Almost daily. She had overlooked the simple Buddhist tenet that there is never a single cause for an event.

A string of causes web together to bring an event to pass. If even one is absent, the event will not take place.

She looked around the room. Just the day before, twenty villagers had sat here listening in on her class. Everything about the room and the approaching evening hour reminded her of John. Her ability to teach a faith other than that of her own upbringing was because of him. Her love of a land alien to her own was because of him. Anna smiled wistfully, her eyes lost in reverie. She seemed to forever oscillate between two memories: how they had met and how they had parted. Today, she chose to remember the first time they had met, as though in the beginnings might be detected the entire skein of events that were to unfold.

After that one chance encounter in the library, she had not bumped into John anywhere on the campus. Ever in need of supplementing her frugal allowance, she was busy applying for campus jobs. One day, she answered an advertisement by an associate professor, John Fletcher, for an assistant to help collate his field notes. Her first impression when she entered his small sunlit office was of books all over—on open shelves, piled on the table, stacked on a small side table. The large desk was strewn with papers, files and folders, like the scattered disrobing of an adolescent.

When she entered, he looked up from his desk. His was an aesthetic face, lean and long, and smoky-grey eyes keen with intelligence; his eyes smiled at her even before his lips did. Anna was surprised. He was the bearded man from the library! But he had not recognized her. Deflated, she reminded him of their meeting.

'Ah, yes. The temple connection! Well, that's an auspicious beginning,' he smiled. 'But will you be able to handle all this,' he said, waving his hand generally in the direction of the room. Not knowing what she was giving consent to, she nodded.

In the days that followed, she waded through his field notes on Kashmir and Ladakh, and taped interviews and diary notations of meeting with lamas, concerning closely guarded rituals centred on esoteric sexual practices. Thinking his interest somewhat weird, she asked him one evening, 'What's this all about?'

'I think we briefly touched on this in the library. Some schools believe sexual intimacy is a form of spiritual discipline,' he replied.

She was far from convinced. 'Is any connection between sexuality and spirituality possible?'

'It is difficult to see the connection as long as we think of sex as inherently bad, dirty, or wrong. Such a view denies sexuality and aims to fill our minds only with "clean" thoughts.' Seeing the curiosity in her eyes, John continued, 'For the last two thousand years, Christian culture has been involved with finding redemption from the original sin of Adam and Eve. Along with Christianity, most religions envisage that when the mind is perfectly calm, it is like the still water of a mountain lake. Any desire will cause a ripple and disturb the stillness; therefore, sexual restraint is essential. Yet another tradition asks: Is it necessary to deny that which is intrinsic to life? Is it necessary to slay the dragon of desire? Instead, can desire not be engaged with, and redeemed? What would happen if that ripple is allowed to intensify and become a wave?'

'Obviously, you will be destroyed by its blind, surging power,' Anna responded.

John smiled. 'It will smash you only if you oppose it with your will. Instead, if you ride on the crest of the wave, it may help shed the ego-personality.'

'That's pretty poetic. But isn't this merely a metaphor?'

'Sometimes, a force is generated between lovers, which is greater than both. It pulls them both ways: irresistibly inwards towards unification, as well as outwards in panic, away from the threat of annihilation.'

'But almost everyone on the planet has sex; how come they don't feel this force?'

'Most people view sex only as the gratification of an instinctive need, and don't realize that sexual attraction can generate a subtle energy. Also, the pursuit of an orgasm may be the surest way to avoid the build-up of this energy, for it appears only in the tension between the lure of union and its restraint.'

'And how much of all this is just an excuse for enjoying sex?' Anna dared ask.

As they continued to debate whenever they worked together, a mild state of arousal seamlessly entered their relationship—in the accidental touching of hands when passing a paper, in looks that lingered longer than the moment asked for. Was this conversation actually a result of their emerging but unacknowledged interest in each other? Or was their interest an outcome of the erotic nature of the subject they were dealing with? Had they ventured to notice, they would have found their lives linked by subtle forces beyond their conscious control. In a synchronicity of events, their pens would run out simultaneously; even their cars would break down at the same time though at different locations. They were like two dancers dancing to an inaudible tune that both kept time to, slowly and surely awaiting its crescendo.

It was not long before Anna began to accept the onrush of her feelings. She was convinced this attraction was different from any of her earlier involvements. In the past, in any adventure with men, it had been a cocktail of his physical appearance, style and talent that had drawn her, made all the more intoxicating by a dizzying guesswork of whether her feelings were reciprocated or not. As for all her friends, it was a predictable progression. She would date, pledge fidelity, look forward to marriage, family and a joint bank account. And, of course, the measure was always sexual compatibility. She smiled ruefully as she thought about her younger self and her childish idea of love.

John seemed to hold out another promise. Would his love have the power to lift her to the heights of some deeply profound union, as promised by the texts he was immersed in? Somehow, she felt he was capable of transporting her to a space where something more than the body would be offered in union. Yet, something stopped her from giving in entirely. Her instinctive feeling was that this erotic encounter could equally plunge her into despair. The passage of days compounded the confusion within her.

Time and again, she asked herself why was she so greatly drawn to this young Harvard scholar researching tiny hermitages on cliff perches, trailing lamas and yoginis in meditation caves hollowed into rocks in Ladakh, desperately trying to gain admittance into esoteric religious events, listening to the faint sounds of conch and drum, and letting his imagination fill in the rest. A man who struggled with a foreign language and physical hardship, and continuously attempted to balance on the precipice of a cultural chasm so deep and wide that he sometimes despaired he had the means to bridge it. Yet, something—perhaps an unfathomable passion to understand—drove him on. But understand what, Anna wondered. Was he searching for something deeply personal while pursuing his academic theories?

One evening, with the wind whistling outside, cocooned in the warmth of his office, she opened the subject again, hoping to elicit something that would rent the obscuring veil of her confusion. 'Is this whole business an Eastern fetish?'

'No. This "business" exists equally in the Western tradition. Courtly love, the troubadours…' She looked at him blankly. He explained. 'Remember the Arthurian legends and the love of Sir Lancelot for Queen Guinevere? In the traditions of courtly love, the knight always fell in love with a woman of higher rank. He dedicated his victories to her and aspired to be her champion. Never would he openly profess his love, but accepted a life of longing instead, because she could not be possessed. He could be with her only in the imagination. In short, it was about the love for the unattainable woman. The idea is to separate genital satisfaction from Eros and focus on longing itself.'

'Wow. That's thrillingly romantic. But surely that's only legend,' Anna said.

'Can you be sure it doesn't happen any longer? You may have your own knight who holds a candle for you without your knowing it.'

John's direct gaze sent heat rushing up her face. Was he flirting with her or was she projecting her feelings on to him? The moment passed, and John switched back to his impersonal, scholarly mode. 'The development of longing is also at the heart of another Western practice, Carezza, where the man withholds from orgasm to experience a state called the "glide". If the heightened bodily arousal is restrained from reaching its goal, an erotic consciousness begins to arise. This state goes far beyond the immediacy of sensory pleasure; it allows you to remain afloat on the ocean of passion. It is subtler, a more overwhelming state that dissolves everything in its wake—the body, the mind, the other, even the world.'

John paused, his face flushed. 'Admittedly, it is easier to bind an elephant's leg in a spider's web than to achieve this kind of love. Others have compared it to the difficulty of making a frog dance in front of a snake.' His smiling eyes danced upon her.

Anna sat mesmerized. He was speaking softly, passionately, as though every word was meant for her. 'Similarly, the accent of the Sahajiyas in India was to focus on longing. They frowned on seminal emission but not on sexuality. The disciple aimed to acquire perfect control of his senses, and to this end, he approached his beloved in stages, in the process transforming her into a goddess. After falling in love, he did not immediately leap into her arms, but spent nights with his imagination fixed on her balcony. Through this longing, he hoped to vivify her face. Night after night, he visualised the curls and waves of her hair till it was all a blur. Then he proceeded to spend a few hours every night outside her house, rekindling his longing, believing that her aroma was suffusing him.

'Gradually, he would enter her home, his desire for her burning ever more fiercely. In time, he would enter her chamber and spend the night feasting his eyes on her but still denying any physical contact, every night inching closer to her bed. And, when he could no longer hold it, he would stretch out his arm, begging her to gratify him with her touch. The months of restraint had purified his longing, and this purified desire would travel down his arm and reach his quivering fingertips, aching for union. And it would be held there, hoping to prolong the thrill of contact.'

John's hand stretched out towards Anna, throbbing with as much expectancy as the lover in his story. The room pulsated with the unspoken, and Anna responded naturally, cupping his hand in hers and drawing her lips to them. In some mysterious way, he had let her reach him. Encircled in the vision of love that John held out, Anna felt exalted. Her whole being felt awash with love. He sensed it, and said, 'What a paradox. I am searching for the very thing I may not believe in if I do find it.'

He held her hands to his cheek, and very simply said, 'Walk with me all the way.'

It was the simplest marriage proposal she had ever heard. Tears filled her eyes as she nodded in silence.

Paradoxically, his death had imparted an odd clarity to his life. She felt she had never seen him so clearly when she was close to him. Who was John? He was a man whose thinking was alien to his colleagues at Harvard. He had often been accused of going native. Was he an Easterner born in a Westerner's body—another of his dead ends? Was he the man she had lived with or the man she was remembering now? Memory is an unfaithful mistress—it embellishes and detracts. But if John had been alive today, she would have asked him, 'How do you judge your life? By what you achieved or by what you did not?'

Anna opened her eyes to the quiet of the room. Her heart was warm with memories, but her body was cold to touch. She shivered with an aching kind of loneliness. There was a void left in her life in the absence of what John and she had shared. For months after his death, like a phantom limb, she had felt his presence near at hand. Had guilt and loss provoked her imagination or was it the reality of John's need to communicate? It seemed he had wanted to say something to her. About them or about his unfinished work, she could not be sure. His search had been more like a symbolic act to bridge the religion of his upbringing with the beliefs of another land he had grown to love. Two diametrically opposite areas of work had engaged him in Ladakh.

Let my dead ends be your beginnings. And I will help you from the other side, he seemed to be saying to her. Search in the very places I could not find.

The evening had slipped into dusk. Anna got up to switch on the light in the room. At that moment, Ajay walked in.

'I was just leaving,' Anna said quickly, taken aback by his sudden appearance.

'I was thinking that we could give that elusive manuscript another shot. Maybe I could help.'

Anna stared at him, taken aback by the uncanny timing. Earlier, he had talked about Jesus's coming to India, unaware of her interest in the subject. And now, he had not only intercepted her thought but carried it forward, just when she was contemplating doing so.

The Hill of Meetings

19 August: Night

Ajay did not see Anna in the monastery the entire day, and he was troubled. She was usually there each day, from the morning prayers to sundown. Could she be unwell? The scab had been peeled off, exposing the bright angry flesh beneath. Death, he thought, is a gaping hole nothing can fill. The expression on her face when he had chanced upon her last evening, edged with fatigue and melancholy, had stayed with him. He had wanted to comfort her, but did not want to invade her privacy. She was such a solitary creature.

The hollyhocks, flushed pink in the sun, swayed in the courtyard. Often, he had found Anna standing in front of them. A dead flower drifted to the ground. Soon, winter would dry and wither the stalks, to be followed by the renewal of spring. Would she also shed her deadness and allow the sap of life to fill her? He had believed her search for the Jesus manuscript was an expression of her love for John. But now, it seemed to be overlaid by guilt. She was a person in search of atonement. So strongly had he wanted to protect her from self-blame that he had readily believed that John could have committed suicide. But why would John want to opt out? Had they not been happy together?

He wanted to ask the abbot about her absence but worried that he would read other reasons into the simple enquiry. Never mind, he told himself, he would still ask. He would feign an air of casualness, yawn as he spoke. He waited all afternoon for the abbot, who usually went down late in the afternoon to check the hydraulic ram. But today, he was busy with visiting officials. Ajay paced the courtyard, watching the hill where Anna lived.

At dusk, he went to the row of prayer wheels and slowly turned them one by one. Each turning was a remembrance. Or was it a prayer? For whom? Even before the question was fully formed, he knew the answer.

The gong for the evening service pealed. Ajay could wait no longer and decided to walk up the hill to Anna's hut. A rough path, no more than three-feet wide, wound its way through stones and rocks, up to a small cluster of cottages. With grey-slated roofs and whitewashed stone walls, they were much smaller in size than any building in the main monastery. Halfway up the hill, he saw a monk gliding down like a moving shadow, his wine-coloured robe the shade of crushed black grapes in the evening hour. He carried a staff to negotiate the descent. He was an old man, his face and forehead cratered with liberal wrinkles. His shoulder-length hair gleamed silver grey in the fading evening light. The eyes were gentle, almost dreamy. Ajay had never seen him before. The man stopped and Ajay bowed reverentially before him.

'You are climbing up the mountain rather late,' the old man said, his English clearly enunciated.

'I wanted to visit Anna, the lady researcher.'

'At this hour?' The old man raised an eyebrow.

'She comes to the monastery every day. Today she did not. I was worried she may not be well,' Ajay said, a little fazed.

'She has withdrawn to her cottage,' the man said, pointing towards the darkening peak of the mountain.

'This is sudden. Why?'

'What do you do when you want to clear your room of clutter and unwanted stuff? You take a broom, sweep and discard. She's doing that,' the old man said, with an uncanny knowledge of Anna's situation.

Ajay looked at the man again. Who was he?

'You live on this mountain, Sir?' Ajay asked.

'Yes, in one of those huts up on the hill.'

'Are you in retreat?'

'Since the last three years,' the man said softly. 'You are the first person I have spoken to in a long time. Because Anna would have wanted you to know.'

'You know Anna?'

'Yes.'

The brief answer left no room for pursuing the matter further.

'How long will she stay withdrawn?'

'Till her room feels clean and quiet. In the meantime, I don't think she would want to be disturbed,' the old man said firmly.

Wanting to linger with the conversation a little longer, Ajay asked, 'What is done in these retreats?'

'Done? You finally stop "doing" and let go,' the man replied, looking amused.

Ajay wondered if he was dreaming. Was this man, coming down a stony mountain path, staff in hand, the archetypal wise man who, like the mountains he lived amidst, would still be there if Ajay came back a thousand years later? Even the landscape belonged to another world, with the rising moon turning the darkened rocks silver, lending a mysterious aura to the evening.

He mused how powerful this goal must be in the hands of the few who could control the mind and step out of time, recognizing that time was nothing but the confines of thought. In amazement and reverence, Ajay bent his head to a goal antithetical to every belief he had held.

Part of the magic of that evening was that the old man with the staff seemed to pick up his thoughts. Softly, he said,

'Sometimes naked, sometimes mad,
Now as a scholar, now as a fool,
Here as a rebel, there a saint,
Thus they appear on earth—the Freed Men.'

Ajay's head jerked up. The old man smiled faintly at him. 'Yes, I know what you are thinking.'

'How?' Ajay asked bewildered.

'Since my mind is still, the thoughts that come to me must be yours. One day you will also know.'

Overwhelmed, Ajay asked, 'Will I?'

'Yes. Through love. That will be your way. Not through the body, not through the mind, but with a heart soaked in love. Don't you know this mountain is known as the Hill of Meetings?'

A flush stained Ajay's face and he dropped his eyes.

When he looked up again, the man was gone. He turned around to see a shadowy silhouette near the rocks below. Such agility in an old man! Was he real or just a figment of my imagination, Ajay wondered as he turned back towards the monastery.

That night, he slept fitfully as Anna's face, her smile half humorous, half melancholic, threaded his sleep. He woke to a darkness that could not erase thoughts of her—her long legs as she strode along next to him; the sensuality of his own response when she carelessly ran her hand through her short golden hair. Somehow, after a long, long time, he did not feel alone, because there was Anna, first outside and now within him, warming him with her presence.

He had saved two apples from his meals for Anna. He sat up in bed and laughed. Two precious apples saved as a gift from a life of privation instead of big gifts given from a life of plenty. He recalled the abbot's tale about a monk who led a very austere life. Half his waking hours, he meditated, and he lived for weeks without exchanging a word with anyone. He ate frugally, just one meal a day, sometimes only an apple someone had left for him. But he meditated upon that apple until it was bursting with juice, redness and crispness. By the end of the day, he looked forward passionately to his meagre meal. 'The point is that you do not have to relinquish passion. You have to get into the right state to receive and hold passion,' the abbot had concluded.

The apples were not merely a gift for Anna; she had become the fruit itself, longed for with an ascetic anticipation that would not succumb to the temptation of fulfilment. He could hardly contain himself. He wanted to see her, give her the apples. Without thinking, in that pre-dawn hour, he wore his shoes, took the apples from the table and hurried out of the door like a squall of wind. As he reached the Hill of Meetings, he wondered if he would meet the man with the staff again. Would he stop him again? Was he the monk in the abbot's story who lived frugally and in silence, meditating and anticipating his meal with passion? He would give the old man an apple if he met him.

The very first light of the morning was draped like a silver raiment over the shoulders of the night. The morning bugle for prayer had not sounded yet. What is prayer? This silent tread of concentration bordering on self-forgetfulness.

He reached the stone steps of the first cottage and stood uncertainly. How would he recognize Anna's hut? It would be beyond embarrassing if he knocked on the wrong door. And what if he knocked on the right door? How would Anna react? Would she be annoyed or pleased to see him?

Then, from nowhere, the air carried her fragrance to him. It was a mixture of wild thyme and dust. It stroked his hair and shot right through his nostrils in a jolt of recognition. He turned towards the door to see if she was coming down the steps. There was no one there. Only the fragrance, a signature of her, a presage of his having held something in the inner crucible of his thoughts.

He climbed to the next hut. It had a small wooden door, old with age, as if it had stayed shut far longer than it had remained open. A steel glass and a pot lay upturned on a stone slab, and a pair of old rubber chappals lay by the door.

He sat down on a stone, his heart beating rapidly from the climb and the anticipation. Maybe he would just sit here and feel her presence. Maybe his very longing would make her open the door. Minutes passed. The air was cold. He had forgotten to wear a jacket. He rubbed his arms, then wrapped them around his chest and looked up.

Something caught his eye. It was Anna's blue T-shirt, hanging from the clothesline outside the cottage just above. He climbed with his heart thudding rhythmically to the tune of his longing, and stood outside her door. He raised his hand to knock and then stopped. There was no sound from the cottage. He turned around and sat down on a stone slab in her sparse, tiny courtyard, lost in thought. He imagined her breathing softly as she slept, and tried to synchronize his breathing with hers. As his concentration became totally focused on her breathing, he forgot his own breath. Not only did he breathe through her, he became her very breath. Minutes passed as he surrendered his body to live in hers. The unhindered radiance of desire no longer spoke the language of the flesh. Just two breaths uniting, neither feeling nor hearing, save the deepening joy of knowing that she was near.

Gradually, he opened his eyes and rose with slow movements. He looked at the closed door and felt the silence beyond. He put the two apples at her door, and without a backward glance, returned to the monastery. It was an offering cleansed of him.

20 August

He worked until midday in the greenhouse, mixing manure and mud and filling rows of empty pots so they could be ready for planting. Whenever he took a break, he came out into the courtyard, just in case she had arrived. But he did not see her the next day either. And yet, behind every thought, her face shone.

Look, Feel, but Don't Touch

22 August: Morning

As Ajay emerged from his room, a young monk bowed to him and said the abbot wanted to see him. Seldom had he been summoned. Ajay quickened his step. Perhaps it was news of communications having been restored with the outside world.

He stopped short, struck by the ambiguity this created in his mind. Did he want to return to his old life in Delhi? Was he going to continue to run away from Swati, especially now that his heart had opened elsewhere? At the same time, he felt an overwhelming tenderness towards his wife. Perhaps the rhythm of his new life was permeating the old with empathy.

'Look here, what is happening?' were the abbot's first words as Ajay entered the room and sat opposite him.

His no-nonsense air was faintly unsettling. This could not be about the airport. Ajay blurted out the first thing that came to his head, 'I am concerned about Anna. I hope she surfaces quickly.'

'That's about her. I am asking about you.' The abbot said pointedly.

He squirmed. Did the abbot know about his being besotted with Anna? But how could he?

He got a grip on himself and, deflecting the abbot's thrust, said, 'I had a strange dream last night. Where the wall and the roof meet, through an opening, hot burning coals are streaming down, like a river of red glowing embers. They pour in so fast that soon, I have no place to stand. I am awestruck and overwhelmed by the sight.'

The abbot muttered, 'If ever there was an unconscious confession.'

'Pardon me?'

'Coals can be read as emblazoned desire. These coals overwhelm you. So it seems the surge of sexual desire is upon you.'

Ajay could feel the stain of a flush seeping down to his neck. He did know. What a fool he was to think the abbot would not pick up his feelings for Anna. Is he going to read the riot act, tell me that the monastery is not meant for entertaining such feelings? Will he send me away? How will I face Anna? The abbot continued to look at Ajay for a long time; his gaze was steady, intense. Then, he slowly and clearly enunciated, 'Look, feel, but don't touch. Nahin toh sab matti ho jayega.'

The words contained no censure, no blame. The wagging finger of morality was nowhere present in them. The man sitting opposite him was viewing his feelings for Anna from an altogether different criterion.

'This is confusing. You do not judge my feelings, in fact, you tacitly encourage them. Then why the embargo on touching?'

'Because you must build the charge rather than dissipate it.'

'Just a minute, Sir. You are allowing me to "look". You are asking for no restraint there. You are allowing me to "feel" the attraction. Then you erect an artificial barrier by instructing me not to touch, or everything will turn to dust. Why should it?'

The abbot said nothing.

Ajay rushed on, 'Remember, I told you, Swati says unfaithfulness begins in the mind and then expresses itself in action. If you allow me to look and feel, then touching will follow. It is as inevitable as it is natural.'

'Precisely.' The abbot pulled himself out of his reverie. 'Everyone is familiar with the gross genital sensation. However, often something more is evoked, a subtle charge that floods the whole of one's being. That charge is the secret you need to discover, to steal. Like Prometheus stole the divine fire from the gods.'

Seeing Ajay's perplexed expression, the abbot added, 'You remember your Mauritius experience, where only a heightened moment of awareness remained. In fact, there was neither you nor Swati, but something greater than both of you. You had spontaneously "stolen" the charge. That was extraordinary.

'This heightened charge comes to everyone at some point in their life—usually when they fall in love: You may go to the office, meet people, work out in the gym, but at the back of your mind, a glow for the beloved remains.'

Ajay shot back, 'A byproduct of body chemistry and sexual discovery, I dare say.'

'The charged state doesn't occur only with genital stimulation, just like sex is not limited only to the body.

When two people love each other, the sexual act is the physical outpouring of their emotional intimacy. Also, it often becomes a vehicle of their self-worth, overlaid by a striving to be loved, or to dominate the partner, to compensate for hurt and unlived desires.'

'"Don't touch" is a strange edict. Should married couples refrain from sex? Is that what you are suggesting? That itself would destroy their relationship. Not to speak of what would happen to society if the reproductive instinct was not acted upon. It's okay if a few monks live celibate lives. Not everyone can do that.'

'Celibacy and building the charge are entirely different efforts. Sexual attraction is like the crude ore from the mine. To obtain gold from the ore, you refine it. You aren't expected to bury yourself in the mine; yet that is exactly what most people do. Others refuse to mine the ore because they consider it dirty work. If you want to indulge in the sexual act indiscriminately, who can stop you? What I am suggesting is that rather than give release to desire whenever it is aroused, restrain it, sublimate it.'

'Why? Why suppress or quell this natural urge? People have sex because they enjoy it,' Ajay protested.

'But does that enjoyment last? Your marriage reached a stalemate even though both of you still share a basic bond. Where did the charge disappear? Could it be that you needed to work on keeping it alive?'

Ajay evaded the personal question and instead asked, 'How can sex be anything more than a desire for the partner, desire for pleasure, or a release?'

'That is because you think it is purely a matter of attraction, chemistry. It is one power experienced in two ways. The attraction, the desire makes sex a compulsive drive. Seen differently, it is the "charge". Sex is merely sex if it cannot generate something more than itself. Is sex the desire to possess or the power to create?'

Silence filled the room. The abbot's personality, rather than his words, had marched in to take possession of Ajay. He wondered whether the monks here had been told about the charge. Or was he being singled out? All Ajay could ask was, 'How do you know all this?'

Eyes twinkling, the abbot wagged his thumb. 'Me, no tell.'

Doubt

22 August: Afternoon

Ajay walked out of the abbot's room feeling like he had taken part in a secret initiation, the impact of which would vanish if he tried to grasp fully its mystery. He started down the stairs and was startled to see Anna, very much in the flesh, making her way up. A surge of gladness filled him. He moved towards her.

'Hi there.' Anna's eyes were guarded as she stopped a step below him.

'Oh, hello! How have you been? I have been wondering…' Ajay's hand moved down towards hers, where it clasped the banister. He bent forward and for a moment their breaths mingled. Suddenly, Anna looked past him. Ajay whirled around. The abbot stood in the doorway of his room, watching. *This man appears at every inopportune moment,* Ajay thought with annoyance.

The abbot said firmly to Anna, 'I have been waiting for you.'

Anna hurried up like a schoolgirl who was late for class. The door shut and Ajay felt bereft. He touched the banister where her hand had been. Something lingered there, a hint of her smell, the warmth of the imprint of her hand. What lay between them was delicate as the silvery morning dew and fragile as the tightly curled buds in the greenhouse, he thought dreamily.

He longed to gain entry into her innermost world, to trawl the depths of those clear eyes. He thought of all the things he liked about her: how she listened to him with full attention; the way she watched without the compulsion to participate. If an emotion rose to the surface, it was curtailed by a long-learnt discipline of restraint. And he was touched beyond words when, sometimes, she seemed to communicate with him in some unintentional, nonverbal way, her eyes resting on him a second longer than necessary, her tone gentle, her look beseeching.

The abbot had suggested that in these matters, the imagination was far more compelling than reality; the beloved is far more powerful in the imagination than when you indulge in physicality. A charged imagination can extend the arousal far longer than the sexual act.

What was this form of love the abbot talked about where it was not pleasure that was sought but a passionate kind of asceticism, which made denial a purer joy than fulfilment? You relinquished union but cultivated and retained its tension, an active courting of a force greater than the ego. But what did you do when you were overwhelmed by emotion? Could the very power that had stoked it control it, he wondered.

He walked down the familiar staircase with unsure steps, wondering about his attraction to Anna. He didn't know her well enough. Only a handful of shared experiences and yet, irrationally, she was someone deeply known. Why did she make him feel so intensely alive? Did he find her exciting because she was forbidden? There was a surreal quality to his feelings, as if she had already been written into the pages of his life by the ink of predestination.

He breathed in the crisp air of the courtyard. It was a fine afternoon, with the early touch of winter in the breeze. The seasons changed earlier here. Where was his place in this land of frozen peaks, high windy flatlands and the river below with its busy growth of willows and poplars? A land that, legend had it, was once closest to heaven, until a careless king cut down a miraculous rope that was a stairway to the immortals. Some mysterious power reverberated off these mountains. Perhaps it had entered him without his realizing it.

For the rest of the afternoon, he continued to work in the greenhouse, mixing and shovelling manure and soil into drums for the winter. I will not be here then, he mused, but I will always carry the stamp of these days. My life will never be the same again. Not only have my spectacles changed but someone has restored my eyesight as well. And helped accentuate my listening. I can now hear my thoughts and when I do that, I can sense them looking over their shoulder as though someone is watching them.

The abbot's words had aroused a complex mix of emotions in him. He had always been sure he had never felt sexually drawn to Akanksha, yet Swati was sure he had a 'thing' for her. His first experience of sex with Anita, during his college days, had been disquieting. The disquiet lay not just in the stealth of stolen sex but in the feeling of emptiness afterwards. Instead of feeling replenished, he had felt disconnected, impoverished. He just wanted to get away. Was the absence of the mysterious 'charge' the reason for having felt so let down?

With Swati, it had been different. He had felt an immense pull towards her. His body, mind and heart had become one instrument playing a symphony uniquely theirs, music that had reached a crescendo in his Mauritius moment. Now that the abbot had pointed out the perfection and rarity of that moment, the murmur of it would be forever in his ears.

In the case of Akanksha, he reflected, the charge, without the release of any physical expression, was so powerful that it had the potential to wreck his marriage. The abbot had noticed his feelings for Anna much before he had voiced or acted on them. Had Swati similarly sensed his feelings for Akanksha?

23 August: Morning

Ajay stood on the terrace of the monastery, watching the river below. The first light of dawn glinted on its back as it slowly slithered away like a silver snake into some distant horizontal burrow.

He could hear the undze in the temple, chanting the liturgy in a deep rumbling voice, chorused by the rest of the monks. The cymbals clashed, the bells tinkled, the drums beat and the eight-foot-long horns followed in a long-drawn-out note of supplication.

The complex orchestral arrangement, with alternating calm and strident phases, subsided suddenly and unexpectedly into a reverberating silence; the sharp, clear, almost ethereal, light of the early morning, holding the fading vibratory note in the cup of stillness.

Ajay rubbed his three-day-old stubble and smoothed his crumpled shirt. He had changed. At work in Delhi, a midnight blue tie would have matched a powder blue shirt tucked immaculately into the waistband of steel grey trousers, falling arrow straight over designer shoes. Here, not one phone call, no shopping malls, no entertainment, no aphrodisiac of variety. He could not even remember when he last took out his wallet!

Ajay made his way out of the monastery, his thoughts going back to the earlier conversation with the abbot. How did he know such intimate details of sexuality when he was celibate? Or was he? He had not denied personal experience when he said, 'Me, no tell.' He was a full-blooded man radiating an aware energy; not a dried-up, repressed man posturing piety behind his monk's robe. He could not have remained an ascetic all through these years, his energy kept in cold storage. Had he spoken through personal experience, of perhaps his college or Oxford days? Wait a minute, hadn't that monk said the abbot had come here under a cloud? Had he been involved in a scandal that had shamed him, and was that what made him pace up and down the terrace through the nights?

Uncomfortable thoughts hovered at the back of Ajay's mind. The discomfort was not over the abbot having violated the vows of a monk; the discomfort was at the thought of who was the woman the abbot had a relationship with.

Two hours later, when he returned to the monastery after his walk, it had become a bustling marketplace, with monks spread all over the courtyard. It was time for the debate. Ajay smiled, relieved to be distracted from his thoughts. He began to weave his way quietly around a group of monks, but the liveliness of their speech caught his attention.

'A disciple asked the Buddha whether a spiritual friend is half of the religious life. The Buddha replied: A spiritual friend is the whole of the religious life.'

'The spiritual friend need not be a woman but can be a mentor or helper.'

'The texts also state that striving without a partner is as useless as churning water to make butter. However diligently I may churn, fresh butter will not be produced.'

'I thought the churning was the ever-churning mind, and the union of the churner and the churned meant the cessation of thoughts.'

'No one is suggesting a physical partner. Use an imagined partner.'

They were arguing about the very thing he was grappling with! The use of the imagination versus physicality. He was relieved that one of his doubts, at least, was put to rest—the abbot had not spoken exclusively to him of these matters.

The rapid-fire conversation around him continued.

'When two people desire, the force is doubled. With this surge of passion, you can cut through your emotional knots and leave your little self behind forever.'

Ajay recalled the abbot's words, 'The key lies in seeing the partner as divine. Every gesture then becomes an act of worship, every sigh a prayer, the gazing into the lover's eyes a meditation.'

One of the monks declared, 'Sexual union is not mentioned in any of our texts.'

Another monk said, 'In many of our texts, there is no one single meaning that is intended. The nuanced metaphors allow multiple meanings. For example, the image of the churner and the churned. It could refer to a physical analogy;

it could be an emotional analogy for negative emotions all churned up. It could be a mythological symbol of the churning of the ocean by the gods to produce nectar. It could refer to the state of arousal between a man and a woman, or to the circulation of energy thus ignited, that so richly lends itself to the various nuances of sexual union.'

'Sex with a woman energizes the emotions much more. So this makes the case for karmamudra or physical union versus gyanamudra, the path of arousal with an imagined partner.'

A dozing monk woke up to cap the discussion. 'Who can argue with what you have said? But that is a surface view. Would you concede that the degree of excitement varies with different partners? One who is more desirable will generate greater arousal than one considered ordinary. And this arousal is not dependent on face or feature but on your perception of the partner. So sex is first in the mind. If that is agreed upon, then why have a partner when you can turn it on in the mind? When dull, stir it up. When excitable, calm it down. That is why the texts prefer the gyanamudra.'

'What then is the rationale behind a sangyum?' asked a young monk.

Ajay was all attention. They had actual terms for different expressions of sex in the classical texts! But what was a sangyum? He could not interrupt and ask for a clarification.

Moving away from the debating monks towards the far end of the courtyard, he saw Anna coming down the steps from the abbot's room. She was always either going up to or coming down from the abbot's room, Ajay thought speculatively, as she walked up to him.

'Interesting debate I just heard on gyanamudra versus karmamudra. Is it part of the classical texts? Quite disconcerting to hear such an open discourse on sexuality in a monastery!'

'How do you think people in monasteries handle their urges?' she said, watching the burgundy-robed bustle in the courtyard. 'Denial only leaves them to express it through wet dreams.'

'And what is meant by "sangyum"?' Ajay asked.

'She is a spiritual consort, often a secret one. The intimate partner, married or unmarried, of a lama, a Rinpoche or a Khenpo.'

'Khenpo?'

'An abbot.'

'To perform sexual practices?' Ajay asked in a dangerously taut voice.

Anna's answer was an unflinching look.

Unease had lurked in his mind for quite some time, but it was only now that he was acknowledging it. So the abbot could have a sangyum. He turned to look at Anna but she had done the usual—disappeared when he most needed an answer. He bit his lip in frustration. The memory of his first meeting with Anna in the monastery flashed before him. The lights had gone off. When they came back on, the look that had passed between the abbot and Anna was of one of familiarity, of sharing. And how come Anna knew all the details of his marriage, which he had only spoken to the abbot about? In fact, they acted like a couple: one began a thought and the other finished it. The abbot talked about one aspect of the transformation of energy and Anna would explore its psychological aspect as though she was an arm to his body. All tranquillity drained away from him as more thoughts kept in abeyance tumbled out.

How come she was constantly making a beeline for the abbot's room? Why was she with him so often? Was the search for the Jesus manuscript a cover for their relationship? Perhaps there was no manuscript, just a cooked up story by Anna to continue staying near the abbot.

They had taken him for a ride, jollying him along with dazzling, unfamiliar ideas that lulled him into believing them. He was merely a toy, carelessly tossed from one to the other, while they carried on their secret liaison.

Anger rose like blood before his eyes. That which had seemed transparent all of a sudden was now mired in muddy waters. Sex under the garb of religion. Monastic vows with a wide-open bedroom door into which Anna walked unhesitatingly. In any case, she almost lived in the abbot's room, he thought, suddenly infuriated. He ran up the steps to the abbot's room and flung open the door, that banged against the wall in alarm. He looked around to see if Anna was there. She was not. The abbot, standing by the bookshelf, looked up, startled by the noise.

Through clenched teeth, Ajay asked, 'Do you have a sangyum?'

The abbot straightened to his full height and said calmly, 'Yes. But not in the way that you think.'

Sangyum

23 August: Midday

Ajay covered the short distance between the door and the abbot in four angry strides. 'How could you?'

The abbot frowned.

'You deceived me and encouraged me to talk to you about Anna,' Ajay said, his eyes spitting anger.

'You mean I created your feelings for Anna? Why would I do that?'

'To keep a veil on your affair with her. I was the toy meant to distract everyone from the fact that she is your sangyum.'

'Anna? Who said she is my sangyum?'

'Why should I believe you?' Ajay said, weighed down by the dull inevitability of what he was about to hear.

The abbot shrugged. 'That's up to you. Who but I can know the truth?'

Ajay's anger braked in a moment of hesitation. He slumped against the wall and whispered, 'Who then?'

The abbot sighed and turned to look out of the window. 'Yodon. The woman I worship is Yodon,' he said softly, reverentially.

After a few moments, the abbot turned around and chuckled at Ajay's bewildered expression. 'What are you more shocked about? That Anna is not my sangyum, or that I have loved a woman?'

Relief flooded him that it was not Anna. His anger spent, Ajay asked hoarsely, 'Who is she?'

'Where do I begin? It's been many years.' He closed his eyes and immediately saw Yodon's face. Serene, self-contained, ethereal.

'Five years into my monkhood, and a year after joining the Tibetan government in Dharamsala, the department of education sent me to Delhi. This was in response to requests from the Tibetan school to look into the problem of administrative control. The issue was complex, as two parallel administrations were in charge of the Tibetan schools.'

Rigzin had gathered that shortly after his arrival in India, the Dalai Lama had approached Prime Minister Nehru for assistance in educating Tibetan children. His Holiness believed the reason for Tibet's invasion and its subsequent humiliation lay in its isolation from the world. The first step to redress this would be to provide young Tibetans with a modern education. Nehru had generously offered to admit Tibetan children into public schools and to pay for their education. However, the Dalai Lama had declined the offer, and for good reason. It would have provided the children a good education, but at the cost of their own language, history, religion and culture. The only way to ensure a balance between a modern scientific education and the preservation of their cultural identity was to establish separate Tibetan schools.

'The Dalai Lama's sister had mobilised funds to set up Tibetan Children's Village residential schools, administered by the Tibetan government-in-exile, where refugee children like me could be housed and educated. At the same time, day schools were set up under Indian administrative control. The Delhi school wanted to come under the control of the TCV system,' the abbot explained, and walked across to the window. He paused to listen to the voices floating up from the courtyard below before closing the window. 'You know me as the abbot. But this story begins with the younger man.'

A senior lama based in Delhi had accompanied him to the Tibetan day school in Majnu-ka-Tilla. They walked past a tiny unkempt garden, past an open area with a raised platform at one end. One of the teachers engaged the lama in conversation outside the principal's office. Rigzin glanced inside the office and was taken aback at the picture of apathy the office presented. Dusty brown curtains, half of them off the rings, an old sofa with one cushion missing and another with crumbling foam peeping out, a desk with chipped legs and a tea-stained tabletop.

The principal's chair was unoccupied. Three women, dressed in traditional chubas, were animatedly conversing. One of them appeared far better dressed than the other two. Her jade green chuba, highlighted with a white collar and cuffs, and pearls in her ears, made his gaze linger a fraction longer on her. She had a long, graceful neck on which hung a low bun of straight, fine hair. Wisps of hair had broken free from the entrapment to dance on either side of her cheeks.

Pink accentuated her high cheekbones, a colour replicated on her full lips. A comely face retained the vulnerability of her thirty-odd years.

He turned away, trying to dismiss her from his mind. She did not fit in the principal's shabby office. She was probably a richer Tibetan assuaging her guilt by giving a donation, the easiest kind of service to offer in lieu of other strenuous options.

She looked up and saw a man in his early thirties in burgundy robes, taller than most of their race, one hand clasping the other at the wrist. For a fraction of a second, their eyes met, hers curious, his deeply watchful.

Soon enough, the principal and the other lama arrived, and introductions were made. The woman in green was Yodon Chodron. She was, in fact, an active fundraiser who also headed the adult education programme at the school, and had introduced Tibetan dance as an extra-curricular activity. The other two women were teachers at the school. Through the rest of the meeting, he barely glanced at her, addressing primarily the principal, intent on understanding his needs and acquainting him with the funding constraints that dogged the Tibetan government.

The system of education, so useful in the early years, was now threatened by the constant influx of fresh refugees and the existing exiled population. The problem was not only to do with numbers and miniscule resources. The refugee children and the children of the Tibetan diaspora in India had very different requirements. The refugee children could be cared for and educated only in residential schools. In the day schools, the second-generation children were demanding a greater emphasis on vocational training.

'We do not want to become a residential school because most of the parents live in Majnu-ka-Tilla and there is no greater cultural infusion than when children live with their parents versus in residential schools,' the principal said.

'Then why do you want TCV to take over?'

One of the teachers informed him that, increasingly, the Indian authorities were paying attention only to the syllabus, leaving no time for activities centred on Tibetan culture.

'Today, there is far greater pressure on the students. The increased curriculum consumes much more of their time,' Rigzin said.

'We are not blaming the Indian government. Tibetan parents are equally keen on their children acquiring vocational skills rather than Tibetan literature and dance,' the teacher explained.

'We agree that it is important that the exiled population stands independent in the marketplace, but it cannot be at the cost of our cultural heritage. If Tibetan identity is not inculcated in our children in their schooldays, then who will fight for Tibet,' the principal said.

'I agree. But besides saying to you that we need to be dynamic and quickly usher in changes, I don't know how TCV can help.'

The principal and the other two teachers nodded their heads in agreement. After all, he had come from His Holiness's office. Through most of the discussion, Yodon had kept quiet.

Suddenly, she said, 'In Oxford, how did you encourage the Tibetans there to preserve their identity?'

Quiet descended on the group. The principal stared at Yodon. The other two teachers looked down as though an invisible line of propriety had been crossed. Rigzin frowned. How did she know he had been to Oxford? No one had been informed of who would be coming from Dharamsala for the meeting. How did she find out, and why?

He got the distinct impression that something about him annoyed her. Yet she had singled him out with the kind of personal interest that in other circumstances could be termed flattering. He looked at her with assessing eyes. She was neither deferential nor insolent, but her question held the hint of a challenge. Oxford taught me to think and monkhood to feel, he wanted to say. But he kept quiet, smiling slightly, not at her but at his private thoughts.

On returning to Dharamsala, Rigzin set into motion the process of the takeover of the Delhi school by TCV. He drew up a training programme for the teachers to update their knowledge, incorporating Yodon's suggestion of greater interaction between the Tibetan schools and their non-Tibetan counterparts through participative school activities. He emphasized the need for Tibetan music, dance, plays and philosophy to be inculcated not only in the Tibetan schools but introduced as a wider cultural programme in the Indian capital. The idea was to encourage a fusion between the old Tibetan arts and their portrayal of modern themes and dilemmas. After he had made a presentation of the training initiative to the department, it was decided he should make the Delhi school an experimental base for some of these ideas.

Three months after his first meeting with Yodon, he returned to Delhi. It was the month of March, when the last of the petunias, dahlias and salvias still sang in rows of colour in Delhi gardens. In the small school courtyard, Yodon, in a clear, sweet voice, was singing a nursery rhyme to a group of children.

She stopped singing when she saw him and came across, smiling. Transfixed by her beauty, Rigzin stood silent, feeling extraordinarily alive.

'Stopping or passing through,' she asked softly.

'Stopping.'

'What gifts do you bring us?' she asked, looking up at him with her large eyes.

'TCV will take over this school. And I have brought a bag full of ideas to try out.'

'Good. Spring is here,' she said looking around. 'And so are you.'

When and how and why, he did not know, but gradually, Yodon became his collaborator, his sounding board, his alternate pair of eyes.

'We talk of educating our young. But educating them towards what?' she asked one day, as they left Tibet House after tying up the programme for Buddha Purnima with the director. This year, an Odissi dancer would accompany the chants in Pali. Their school would perform traditional dances from the Kham and Amdo regions of Tibet, which Yodon had been practising with the young ones for days.

Something about her stirred his curiosity. Not that he acknowledged this interest even to himself. One day he ventured to ask her a personal question. 'You feel committed even though you were born and brought up here?'

'We feel empty if we don't believe in something. And this was close and familiar enough to grow into and believe in.'

There was an odd poetry to her thoughts, an enticing mix of self-reflection with a dash of self-deprecation.

'Having conviction is something of a privilege.'

'And for you, where did the conviction to become a monk come from?'

'We are such a fragmented, divided house within that when one desire rides strong enough, we give it the name of conviction.'

She smiled. 'You have deflected my question.'

'No, I have answered it in non-personal terms,' he shot back.

She threw back her head and laughed. 'I can't trap you easily, but that does not mean I won't try. A strong desire and conviction are not necessarily the same thing. I may have a strong desire for money, power, acclaim but that cannot be termed conviction.'

Rigzin nodded. 'Conviction usually has consonance with higher values. But for that too, you need a strong desire.'

'And how does that fit in with a monk's avowed aim of desirelessness?'

'Luckily, I am not that desireless as yet!' he said, his gaze fixed on the low bun slipping loose from its knot.

'Really?' she glanced at him sideways with an expression in her eyes that he was unable to decipher.

In his confusion, he felt something transpired between them as they stood on the pavement.

The principal had told him she had been assisting at the school for almost three years. She was married to a businessman who exported Tibetan artefacts and was often out of town. Hence, Yodon would be able to give considerable time to assist him. How did he take the news that she was married? There was both a measure of relief and a strange kind of disappointment. Relief that she was out of bounds not merely because he was a monk but because her own marital loyalty would help her keep a distance from him, and in turn help him maintain his. Disappointment because it was one more reminder that he must not feel for her what he had begun feeling.

One day, he dared to question his feelings. His attraction to her was disturbing, but there was a measure of wholeness to it. It did not seem located in the realm of fantasy or dreams but more in the reality of knowing when two people walk well together. She was warm, vivacious, playful and also serious and reflective, with a large-heartedness that included and expanded him. By her mere presence, she challenged his world of rules, his piety and his impossible quest to live among the gods, one day aspiring to become one. She felt that was hubris of another order. Was it?

She questioned his striving to become an ideal monk. Once she said to him seriously, 'You try too hard. You cannot become a perfect monk before being a man first.'

He had raised an eyebrow at that.

'Very English,' she laughingly pointed to his raised eyebrows. 'Remnants of Oxfordness!'

'You haven't told me what you meant,' he challenged.

'It means you are in too much of a hurry to deny your frailties. You think if you do not acknowledge them, automatically they will be overcome. You want a shortcut to divinity. But you cannot vault over your vulnerabilities.'

'And what will I gain from such acknowledgement?' he asked.

'Your denial of them excites those very tendencies, your acceptance quietens them.'

He stared at her. Who was wiser: he in his monkhood or she in her worldliness?

It was July, the twilight air warm and sultry, as they sat quietly on a bench in Lodhi gardens. A thumbnail moon hung low over the monuments that had just been lit. A light drizzle had left the bench damp. Neither of them broke the silence because something too potent for both of them had arisen between them and they did not know how much to acknowledge and how much to deny. Either option seemed fraught with consequences. A monk and a married woman, he thought wryly. A good title for a short story, or was it that he was helpless to make it a longer one?

Her neck was beaded with sweat from the exertion of the walk, or the humidity, or his proximity. Magnetism radiated from her. Her hands were restless. She refused to look at him. His monkhood and her marriage were always between them. Then Yodon decided to broach one of the two barriers between them.

'I wonder if you became a monk as a form of self-punishment, a payment for being a survivor.'

'Survivor?'

'Being the only one in your family to leave Tibet. Monkhood was your offering of self-denial in lieu of what your family had been denied in staying back and letting you go.'

He had never thought of it that way. She looked at him, eyes alight with understanding.

He said gruffly, 'Are you suggesting that was the main or the only reason?'

'There is no one reason for anything. But maybe monkhood was your grand gesture.'

'And what was yours?'

'Relinquishing the idea that there is a truth to find,' she said provocatively, knowing it would bother him.

And it did. Everything about her bothered him.

'Then what do you believe in?' he asked, genuinely curious.

She stared at the early stars winking through the drifting clouds. Then thoughtfully, she said, 'To climb a mountain high enough, from which suffering ceases to look like suffering.'

'That is as close to spirituality as you can get.'

She shrugged her slim shoulders. 'Maybe. But unlike you, I am after no truth.'

'Oh, I would not name my endeavour in such lofty terms. All I am trying to do is listen to myself more clearly. Whether I will hear better or discern anything through such listening is something I have no guarantees for,' he said.

'Then what keeps you going on this path?'

'A stubborn faith that promises there will be a resting place for a lost traveller before nightfall.'

'I think all truths are lies except when love to love replies.' Her look turned to ashes all his carefully constructed theories about devoting himself to a life of monkhood. Her eyes blitzed his fortress empty of a god he had never seen, and replaced it with a woman whose love was palpable in that moment. What would he choose? A light he may never see or a woman whose love he may always know?

Twilight became a sooty darkness, like tangled desire. He had to stop her. Stop himself.

'I am a monk because it fills a need in me that no human being ever could.'

She flinched at the blow. Her eyes looked at him as though she was desperately trying to imprint him on to some inerasable part of her brain; his dark, intense eyes, a lean and taut face, perhaps sculpted by years of practising restraint over desire. She did not want to break his will, and yet how desperately she wanted to.

He folded his hands over his chest as a protective armour against the dark turmoil that raged within. Her presence filled every empty corner in his heart. I am a man; I cannot be a god. Was it a delusion—this search for a godhead? Maybe the biggest illusion I suffer from is my search for that transcendent emptiness when all I crave is fullness with her. What kind of punishment is this? My feelings for her have put my chosen path into question, pitting one against the other. At their root, both have love. Then why do they have to be in opposition?

He turned to find her watching him. There was a look in her eyes, a doomed look.

'What is it?' he asked softly.

'How can we bear it for so short a time? Every day we will have less. And one day, none,' she said with a catch in her voice.

'Would you rather have had this or nothing at all?' he asked.

'I feel all my life I have been travelling towards this. And when we part, that will be my marker, the mid-point from which everything will be before and after.'

He closed his eyes, his chest hurting.

The next morning, without telling her, he left for Dharamsala. No longer did he have the strength to be with her. A single glance, a casual touch would detonate in him a passion that his will would be unable to control or extinguish. He had already created a whole arsenal of memories out of her and he was afraid. He needed to get away from her to unearth the unaccountable fascination she held for him. A full exposure of its source might give him the means to eradicate it.

In Dharamsala, he went straight to his old teacher, Urgyen-la, now a monk. He needed to talk to a monk he respected to help reinforce his vows. He needed to hear about the subjugation of desire, the overcoming of it, the penance for it. He had realized there was nothing he was in control of. An engine running within him was fuelled by something far bigger than he was. What was he fighting—her, himself, or something else that had taken possession of him and which, in its indifference, seemed frightening and alien to all that he had believed he was and all that he had wanted to become. If he had not been a monk and she not a married woman, would the raging fire have been less of an inferno? Maybe, under normal circumstances, it would have been like a glowing, warm fire, at points sharp and intense but not with this escalation brought about by the torment of denial. Why was the denial necessary for him as a monk?

He entered his teacher's room, so small, so bare, with plain limewashed walls and a window that overlooked a little courtyard. A steel trunk in a corner, a folded camp cot against one wall, an old chair and two thick cushions on the ground—are these the privileges a senior monk has earned,

Rigzin thought wryly. His teacher had put on more weight; his hands rested on his ample belly, his face was more round and fleshy, and his eyes twinkled with merriment, as if he was watching an entertaining game. Rigzin touched his feet and his teacher rose to embrace him. He sat down at his teacher's feet and immediately said, 'I need help.'

Urgyen-la looked at him silently. The merry eyes grew serious as he listened.

'I can even feel her in this room. Her scent is in my robes, my breath inhales her and, as a man, I have found a pleasure in her company that I did not know existed. She has become sacred to me, dangerously more sacred than my vows,' Rigzin ended.

'Have you broken them?'

'No,' Rigzin said with disturbed eyes. 'But every thought of mine has. I no longer know the difference.'

'Oh, there is a difference. Between a thought and an act, there is a choice. You may not have, but you feel you are about to. Is that it?'

Rigzin's gaze was fixed on the floor.

'I know you very well, Rigzin. You have not had an easy life. You have fought every hardship with an ideal in your head. You wanted to change chaos into order, replace it with control and perfection. You thought that if you could be the perfect monk, finally you would bring order to life's disorderly ways. Is it possible you needed this particular lesson to make you understand that you are first a man, neither perfect, nor as exclusive as you think you ought to be? The two closed doors are facing you again.' He smiled and said, 'You thought you would be exempt from desire when the whole world spins on and around it?'

'But this desire contradicts all that I believe in,' Rigzin said, his eyes still downcast.

His teacher quoted:

'One who, possessing desire, represses desire,
Is living a lie. Whoever lies sins and
Because of that sin will go to hell.'

Rigzin looked up with a mixture of relief and disbelief. 'I cannot indulge it. I cannot repress it. Then what am I to do?'

'What do you do when a fire is burning in your grate? It warms and its leaping flames fascinate. But you also ensure that no log or coal falls onto the floor. You don't extinguish the fire, you don't douse it, but you keep a vigil over it so that it is contained in the grate. Hold the fire in awareness,' his teacher said.

'The other two options are easier—to repress or to indulge. What you have said is the toughest.'

'Not really. For with it I have given you the key to open the lock.'

'How?' Rigzin asked.

'If it is not clear, then let me quote from the *Hevajra,* which is assiduously followed by people from your region:

'By whatever thing the world is bound, by that the bond
is unfastened.'

Tender eyes looked down at the bent head of his student. 'Raise them, my son, look it straight in the eye, for you are looking at the dance master of life. You may not understand its lessons the first, second or even the third time. But you will become more of a man because of it.'

Rigzin raised his eyes to his teacher. He felt a power emanating from him that somehow refuelled him. He holds me in the palm of his hand as though he knows the journey ahead is by far the most difficult I have undertaken. He has not given me any easy answers. He has not told me to bend desire with my will, he acknowledges that in the face of desire my will is a bit of straw. Is he suggesting that the only cure for a burn is to put your hand back in the fire?

The silence stretched. Finally, his teacher said, 'You have brought no harm to her?'

'Can such things be measured?' Rigzin asked.

'They can be felt.'

'I am fighting her all the time. That is harm enough.'

'In fighting her, you are acknowledging her hold over you. That should be reassurance enough for her.'

'If I don't succumb, whose victory is it? If I succumb, whose loss is it?

'With any other monk I would have given a dictum, wagged the "no-no" finger. Your mind is too sophisticated for such simple-minded answers. You are up against the age-old war between wanting and relinquishing. You have to walk between the two paths. The middle path!'

'What does it mean, that what one is bound by is also the means to unfasten it?' Rigzin asked his teacher.

'Your feelings for her are also the gateway to transcendence. They are neither wrong, nor something to be ashamed of, or to be dismissed. They can become the boat that ferries you to the other shore.'

'But how do I negotiate its waters?' Rigzin asked, his expression tormented.

His teacher said cryptically,

'He who does not flow, does not grow.
He who flows, drowns.'

To flow and not drown, that is the conundrum. Does he mean that if I do not flow towards her, I will remain a timid creature with a truncated capacity to love? But if I love her without boundaries, will I flow so far afield that I will drown? Drown in the myriad entanglements that love demands, my one-pointed aim as a monk becoming a dim memory?

Something in this thought worried him. He did not want to justify his feelings for Yodon as a means to an end. He did not want to think of her as a boat that might ferry him across to some transcendental shore. She was too real a person and his feelings too immediate to use as a tool to benefit his monkhood. To hold on to his feelings for her under the guise of some higher religious sensibility would be false. In order to be able to sustain the emotional flow and not drown in it, he would have to learn to put his feet down where the current was the strongest and not lose his foothold.

He returned to Delhi a week later, stronger, yet more fragile. He did not know how he would face her. The moment was snatched out of his hands, for she was not at the school. She did not come for the afternoon adult education classes that day or the next. He asked the principal where she was. 'Not well, I think,' he said vaguely. He dared not find out where she lived and visit her. So this is what she must have felt when I left. This hollow sense of desertion, loss, emptiness within the chest.

On his third day in Delhi, he saw her coming out of the principal's office. Her face was pale, her eyes distant. Even the deep maroon chuba she was wearing did not lend any colour to her face. Her hair was pulled back in a rather severe bun that made her cheekbones stand out. He walked up to her. They stood outside one of the classrooms, speaking over the din of children repeating their lessons indoors.

'You have not been well?' he asked, searching her face.

'Well enough,' she said briefly.

'I am sorry, truly sorry.'

'For what?' she asked, and for the first time, raised her eyes to meet his.

'For only thinking of myself. For leaving without telling you.'

'We don't owe each other anything except what is given willingly.'

'I can't afford to give.'

'I know that. But you must leave me the choice of how to deal with that.'

He admired her for making a decision far superior to his own. She understood the constraints of the situation, took full responsibility for her emotions and asked for no help from him.

How could he forget that summer of a single passion where they had worked on so many things together? They took their first batch of children to Bal Bharti School for a quiz contest. They organized a recital at the India International Centre on Milarepa, the renowned Tibetan yogi. They planned an inter-faith tree planting day titled, 'Living in Harmony with Diversity'. The school performed its first street play, depicting the Tibetan struggle. They did so much together in such little time.

But how is time measured? By events, by feelings, by the impressions they leave or by the knowledge that it will run out on you? They struggled daily with that which was felt but left unsaid. It was always there, a look across a room, a moment of shared joy when the children won a prize in the quiz contest, when she planted a sapling and he covered its roots as though they had created something together which the earth bore witness to.

If she went out of the room, it felt empty. If she was there, he could not concentrate. How much did all this mean to her, he wondered. They dared not ask each other. So many days he had fought this feeling and she had fought it alongside, so that he no longer knew whose fight it was anymore. Sometimes he imagined his great relief in relinquishing the struggle, giving in. Would he find greater peace in losing, finding the surrender far sweeter than the battle?

'How hard you fight it,' she said, as they sat alone one evening in an empty classroom.

The Dalai Lama's picture hung on the wall. A few hand-painted cards were stuck on the pin board and the empty wooden desks looked like abandoned posts of learning. Yodon sat on the teacher's desk and he on one side of her. Their arms rested on the table barely inches away from one another. All he had to do was to move a little to the left and hold her hand. He watched the whiteness of her hand, the softness of her fingers clasped together. Then he raised his eyes, his hands clammy, his heart an altar to her face.

'You are a married woman. How do you deal with it?'

'I don't have harsh boundaries like yours. I feel, I flow and am fulfilled. A woman is always loyal—loyal to love.'

He got up and stood by the window that overlooked the small playground.

'Don't fight it,' she said softly.

He turned around and smiled. It was a smile of a man who had let go. He was not fighting her but flowing like a river that had broken its banks. His life seemed to have been leading him to this moment, to this woman, to her impenetrable mystery and to his own true moment of faith, not faith in the intangible unseen but in love's recognition.

What had he hoped to achieve in his aloof monastic citadels when his search seemed to have begun and ended in the faith she held for both of them? The darkness of her hair against the paleness of her skin, the smile that was tremulous with joy and the face lifted up to him as though the sight of him was all she had ever wanted. All the power held dormant in him rose like flames of feeling that licked his body and extinguished his mind. In that moment, he became her. All that was there was Yodon, a benediction, a sacrament of a different order. He no longer knew who was the worshipper or the worshipped. There was only worship.

He moved towards her as though his body was a poem written for her. He crossed a full lifetime in those six steps. 'Tomorrow we will meet. Come for dinner to my house,' she said, as though a promise long given was ready for fulfilment.

Throughout the night, he had recurrent dreams of drowning, sinking deeper and deeper. He could neither rise to the surface nor find the ocean floor. With arms and legs flailing, he struggled between the two. He awoke with his teacher's words resonating in his head: 'He who flows, drowns.' Was he drowning in his desire for Yodon, in his love for her, and no longer had the power to separate one from the other? Tonight, he would meet her. Tonight, love and desire would become one.

Unexpectedly, the next morning, he got a message that the Minister of Education, Venerable Geshe Tsephel, chief architect of Tibetan educational policy, was in town and wished to meet him at Tibet House.

Rigzin made his way to Tibet House. When he entered the room where the Geshe was sitting, he prostrated in front of him. As he rose, his senior clasped his hands and beckoned him to sit on the green upholstered sofa. Outside the window, the garden was visible. Everything was green within and without, Rigzin thought. He studied the face of the Geshe, who had spent fifteen years in the Namgyal monastery in pursuit of superior scholarship of the Buddhist texts. He was in his late fifties, with a strong square face, small deep-set eyes and a head crowned with a stubble of grey-black hair rising from a broad, well-furrowed forehead. He had earned respect, and subtly enforced it.

Rigzin waited for his superior to state the reason for the meeting. Presumably it had to do with the school and its programmes.

'Only the other day, I was reading a text.' Very softly, the Geshe quoted from the *Cittavisuddhi-Prakarana*:

'Love enjoyed by the ignorant,
Becomes bondage.
That very same love, tasted by one
With understanding brings liberation.'

Rigzin knew the text. He also knew that the Geshe had been kind to him by translating the Pali word in the text as 'love'. It could as well be rendered as 'erotic attraction'.

Rigzin's heart beat faster to a single thought. He knows. He knows. But how?

'Perhaps I misunderstood the texts where it is said that anyone having desire and repressing it is living a lie.' Rigzin ventured his own answer through another text. Some kind of battle was underway. But was the fight equal?

'Where is the text asking you to indulge desire? All it says is not to repress desire. And we do know that indulgence never leads to the cessation of desire. You will have to find another way that does not repress or indulge,' the Geshe said emphatically.

'What is that way, Geshe?' Even to Rigzin, his voice sounded faint and far away.

The Geshe grew quiet, as though debating the answers in his mind. Then, he said, 'I thought you knew that the superior practitioner practises with an imagined partner, while those of dull capacity, not having the strength or purity of mind, must rely on a human partner.'

Was it the breeze or did he hear a door open? Or did it close? How do you know by the tread whether someone is entering a room or leaving it? The pause in the conversation was not really a pause. It was pregnant with thoughts. The air grew stiflingly still.

Finally, the Geshe said what he had come to say. 'Recently, my attention was drawn to this small monastery in Ladakh that needs young monks. It is tucked away in the Hemis Sanctuary, far away from all distractions, an ideal environment to practise emptiness. The present head is getting on in years and the monastery would be well served by the enthusiasm of youth and the influx of new ideas.'

Can the heart actually stop and yet you live on? Maybe you are neither alive nor dead. Is that what is called the heart's dark night?

The dictate was clear. It was a command cloaked as a suggestion. His life was not his own. His vows were absolute. He would never be released from them. If he could not police himself, the eyes of the monastery would.

Rigzin cleared his throat. His voice wobbled as he said, 'May I be given a few days to think this over?'

'Certainly,' the Geshe replied smoothly and left the room.

Rigzin continued to sit there, paralyzed. He should have expected it, but he had not. Love is an odd bubble that engenders a private reality with only one other as its partner. You forget that the bubble is a very fragile one, only a pinprick away from reality. He could give up being a monk. Ask to be released. Defrocked. A pain clutched his chest. He weighed the other against it. How sharp was the pain when he thought of giving up Yodon? Not a second elapsed between the question and his heart's answer: You will close the door to love's sanctuary and break faith with joy.

He did not remember what he did that day. Perhaps he walked, and walked aimlessly, he did not know where. Did he pray? He could not remember. There was one memory he had of that day—of standing under a tree, feeling the sun had no light and the shade no shelter.

That evening, he climbed up the steps to Yodon's house and rang the doorbell. He could still recall the colour of the door—a deep walnut. Yodon opened it. She looked radiant, her hair open, eyes alight with welcome, her hand outstretched to bring him in. Then she looked at his face. She recoiled, her hand rose to her mouth in shock.

His eyes welled with tears. 'I can never stop being a monk,' he whispered.

Her mouth trembled, her eyes shimmered with pain.

What a strange threshold this is, he thought. A door is open and yet not. I cannot enter even though, past her, I can see a table set for dinner for two, a fragrant candle lit, and the red mats on the table.

'I am going away, Yodon.' His words reflected an emotion too great to be contained.

'No…' she said, shaking her head as though to deny the news. 'Why?'

'Forgive me. Forgive me if you can. My payment and punishment will be lifelong, for I may find that my love for you was far greater than what I have embarked on as a monk.'

Yodon looked at him and from the depths of her pain, gave him a smile of absolute, overflowing love. Nothing was held back. There were no inhibitions, no taboos, only a profound giving. To be loved thus shook Rigzin more than anything else he had endured. This was his undoing. He returned her gaze with the abandon with which it was offered. Then she took his hand and held it across the threshold. In that moment, no two people could have loved more or lost more.

Slowly, reluctantly, he let his hand slide away from hers. He walked down the steps, not looking back. He could not afford to.

She would never know where he had gone, and he would never be able to tell her.

He flew to Ladakh a week later. The pain did not fade. It seemed to grow worse in a colder, darker, uglier way as he paced the terrace of the monastery night after night. Earlier, his aloneness had been impersonal. But now it had a name: Yodon.

Ajay stirred, shaking off the silence that filled the room. When he turned, he saw Anna sitting next to him, listening to the abbot's story. He had no idea when she had come in. Her eyes held tears on behalf of both of them. She rose, bowed to the abbot and warmly clasped his hands before she left the room.

Incandescence

23 August: Evening

Ajay was moved by the abbot's renunciation. But greater still was Yodon's sacrifice. While Rigzin had struggled between his path and his love, she had to live by his choice. What is worse: to give up one of two desires, or to give up the only desire you have?

Though Rigzin's decision had led them away from each other, his life remained inexorably linked to hers. How strange, Ajay thought, you can live with someone and not feel close, or live apart and feel infinitely close.

If Rigzin had not met Yodon, would the abbot be the same man that he was today? She had become his engagement with life. His love for her had softened the sharply defined boundaries of his monastic mantle, making him more empathetic to human frailty. And his renunciation of her had become the wellspring for him to understand love and its vicissitudes more deeply. Was Rigzin's journey a search for the very fount of desire?

How could I have ever doubted this man, and imagined he was in love with Anna? The fires of desire must burn, minus the dross, the abbot had said. And his flame had never gutted. If he could but touch the embers of the fire the abbot had been through, he would be that much richer. So much fullness of passion, so much suffering. Ajay looked at the abbot haloed in the light of the setting sun streaming in from the window, his eyes still blurred with memory. A distant chorus of birds pierced the silence. Then twilight came. The abbot rose to light the lamp.

Ajay asked sombrely, 'How long has it been since you saw her?'

'Seventeen years.'

'And you never heard from her?' Ajay asked.

The abbot shook his head.

'Do you have any photographs?'

'No,' replied the abbot softly.

'If you have nothing, what do you remember her by?'

The abbot smiled, his eyes glowed for a moment, but he did not answer.

'I am sorry I doubted you. It was irrational,' Ajay said contritely. The abbot looked at him with calm, absolving eyes.

Ajay swallowed. So easily accepted, so easily forgiven.

Time seemed to overlap between past and present as Ajay struggled to ask the question uppermost in his mind. Hesitantly, he ventured, 'Did being a monk help you get over Yodon?'

The abbot responded in all seriousness, 'At first, the pain was very intense. The only way I could deal with it was by trying to banish her from my thoughts. Deep into the night, rosary in hand, I would struggle to quell them.'

'It couldn't have worked?' Looped into the question were Ajay's own struggles with his yearning.

'My will was powerless in front of her face. I then let her memory sweep over me without any restraint. The indulgence inflamed the fires further. The irony was that if I left myself unguarded in my feelings towards her, I became lost. If I erected barriers, I felt trapped within a hard shell. I often thought I might have made the wrong decision.'

It was Ajay's turn to look at the abbot with compassion. 'After many months of yo-yoing, I realized what I was doing.'

'A monk had loved a married woman,' Ajay said.

'Reprimand myself with guilt? Oh, no!' the abbot said, shaking his head. 'She was my truth. Denying love would have denied my internal reality. Whichever way I swung, indulgence or resistance, my dilemma would not resolve. I had to try something different. I cannot say why, but I took to visualizing her face in as much detail as I could. One night, I actually saw her shining presence. No, it wasn't a dream. She spoke to me gently, reassuringly. She encouraged me to accept suffering and not resist it. In her compassionate face, I saw that my salvation was in love and through love.'

Ajay was startled, remembering what the old monk had told him: Through love. That will be your way.

'That's inspiring, but I am not sure what you mean,' he said.

A fleeting smile crossed the abbot's face. 'The process is tough to describe. Perhaps the simplest way I can put it is that I learnt to "train" my yearning. I allowed it to flood me, and simultaneously I watched it. Unwittingly, I tried to empty my "mad" mind. Gradually, I realized I had to let Yodon in consciously, not blindly and self-centredly. It was then that I began to experience love fully.'

'I don't understand. When you pined for her, you were held captive. In fantasy, you found release.'

'Visualizing is not fantasy. Fantasy is the need to possess the person.'

'What do you mean by visualizing?'

'In it there is only the longing of love. There is nothing to achieve. No demands or expectations. I had lost everything, but I didn't feel empty. Many months passed before I realized that love goes far beyond the physical presence. Of course, I grieved, and of course I missed her in immeasurable ways. Slowly, it dawned on me that what I was missing were aspects of her personality. The essence that shone through the personality had never left me.'

In the long silent moment between them, twilight quietly melted into a moonlit night. To Ajay, the abbot with his eyes closed in remembrance, his face glowing warmly seemed like a priest touched by the fire he had offered in oblation.

'Night after night, I found myself in front of the Beloved, not in the hope that she was attainable or would become mine if I waited long enough. No. Abiding just so, expecting nothing, wanting nothing, every now and then the door would open when "I" was not there. Over time, I learnt to absent myself.'

Confronted with loss and suffering, Ajay thought, the monk had not asked the usual questions: Why me? Did I deserve it? By keeping himself out of the way, Rigzin had tried to look beyond his personal angst and set out on an extraordinary quest.

'In those moments, I had known bliss, momentary though it was. However, it gave me the courage to persevere in naughting myself. A fire had been lit and an all-consuming blaze began erasing the boundaries that defined and bound me. No longer was Yodon a woman separate from me; she was the charge that had reached incandescence. There were no distinctions left; no me, no her, no here, no there, no now, no then. Only oneness.'

'Was it like my Mauritius experience when everything disappeared?'

'Deeper. The mystery is how that void paradoxically becomes fullness: radiance that blazes like a thousand suns.'

'Is that the end of the road?'

'I am afraid not. To taste a strange fruit is not to possess it. Much work has to be done to bring one's whole nature into harmony with this numinous experience. I began by paying attention to the charge, not letting it churn in a cauldron of chaotic thoughts and emotions. Instead, I built up the energy and then consciously directed it.'

The air around the abbot was charged, startling Ajay's consciousness awake, opening him to a new attitude of mind.

Finally, the abbot looked him in the eye and said, 'There are no guarantees. But, if you decide not to take that road at all, you will be the lesser for it.'

Guilt

25 August: Morning

Ajay found the abbot, his tall frame bent low, broom in hand, sweeping the temple steps rhythmically and slowly as he descended. There was absorption in the act, a concentration that spoke of his total involvement in what he was doing. With this simple act of attention, Ajay thought, the gains in contemplation were being returned in work, and the difference between the two erased.

'Need something?' the abbot asked without turning around. He finished sweeping, washed his hands, and looked at Ajay enquiringly.

'Is this a good time to talk?' Ajay asked hesitantly. The abbot nodded and walked towards the courtyard, the sleeves of his robe catching the breeze and flapping like a prayer flag. Ajay zipped up his windcheater.

Not knowing how to begin, Ajay said falteringly, 'It's not working. Something odd is happening. Each time something stirs and starts to build, Swati's face swims in front of me.'

'That is to be expected,' the abbot said.

Ajay rushed on, 'When I try to look or feel, I hear Swati accusing me—not even three weeks and you are onto another woman; disloyal before, disloyal now. Pulled in opposite directions, I stand paralyzed.'

'Perhaps you are unaware that there are two forces operating within you,' the abbot said.

'I thought there was only one force, one thought, one person that was occupying my thoughts recently,' Ajay smiled self-deprecatingly.

The abbot nodded without smiling. 'When something has been ignored, it will force its way through, demanding recognition.' Ajay's silence prompted him to continue. 'You do realize that the two women in your thoughts represent desire and guilt, two forces that are constant companions and a source of lifelong conflict. It runs through my life as well. The opportunity given to me allows many kinds of desires. But guilt—obligation to my family, my school, my community, restrains me from exploring them wholeheartedly.' Coming directly to the heart of the matter, he added, 'But that aside, when you first came here, you were in a dilemma, which it seems has reinvented itself.'

'I beg your pardon.'

'Swati is an unresolved issue. Perhaps, you are asking: Did you do her an injustice by not accepting your feelings for Akanksha? Your guilt could also be a reminder that your feelings for Anna are connected with your buried feelings for Akanksha. I think it would be equally true to say that your denial of any feelings for Akanksha has created your present state. An emotion intensifies in proportion to its denial.'

'I don't think so. You asked me to focus on desire. I am bound to feel disloyalty to Swati,' Ajay defended himself.

'All I asked was that you separate the charge from raw desire.'

'Comes to the same thing,' Ajay said quickly. Too quickly.

'Your attraction was not the result of my suggestion, it was prior to it. In fact, it had built up enough for me to notice it,' the abbot stated calmly.

'But you abetted it by asking me to look, feel…'

'If I had chastised you, would you have stopped?'

Ajay thought for a moment and took the easier option of not replying.

'Tell me, is desire to be viewed only through the prism of morality? Or, put differently: Is morality the truth of sexuality?'

'Sex is meant for procreation.'

'When Swati rebuffed your advances, you didn't feel she was saying no to having another child. You were convinced she was rejecting you. Sex is usually a measure of our self-worth.'

Skirting the monastery, the abbot took the road to the hydraulic ram site. 'Guilt may be a moral check but it is also an obstacle because it blocks the erotic flow,' the abbot said.

On reaching the line of black drums, he muttered, 'Not enough pressure built up as yet.'

He is ambidextrous, Ajay thought in amazement as he hurried to keep abreast with him. How easily he switches from the rise of sexual energy to the rise in the pressure of water!

They continued downhill in silence. A little umbrella of clouds blocked the sun, as a monk and a man traversed a little known path in the belly of a mountain in search of a water source. One knew about it and the other trusted him enough to lead him there.

After a while, a little breathless, Ajay stopped and rested his back against one of two large boulders hugging each other. 'How do I reconcile my flow for Anna instead of Swati?'

'The spark lit by Anna may open your locked feelings for Swati. When you have collected enough honey, take it back to where it belongs,' the abbot's reply was swift. 'But to do that, first learn to separate the charge from the instincts.'

They soon reached the small open hut with the hydraulic ram, a cylinder of steel in the shape of a tall Shivling. The abbot adjusted the waste valve and tried to prime the pump. 'The damn thing stops too often,' the abbot muttered, and primed the pump several times. 'It's probably trapped air.' He opened one of the inlet check valves and cleaned it of debris with the cloth tied around his waist. Then he primed the pump again. After a while, the hydraulic ram spluttered, coughed, cleared its throat and started. The sound was of the rhythmic clang of a hammer beating on steel.

'Music, sheer music. This sound promises our morning bath!' the abbot smiled as he wiped his hands on the side of his robe. He checked the inlet pipe and the pressure vessel after a while. 'Our real problems will begin when winter comes. The pressure of water drops, and we have to restart the ram at least three times a day.' The engineer was at work, the abbot had disappeared. A little later, he declared, 'Let's head back. It's unlikely to stall again today.'

Silently, they trudged uphill, the abbot climbing with his hands behind his back. Ajay's thoughts stayed on what the abbot had said before they reached the ram: restrain the outflows, plug the leaks and let the energy build consciously. And how many can handle such a build-up? Ajay wondered. Perhaps the real test comes when the fire roars and the fireplace is too small to contain it. He could claim little control over his own flame of attraction.

Tung…tung…tung, faint and far away, the ram chorused its agreement.

Yab-yum

25 August: Afternoon

After lunch, Ajay decided to visit the tiny chapel, near the library, that he had not seen so far. He bent his head to gain admittance into the dimly lit structure. It was painted red inside. His eyes dilated instinctively and took in the murals of four-armed gods receding into the wall. On a shelf were set enormous copper pots, most likely for use during festive occasions. They were undecorated but beautiful, a rugged and imposing testimony to the ancientness of their origins, symbols of rituals and rites of passage.

In the centre of the chapel was a brass statue of a deity seated in the lotus position, with half-open eyes looking down. His hands, loosely crossed over his chest, held a dorje and a handbell. The deity looked rapt. Fleetingly, Ajay got the impression that the god was looking down at a woman he held in his embrace. His hands were supporting her slender form astride his lap. His gaze was intimate and full of enjoyment, and her eyes were drunk with arousal and love. What was the nature of this passion, this musk of desire that he could actually smell, Ajay wondered. The deity's arms were cupped around her back, his lips touching hers, her naked back glistening with sweat, her breasts flattened against his bare chest. The energy between them synchronized, their breaths attaining a single-minded absorption. They were ablaze. Then, as suddenly as they had appeared, they vanished from his view.

Ajay stepped back, and his foot hit a stone. He looked around dazed, clutching the wall with one hand. When he looked back again, everything was the same as before. The deity appeared bathed in the pale sunlight filtering in through the latticed windows, with hands folded across his chest. There was no woman there.

What is wrong with me, Ajay thought, shaking his head remorsefully. Did his feelings have no boundaries? He was prepared to defile an object of worship in his current state of fantasy.

He folded his hands in forgiveness and stumbled out of the chapel.

He sat down outside and tried to calm himself. He was becoming delusional. Too high an altitude, too little oxygen, too much sexual energy swirling around, too few releases. He rose and tried to consciously inhale and exhale. Head bent, he walked on until he bumped straight into Anna heading for the library.

'I don't know what is happening to me. I am beginning to see things,' Ajay exclaimed. He told her of his flight of fancy in the small red chapel, once again making her the recipient of his forbidden feelings.

'You have accurately described the Yab-yum position,' she said matter-of-factly.

'What's that?'

'Yab-yum is a common symbol in Buddhist iconography, portraying the male deity in lotus posture embracing his consort, who is seated on his lap. Often, the consort is invisible, as in the statue in the gon-khang you just saw, so the deity appears with hands crossed in mid-air. Yab-yum means father–mother in Tibetan, and their embrace represents the power that brought you into this world.' She spoke as if all this was self-evident.

'Thanks. I thought I was losing my mind and had profaned something holy,' he said, recovering his composure.

'On the contrary, what you thought was a private fantasy is a collective experience represented in a well-known art form.'

What are we really talking about, Ajay wondered. About the lovemaking he had imagined in the chapel, or his feelings for Anna? He looked at her flushed face. What was she thinking? As if on cue, she said, 'You know, the Yab-yum symbol is often recommended as a practice to control one's sexual energy.'

He sat down on the library steps, still under the spell of his experience in the little red chapel. Or was it a consequence of being with Anna? Her eyes were warm as she stood looking down at him. The warmth of a lover; the affection of a friend; the fleeting consideration for a fellow traveller; or was it the effect of their conversation?

'Sometimes I can't handle all this,' Ajay murmured. 'Why am I here?' Finding no answer, he looked at Anna and asked, 'Why are you here?'

'What are you finding so difficult?' she asked.

'Feeling so much and not knowing what to do with it.' It was the nearest he had come to confessing his feelings.

For a fraction of a second, her expression told him that she knew. Then acknowledge it, heart to heart, he wanted to tell her. The wind ruffled her hair as if threading the ancient secrets of the land through it, whispering that this feeling was too potent to be carelessly used: *You are mere novitiates under its tutelage. Do not squander it before you have earned it.*

Ajay sighed. 'Just when I feel I have a grip on this place, something new is sprung on me. What's really going on here?'

'Do I need to tell you that sexuality has a vertical dimension, it is a ladder with rungs. The experiment here is to recognize the rungs,' Anna said, looking him straight in the eye.

They smiled at one another. Ajay felt the warmth of his blood wash his body. The strange experiment was under way within his body. 'I thought desire and monkhood did not match!' he said.

'You distil desire and it turns into spirit. No pun intended,' Anna said impishly.

'Aren't monks expected to extinguish desire rather than inflame it?'

'Inflamed or extinguished, I hope you realize that, ironically, one way or another, all of religion is concerned with sex,' Anna said.

'I don't believe it!' Ajay said, and then teasingly added, 'I thought the whole of life was about sex!'

She laughed delightedly. 'I used to wonder too, when John introduced me to these ideas. Remember I told you about Khajuraho? I learned that some schools believe it is unnatural to suppress desire completely; a more natural path would be to surrender to the beloved. The relationship is the altar where personal desires are sacrificed.'

Both sat lost in their own thoughts.

When Ajay spoke, his tone was soft. 'And you, what do you believe?'

She did not try to deflect or pretend to misunderstand the question. 'Most of my life, I followed the herd, believing desire had nothing more to offer than flashes of pleasure. John introduced me to its larger reality. I had oscillated between curiosity and disbelief. But through my relationship with him, I learnt to love, I felt love. I also realized that love was not about satisfaction, his or mine. On occasion, it transported us to a realm where time was not, space was not. Those were our moments of epiphany. I never speak about it as it is difficult to convey its essence. Somehow, I get the feeling you would understand.'

It hit Ajay that she was talking of her 'Mauritius' moment. Deep down he had felt his experience was an anomaly, even though the abbot had sanctified it. Her affirmation imbued it with greater authenticity. She had been privy to it too. Perhaps that was their bond.

A glow-worm flitted through his body and paused everywhere before lodging in his heart and asking him if it belonged there. Would touching Anna have been a greater pleasure than feeling this glowing dance in his body, he wondered.

The Flying Power

27 August: Night

He looked around her small eleven-by-nine room, simple and spartan, a table serving as her kitchen. On it rested a kerosene stove, a few pots and a clean upturned plate, a glass and two spoons. A jerry can of water lay beside the table. A low bed with a thick mattress ran along the wall opposite the door. Near the bed was a picture of John, chin in hand and eyes laughing. Along the left wall, books rested in cartons stacked one upon the other. Beneath the window, almost hugging the door to its left, was another table on which her laptop lay. The room had the air of a Harvard researcher turned ascetic.

Anna sat on her mattress with her eyes closed. The wrap had fallen from her shoulders to show a peach-coloured shirt tucked into a white skirt. Next to her was a book, *The Universe in a Single Atom,* held open with a small river stone. Home is not the place where we live but where we love, Ajay thought with a pang. He wanted to talk to Anna but did not want to disturb her moment of repose. Could she sense that he was looking at her?

Without conscious volition, he walked up to her and sat on the mattress, his knee almost brushing hers, and slowly raised his hand to touch her face. Longing rippled through his fingers as they neared her face. Then he could not think any longer. Feelings, expectations, hope drenched him. She would open her eyes soon. He rested in that exquisite moment of anticipation, so perfect that his heart sang. He moved closer to kiss her, his body throbbing with anticipation. She stirred. He put his arms around her, feeling on fire. Her face was warm, her eyes opened slowly. They held surprise, and then uncertainty that melted into something that was as vulnerable as it was trusting.

A thud like an airplane touching the ground. Darkness. A sea of shadows. His beating heart. The first glimmer that he was waking. A sharp disappointment, as though he heard the clang of prison doors closing behind him. He was no longer holding her. She was receding from him. Her open eyes did not see him, even though he saw the last of her face disappearing in the opaque mists of separation. The hand he held out was not met by hers, but by his own lying on his chest. He was so near touching her, until wakefulness came as an intrusive enemy, denying what it could not replicate in its own world. Why did the awakening appear a dream, while the other state had seemed so very real? In this twilight moment, he felt a denizen of two worlds. Anna, in dream, as real as flesh yet without the distractions of flesh.

What remained was an intensity of focused feeling, distilled of all imperfections except the desire to merge with her. What was this wild crisis of passion, like an acute nervous disorder, waiting to flare out of control when he thought of her? Was Anna merely an ideal figure fleshed out of his need?

He sat up with his arms around his knees, pondering on the experience. Certain beliefs seemed to have dissolved as though they had never existed, and in their place had come a new tentative emptiness in which other certainties could enter. And one of them was this extraordinary throbbing power that invaded him.

He wondered if it belonged to him or to her, or was it theirs working in tandem. A new life seemed to have begun for him that might, at any moment, burn its way to her, and light up his very soul before her. All his energies were now gathered together like a bundle of loosely held sticks entwined by the rope of thoughts around her. He smiled. What he had ignored and denied all his life, he was now enacting. He was leading a disciplined life, a focused life, a one-person, and one-thought life. Anna. He may call it love, but was its other name prayer? That was his last thought as he drifted into sleep.

28 August: Morning

Before the morning broke fully, Ajay headed for the abbot's room. The Yab-yum deity yesterday, and this early morning visit…he had to discuss this fantasy world he was being sucked into. No sooner had he entered than he declared, 'My mind is playing tricks with me.'

The otherwise rational abbot was singularly interested in the description of his visit to Anna. 'Did you notice which page she was on?'

'Yes,' Ajay said. 'Emptiness, relativity and quantum physics on page 43.'

The abbot looked surprised at the detail.

'I remember it clearly because I'm forty-three and I've always been very interested in quantum theory. My teacher made an abstruse subject come alive.'

Brushing aside his explanations, the abbot asked, 'Have you seen Anna this morning?'

'No. Why?'

The abbot remained motionless, his eyes alive. 'Are you familiar with astral projection?'

'No. What does it mean?'

'Travel without the body.'

'Perhaps my dramatic description gave that impression. I'm sorry, but it was just a vivid fantasy. Why the hell am I having these outlandish thoughts when I am a nuts-and-bolt character?'

The abbot sidestepped his concern. 'Your description of the room, her appearance, it's all too accurate to ignore.'

'Well, I must confess it seemed completely real while it lasted.'

'Have you ever been to Anna's room?'

'Not inside. I did walk up one night and sat outside what I presumed was her cottage,' he confessed a bit sheepishly. 'I thought you knew.'

'How would I? We don't have CCTV cameras,' the abbot replied drily.

'I thought the old monk would have told you. Isn't that why you asked me the other day about my feelings for Anna?'

'Which monk?'

'The one who lives up on the hill near Anna's cottage.' How can he not know, Ajay thought.

'Only women live there,' the abbot said. 'And as for the old monk, you must have been thinking of those archetypal stories in which someone is lost and out of nowhere a helper appears and leads the person to his destination?'

'Like Forsyth's *Shepherd*?'

'Perhaps the old monk was shepherding you? Remember I told you that those who take the steeper path are met, guided, given assurance.'

Ajay had felt a sense of reverence for the old monk, but had certainly not thought of him as a guide. Why was the abbot lingering on him rather than the real issue of his fantasy? He hadn't disclosed how he knew that his description of Anna's room was accurate. He must have been there. But how and why, if it was part of the 'nunnery'? Once again, the same bandwagon! He knew the abbot was clean, then what had triggered the doubt? Oh, yes! Of course, because of the astral theory, which he, for one, didn't buy.

A breathless Anna entered the room. She was dressed exactly like in his dream. The abbot looked pointedly at Ajay, eyebrows raised.

'I am sorry for barging in a second time in one hour but I need to confirm the instructions for Tsering. He is busy holding forth in his inimitable way with some refugees. Sorry for this interruption, Ajay.' Her cordial tone contained not the slightest hint that she had seen him earlier in the morning.

Ajay was battling his own thoughts. So that was what had aroused the abbot's interest on hearing his account. He knew what she was wearing this morning, and wanted to confirm whether Ajay had already seen her and had unwittingly embroidered her dress into his dream description.

'Yes, yes, the instructions are the same.'

'Oh, thanks,' Anna said and turned to leave.

'Anna, one moment please. Which book are you reading these days?' the abbot asked.

'Oh! His Holiness's *The Universe in a Single Atom*. You know, he has so many interesting points to make about emptiness and quantum physics. I do want to discuss it with you sometime soon. But right now I have to rush, or Tsering will be mad at me.' She shut the door behind her and sped towards the courtyard.

'Proof for you that the book you saw was really open on precisely that page. Secondly, her clothes were what you saw. And we can go right now to her cottage and see for ourselves what it looks like. Please tell me, Sir, why I shouldn't reprimand you for violating the monastic rule by visiting the women's section?' The abbot's eyes twinkled.

'I know everything points in that direction. But I couldn't have defied gravity and flown to her on a broom?'

'It's your own experience, yet you disbelieve! Why? Because you have a fixed idea of what reality is.'

'Reality is my two feet, which earlier had taken me to her cottage. How else can I get there? And, since I was lying flat in bed, I presume it was a wishful dream.'

'Not all journeys are of the feet. Can't you see the pattern? You believed Akanksha was only your friend and you journeyed to Ladakh. You believed Jesus died on the Cross and you were fascinated by Anna's journey. You believed only a lithotripsy can relieve painful stones, and yet, in front of your very eyes, one man was cured and a woman's past unveiled. You know the insides of Anna's cottage without ever having been there physically. So, what do you believe in?'

Ajay felt miffed. The abbot always managed to change the terms of the discussion by asking new questions. The abbot continued, 'Perhaps it was ESP, where you didn't journey but saw by another mode of seeing. But is ESP any less of a challenge to our rationality than astral journeys? How did you see the book she was reading through stone walls?'

Unable to deny the question or accept it, Ajay fumbled, 'But still—'

'If your objection is to the term "astral", then call it an out-of-body experience, an OBE, which is not a freak occurrence. I read about a survey in Britain, the rational West, in which over 400 people responded with authentic accounts of OBE. You may have heard of how surgeons, now and then, have come across a patient who, after the surgery, accurately reports some incident that had occurred during the operation—the assistant had handed the surgeon the wrong instrument; the conversation between the doctor and his junior, and so on. As if the patient had been watching from the ceiling.' The abbot pointed upwards.

'At least that gives some respectability to my fantasy. As the British would say, I thought I was going native in this wilderness. On a more serious note, what causes this strange phenomenon?'

'You had a great desire to visit Anna's room, to be with her. There were restrictions, so you went to meet her without the body. The flying power is called Eros, Ajay. It knows no barriers,' the abbot said gravely.

'What's disturbing is that I don't seem to have any volition in this,' Ajay said.

'Perhaps very few realize that sex is energy—psychic energy, rather than just physical stimulation. You, as an engineer, are aware that there are grades of energy, and that one form can be converted into another. The transformation of physical energy into psychic energy is closely connected with sexuality.'

'Excuse me, Sir, isn't that a jump?' Ajay intervened.

'Is it? Tell me, why do we prefer to keep children ignorant of sex? So that their psychic energy stays focused on their studies. Once this channel of energy flow is established, sufficient psychic energy will be available after puberty to support both sexual interests and studies.'

Ajay said, 'I always thought that was old-fashioned morality.'

'From the earliest times, psychically gifted people have found that the spontaneous flow of libido bestows greater powers—an ability to heal, to be precognitive and produce strange phenomena. Isn't that what the lhapa did with Anna? And perhaps it was your aroused state that made you see which book Anna was reading. Not only that, this flying power may help you discover a level of awareness that is not just consciousness of hunger and sex.'

'The only explanation for this must be quantum entanglement?' Ajay said.

'What?' the abbot asked.

'The concept that two distinct particles can interact as if connected despite being spatially apart. If one particle turns, the other turns too,' Ajay said.

'Are we any wiser than we were with OBE? Except that we are now using scientific terminology,' the abbot remarked.

'Well, something else happened this morning. While sweeping my room, I spotted some hair in the dustpan.'

'Nothing unusual about that!'

'They were very fine hair, certainly not mine. My hair is thick. No one had come to my room. In any case, all the monks are clean shaven! Out of curiosity I examined one strand of hair. It was blonde, a couple of inches long. I picked up a few and stored them in an envelope. The modest quantity was enough for me to ask, what's going on? Did Anna come to my room when I was not there? She never breaks rules. Then how?' Ajay frowned.

'I am wondering...' The abbot was clearly intrigued.

'Did she come when I was fast asleep? Returning my call astrally, as I had?'

'But can you leave behind physical evidence in such a journey?'

Ajay was surprised to be taken seriously. 'I have not known this to happen. Must ask some senior lamas when the opportunity arises,' the abbot said pensively. 'We do know that some things can be brought from the dream world.'

'That's not possible!' Ajay said emphatically.

The abbot dilated his eyes.

'You mean it is?' Ajay said.

'Have you never woken with your heart beating faster after a nightmare? Something tangible—the fear—was brought into this reality from the unreal world of dreams.'

'Even more compelling is the wet dream, the sheer power of desire converted to reality. But the blonde hair does not belong to this category of objects. I am puzzled.' The abbot kept shaking his head, 'I don't know how...'

After some time, with the abbot still lost in the puzzle, Ajay stepped out of the room, needing to be alone to comprehend the incomprehensible.

Precognition

28-29 August

He searched for Anna, hoping she might give him a more down-to-earth explanation. But she had gone with Tsering on a three-day field trip to settle the flood-hit people who had arrived that morning at a village near Lama Napa, a monastery reputed for its library of ancient texts. Would she visit the monastery in search of the Jesus manuscript, he wondered. He felt a pang of exclusion. How quickly an expectation develops from a relationship that may not have offered him that privilege yet.

He still couldn't accept he had 'visited' her last night; nor was he prepared to call it a fantasy. He would rather believe he had entered a separate reality because of his intense longing. Perhaps he had been transported to this other realm because he had stood in the gap between physical and imaginative intimacy. His longing to reach Anna had aroused in him a feeling that was not merely physical, yet so potent that it could even dispense with the body.

Not by indulgence but by restraint is the charge built, the abbot had said. Guilt douses it. What would his feelings have been towards Anna without the guilt of betraying Swati? Build a dam not merely to curtail the water but to generate electricity from it, the abbot had suggested.

Another day went by, and Ajay blindfolded his body with work, all thoughts subservient to her return. Late in the afternoon, he went to the abbot's room. 'I think we had better put an extra plate for dinner tonight. I think Anna will be here,' he said.

'Have you heard from her? Today is only the second day; she is supposed to be away for three.'

'No. But I think she will be here.'

The abbot looked at Ajay quizzically, shrugged his shoulders and continued writing.

At 5 p.m., Ajay went to the abbot's room with a flask of tea, a ritual he looked forward to. He put the flask down on the small copper plate next to the abbot's rug. Just then the door opened and Anna entered. The abbot looked up in surprise.

She pulled out a mat and collapsed on it. She looked dusty and distracted.

'You are here early,' the abbot commented.

She nodded. 'My work finished early.'

'Tea?' Ajay asked.

'Love some,' Anna said, and with a touch of asperity, asked him, 'Why were you calling me? What did you want?'

The abbot looked from one to the other. Anna was frowning into her cup of tea and Ajay was trying to look at any place but at her.

'Did you manage to settle that couple?' Ajay asked, making an effort to meet her eye.

'We could do no more than manage some basic survival needs. May have to check on them again. I am a little tired with all the walking, so if you both will excuse me, I'll go to my room now.' She looked at Ajay and smiled. The space between them hummed. The abbot watched the silent exchange. Anna folded her mat and left.

The abbot turned to Ajay and said cryptically, 'Sir, when will you accept what is happening to you? How much more proof do you require that you are dealing with energy? Things have happened very fast. First the OBE, then the hair, and now precognition. All in the last few days.'

'I can't understand it myself,' Ajay mumbled. 'It's like a… quantum event…a different time scale.' He grappled for a plausible explanation. 'In the quantum world, there is no discrete past, present and future. Everything is happening all at once…now! Perhaps that's how I knew of her return.'

'Really?' The abbot looked innocently at Ajay. 'Well, time did not collapse for me. Do you and I live in a different time?'

'I don't have answers to everything,' Ajay protested.

'My dear Ajay, why can't you accept the simple truth—it's a mystery. We do not know. You, at least, know that events beyond the plausible do happen! By practising restraint, it may seem that nothing particular is being done but you *are* storing power.'

The abbot smiled enigmatically. 'Please accept that sex is not only sex, it is a power. By restricting its wasteful outflows, very unusual states may be experienced. Irresponsible desires are not permitted. All that can be said is: Catch fire and get out of the way.'

Anna's Search

30 August

Ajay hurried to keep abreast with Anna's long impatient strides as they walked towards a little-known monastery in search of an elusive manuscript.

This search had reversed the gains of the last few days; her shoulders drooped again. Her face was lined with tension; her eyes glistened with the ache of lost moments; and the reserve was back in place. Ajay realized that unless the big issue swirling around her was addressed, nothing else could be spoken of. He decided to begin on neutral ground by asking her something he felt she could deal with.

'Is the original manuscript still at Hemis?'

'Oh no. The abbot of Hemis let slip to John that it was a controversial manuscript. Too many far-reaching implications, he said, rolling his eyes upwards. Jesus learnt from Hindus and Buddhists!' Anna's voice trailed away, and she seemed to fall into reverie.

After a while, she surfaced again. 'He had relented somewhat, after John sought interviews on three separate occasions. He even offered a clue: Where do you hide something, you don't want anyone to find? Put it where no one will think of looking.'

'You mean, it could even be in our monastery!'

'Who knows?' Anna's tone was non-committal.

'Did John suspect it was in any particular monastery?'

'The Hemis librarian told him that the head lama of one of the smaller monasteries had come to visit the abbot of Hemis, and they spent the evening with each other. The next morning the manuscript had disappeared!'

'Have you tried talking to the librarian?'

'I did, but he just clammed up. John suspected it might be in this tiny monastery that we are headed towards. I have made many attempts to meet the head lama, but the old rascal—that's what John called him!—just won't see me.'

'This manuscript, it meant a lot to John. Is that why it is important to you?' Ajay asked, persisting in his attempt to separate her story from her guilt about John.

'That's an oversimplification,' Anna retorted.

Ajay was silent for a while and then said, 'How long are you going to atone, Anna?'

'As long as it takes,' she said fiercely.

'For god's sake, Anna, it's been five years since John's passing on! How much longer? Another year? Four, five? Or is it to be lifelong?' Ajay exclaimed.

'How dare you tell me how long I should mourn? It's none of your goddamn business,' she shouted at him and walked ahead.

Ajay marched up to her and caught her arm. 'It was not your bloody fault! Can't you understand that? You feel you could have done something. Such feelings merely mask our helplessness in the face of death. The person who was meant to go, went. You, however, have decided that the wrong person went. And each moment you live, you punish yourself for being alive. Perverse logic, isn't it?' Ajay asked angrily, shaking her by the shoulders.

Listlessly, she whispered, 'I deserted him when he was dying; I'm not going to desert him again.'

'I am not asking you to desert him or forget him! All I am saying is, let him go. There is a huge difference between the two, Anna. Letting him go would not be abandoning him, or prove in any way that your love is fickle; just the opposite, in fact. You love him enough to let him go where he now belongs.' Ajay was taken aback by his own words. Had the alchemy of the monastery opened the unvisited rooms within his own psyche?

He stared at her, wondering if she had been listening. Then she did the unexpected. She rested her head on his shoulder. He drew her close and folded her in his arms.

'I have not permitted myself to be touched by anyone for so long,' Anna tilted her face upwards, gazing directly into Ajay's eyes.

'We both have been frozen. It's time for the thaw now,' Ajay said, smiling back into eyes that suddenly looked freer of the dark undertows of memory.

'Then let's walk to that,' Anna said, a tremulous smile lighting her face. The road was the same, but this time the footsteps of the travellers were imperceptibly firmer and surer.

'I've often asked myself, why was he alone in his last moments? What did he think? When he was dying, did he think of me? God knows how long he suffered. You're right. The knotty issue for me is guilt. Am I not responsible?'

'Would John want you to remain immersed in sorrow? Would he feel you have betrayed the specialness of your love if you reinvested in life? Would he think it's unfair if you were to find happiness?'

'The rational part of me knows that I couldn't have done what he did for me. I was in a coma. There is no explanation for why his injuries were fatal and mine were not. But how do I get away from the fact that I was the one who was driving?'

'Maybe you are punishing yourself for all the regrets you had before the accident: you should have been more thoughtful of his needs; not have fought with him; you should have been more receptive to him; expressed your love more openly. Just for a moment, imagine what it would be like if there was no guilt. What remains?'

Anna inhaled deeply and said, 'A big vacuum.'

'Perhaps you needed guilt to obscure your grief. Guilt shielded you against missing his companionship, the stimulation he provided.'

Anna looked startled. 'I never thought of guilt as a comforting quilt shielding me from aloneness.'

'You don't need that quilt anymore. Winter is over,' Ajay said gently. 'Mourn John properly, Anna, but not with guilt. If you reflect on it, guilt is about self-concern. I should have been the caretaker, the life-giver. I should have done something more. Aren't those your expectations from yourself? They have nothing to do with John. This overpowering guilt made you mourn yourself, not him.'

Anna stopped in her tracks. Then, after a long moment, she nodded slowly. They continued walking on a dirt track down the hill that led to a miniscule stream of water. There they sat down and rested against the slim trunks of willow trees drooping over the water. Periodically she looked skywards, as though searching for something.

Touching her hand lightly, he said, 'Maybe you never had a closure to your relationship with John. One minute he was sitting next to you, talking animatedly, and then he was gone forever. You could not attend his burial or speak at his memorial. You had no preparation for his going, as most of us do when faced with illness or old age. The abruptness of his departure made it utterly unreal. It is possible that you are still waiting to say goodbye to him.'

'How do you say goodbye?' Anna whispered to herself.

'Did you think the manuscript would be your farewell gift to him?' Ajay asked gently.

Anna sat silently gazing at the flowing water.

'Only if he were "alive" could I say goodbye,' she said wistfully.

'You can bid farewell to him even without finding the manuscript, you know. Without bringing him back to life.'

'How?'

'Thank him for what he gave you. No one, not even death, can erase that. You shared a special relationship. How many people have that? Celebrate it without the guilt.'

Ajay looked at Anna. Her gaze had softened, her mouth had lost its tightness. He knew she was listening.

'Maybe you never mourn just the person. You mourn the love you shared. You mourn the loss of being able to love and be loved. You mourn the fact that you may never again find it with another,' Ajay said pensively, cupping his chin in his hands.

They fell into a silence that held the solace of quietude.

Seen from afar, they looked like a Japanese painting on rice paper. Two small figures perched on rocks with the overhanging willow tree eavesdropping on their conversation, while the little stream at their feet sought the whereabouts of the river it belonged to but had never seen.

Eventually, they got up. A half-hour trek from there brought them in sight of the Thangse Gompa. The residential building cleaved to the ledge of a mountain. A small side-door led into a courtyard, in the middle of which stood a high pole of poplar wood with a yak's tail flying on top. The whole place, sorely in need of restoration, was reminiscent of a faded, forgotten era.

The indistinct frescoes on the walls of the anteroom, with just a hint of blue and red in them, were barely visible through the soot and grime. The blurred Wheel of Life painted on the wall was like a hazy memory struggling for recall. Ajay noticed that the doors and windows were not aligned, either because the floor was not quite level or because the windows themselves were a bit askew. A black dog leapt out of nowhere and began barking. A young monk came out, restrained the dog and looked at them enquiringly. Anna requested an audience with the abbot. The young monk vanished into the interior of the building.

Anna said, 'This is the first time I have entered this far into the monastery. We'll probably be sent back.'

The monk returned after a few minutes and said the abbot would see them. Anna sighed with relief. Ajay teased, 'You should have come with me earlier.'

The monk took them up a dark staircase to a small room. They paused on the threshold of the room, a lone candle guttering in one corner. The air was heavy with incense, and the flickering flame teased both light and shadow. Heavy hangings and pillars of dark wood accentuated the darkness in the room. As Anna tried to focus her eyes, Ajay stared at the octogenarian sitting on the floor, with a faded lacquered desk in front of him. The abbot's eyes were heavy lidded and shuttered. His long beard was completely grey, plaited and tied at the end with a tiny black ribbon. Cheekbones jutted out from a gaunt face, and his thin arms and long bony hands motioned like a conjuror's, inviting them to sit on the two folded yak wool blankets on the floor.

Anna felt a gust of uneasiness, much as one might feel on entering a mausoleum. Addressing the abbot in a low and respectful voice, she thanked him for the meeting and told him she was searching for the Buddhist texts that spoke of Jesus's stay in India and Ladakh.

'For that you will have to go to Lhasa. They say the original lies there. That is, if the Chinese have not destroyed it already!' The abbot chuckled malevolently.

Clearly, the lama knew about the Hemis manuscript, which was a copy of the original in the library at the Potala Palace. Anna's shoulders sagged with disappointment.

The old lama, his eyes narrow beady slits, looked at Anna speculatively. 'I know you have tried many times to meet me. Why do you want the manuscript?'

'For various reasons.'

'And why should I give it to you if I had it?' the abbot asked.

'Because it could alter human thought. It could remove false perceptions. It could open the way to reinterpret Christian theology.' Anna never took her eyes off the man who barely looked at her as she spoke.

'Clever. You flatter me by suggesting that I could be that instrument of change if I gave you the manuscript,' the abbot said, stroking his beard.

'Would you show it to me if you had it?' Anna asked.

The abbot smiled a secretive smile.

He is playing her, Ajay thought. He loosens the string and then reels it in. But is the bait really there?

Anna was about to say something when the abbot said abruptly, 'The manuscript you are looking for is not in this gompa. You may have to search elsewhere.' He gave her a sharp look before continuing, 'I said the same to another very persistent foreigner five years ago. He pleaded with me, saying that his time was running out. Unfortunately, I couldn't help him.'

Anna's gasp echoed in the room before she asked urgently, 'Did he have a beard?'

'I am an old man. You can't expect me to remember such details,' he said, pointing a long bony finger with a curling, sickle nail at her.

'What else did he say,' Anna asked eagerly.

Oh, hell, she believes it was John, Ajay thought.

'He said something about a past that was pulling him and a future that had no face. Curious fellow,' the old man mused.

'Where was he from?' Ajay asked.

'America. I think he was teaching at Havad…Harvard.'

Anna stumbled out of the room. Ajay found her sitting on the courtyard steps and settled down next to her. They had come in search of a manuscript; instead, they had become enmeshed in the memories of an old man. Weird, he thought, that out of any number of possibilities, the old lama had chosen to narrate his five-year-old conversation with an American professor. Stranger still that the octogenarian had chosen to relate information that had nothing to do with the manuscript but was most significant to the professor's wife. Almost as though the dead could speak through the living.

Anna's quavering voice broke into Ajay's thoughts. 'How did John know of his impending death? How, how?'

'Did he ever mention anything to you?'

'No, never. But he chose to tell a stranger about it.'

'You may not have believed him, if he had. He did tell you that "death rides on your shoulders". I suppose he felt it was only a hunch, too alien to express in a rational setting. Maybe he found it easier to voice it in a monastic setting, to a stranger.'

'It must have been a terrible burden for him to carry alone,' Anna said in a low whisper.

'If he sensed his approaching death, then in some manner, it was fated,' Ajay said gravely. 'It would have happened in any case, whether he was driving the car or you were. Even if he was on a bus, he would have died. Inevitably, someone or something has to execute death's bidding.'

Anna nodded her head slowly. Perhaps, for the first time, it was sinking in that she had not killed John. Death had.

'A past that was pulling him and a future that had no face,' she repeated John's words to the lama. Standing with her hands on her hips, she looked at the broken courtyard with the early afternoon light deserting it. A sudden gust of wind made the monastery flag flap fretfully. 'Let's get out of here. This place is giving me the creeps.'

They walked out of the monastery, and from a past that had been spoken of and had received a hearing.

It was evening by the time they saw the familiar warm lights of their own monastery. Anna opened the latch of the abbot's door, and they walked in unannounced. Startled, he looked up from the leaves of a much-yellowed manuscript. A magnifying glass lay on top of a faded old maroon cloth, probably the binding cloth of the manuscript. Quickly, he slid the manuscript under his leg, covering it with his robe.

'Oh! You are back. I did not expect you till later,' he said in a tone that was a little too rushed and shifted his weight on to the manuscript, as though to conceal it further. 'So what did the trip yield?' Without waiting for Anna to answer, he said, 'Something is different. Your eyes. They have shed some of their sadness.' The abbot nodded his head. 'It's visible in your shoulders. Is the lhapa's magic working?'

That's right, Ajay thought. She had not once rubbed her shoulders on their walk back.

Anna related all that happened, looking to Ajay to add or confirm some of the details. When she had finished, the abbot said, 'So, it seems you discovered John there, not the manuscript.'

Anna nodded. Ajay's eyes narrowed as he watched the abbot again shift his weight.

'Why not look for the truth that Jesus found within you rather than in a manuscript,' the abbot said, his eyes holding Anna's gaze.

Powerful eyes, Ajay thought. Almost hypnotic. You could lose your will in them. Today, he didn't want to.

'It's easier to look for a manuscript than to find the truth within,' Anna smiled.

'True. But why go for the substitute when the real thing beckons,' the abbot said quietly.

'I still hope to find it, even though many of the earlier reasons have lost their compelling hold.'

'Did we interrupt your reading', Ajay asked.

'No, no,' the abbot said casually.

'Anything interesting you were reading?' Ajay persisted. 'May I take a look at it?'

The abbot shifted slightly, took an unopened book lying next to him and gave it to Ajay.

As soon as they left the abbot's room, Ajay turned to Anna and asked, 'Did you see that?'

'Yes. He hid a manuscript under his knee when we entered. He was quick. The script could have been Pali or Tibetan, I couldn't be sure.'

'You think he could be hiding the manuscript we are looking for?' said Ajay, disbelief and conviction pulling him equally in opposite directions.

A Joyful Madness

2 September

He had not seen Anna for two full days. She had gone into
retreat. He missed her, but in a gentler, less intrusive way.
Earlier, when she had withdrawn after the lhapa's disclosure of
her past, a strong compulsion to meet her had seized him, and
he was resentful at his powerlessness in the face of his feelings.
Not that his desire was any less intense now; in fact, its flame
had warmed him exquisitely when he held her for the first time
in his arms on the way to the monastery: the softness of her
body, her breath warming his chest, the fragrance of her hair.

Should it not have inflamed his desire for more? And yet,
it had not. That is why this was a path of restraint but not of
repression, Ajay said to himself. You looked, acknowledged,
watched, but you did not enact. Different kinds of rules here.
They were not of right and wrong, but of awareness and
unawareness. I am the laboratory. I am both the experiment
and the experimenter. The materials are my own thoughts and
feelings, the process is the observing, and the transformation
is the letting go. Everything within this laboratory belongs to

me. How come I never took ownership of it earlier? Why did I ascribe it elsewhere, to the other? Why was I an alien to myself?

And you, as the other, were known only through the filter of characteristics I ascribed to you. I am Akanksha, the unacknowledged; I am Swati, the unresolved; and I am Anna, the fragrance of life. Do I know what they are in themselves? They are what I have created of them. They dance because my thoughts keep them alive. They came into being because of my need. Would they stop existing if I no longer needed them? And, will love die if the other is not needed? 'Desire can be distilled without it being repressed or eliminated,' the abbot had said. The flame burns steadily with less of 'me' rather than more of me'. Like a sunset that no longer burns with the heat of the sun, but lives under its glow. Even the guilt was missing. Ajay felt cleansed, unburdened of himself. A delicious lightness filled him.

He worked with the children of the families displaced by the floods in the afternoon, showing them how to make a ship from a carton box, strings and willow sticks. He fixed his once-white handkerchief as a sail and the children clapped with joy. He lifted his favourite six-year-old monk onto his lap and taught him how to whistle. The others joined in, trying to make Os of their mouths, giggling and laughing at the odd sounds that came out. They jumped up and down, ran around him and the little ship sitting on the courtyard floor. He threw back his head and laughed with the sheer joy of it.

3 September

He woke late that morning, having slept through the morning service and breakfast as well. It was 7.45 a.m. In need of a cup of tea, he went in search of his favourite tea stall that served Darjeeling tea for the uncivilized few who could not swallow the normal brew of tea leaves, salt and yak butter boiling in the copper churn. Ladakhis called it gur-gur chai because of the bubbling sound it made while brewing.

Going down the road, he met a woman bent under the weight of a load of long, dry twigs tied to her back. A red scarf tied around her head highlighted her ruddy cheeks. She looked up and smiled at him. An open generous smile, sharing a moment of well-being, without asking for anything or being conscious of giving something. She spoke no Hindi or English and he no Tibetan or Ladakhi, yet the communication was real, as though the beauty of the world was being mirrored back to him. The music of the moment strummed between them, life tugged at his sleeve to give him pause. Somewhere he heard a clear mountain stream singing and cascading down from some immaculate source. In the sunlight, the stones on either side turned into shades of dull copper, the glistening mica in them making them appear more rounded and less jagged than usual.

A short while later, he sat on an old wooden bench outside the tea shop. Within, he could see the owner's wife roasting large but not-so-round chappatis on a wood fire. A woollen goncha tied with a shocking-pink cummerbund, a grey headscarf the colour of her eyes, and a worn-out windcheater completed the mix of traditional and modern wear.

Ajay pointed to the chappatis and the tray of eggs lying on the mud floor. She smiled and nodded, understanding his breakfast requirements. 'No gur-gur chai. The other one,' he indicated, lifting an imaginary cup to his lips. The woman nodded again. The language of food is understood easily,

Ajay thought with amusement. The wooden logs burnt in the grate, flushing the woman's face. Her rough cracked hands, sprinkled with flour, turned the browning chappati in deft circular movements on the dark iron plate. She turned to her left where, curtailed by a stick, onions were spread out on the floor. She picked up two and began peeling them. She sensed he was watching her and looked up with calm eyes. The moment had a sharp clarity to it, a reality so different from his normal state of divisions and dualities. He had stepped out of the habitual way of being in the world, woken up for just a moment.

With great satisfaction, he ate his scrambled eggs and chappati, interspersed with sips of hot tea. The other two men on the bench were sipping their yak tea with just as much satisfaction. Like him, did they too hear the sounds of cymbals and gongs, chants and prayers as the living heartbeat of this unending vastness? Even the morning light hummed like the receding echo of a prayer gong.

What is different today, he wondered. Every small thing is alight. Everyone is aglow: the woman carrying the bundle of sticks, the tea shop owner, and even these two unknown men he shared the bench with. Everyone and everything seemed imbued with a poignant beauty.

The sunlight never left his side as, breakfast over, he walked down a brown track with tall poplars on either side, like lit fires across the horizon, each leaf a pendant of gold. Who was this jeweller who had left his craft on display and disappeared?

Further on were a few bare brown trees, just bark and branch spreading thin fingers to the sky in a plea for spring's rejuvenation. Tall golden grass burst through a broken fence, spilling on to the muddy road. He lifted his eyes to an avenue of trees with deep maroon leaves, the colour of a monk's robe, that had perhaps seen more seasons than footfalls. He leaned back against a tree, his body nothing but a flute on which Nature played its haunting notes. A deep joy coursed through him. Not only the people but the mountains and the trees, the bird spreading its black wings, were sharply alive and lustrous beyond measure. Never had everything looked so radiant.

For a moment, he felt puzzled. Was this what the world actually looked like, or was it his own state of heightened emotions that made him see it this way? Was the very thought of her the reason for this joyful madness? No. He couldn't claim that his longing for her was acute, or that his thoughts of her were obsessive. Yes, she was present in the background. But the feeling in the forefront was not of her but of the current of life that made him see angels dance on fallen leaves, turning this barren and empty land into the plenum.

He was two people: himself, and an attentive quiescence that watched his thoughts float past him without immediacy. The usual strong currents of the mind were receding and in its place something poured in so copiously that the very act of breathing became intensely pleasurable. The fundamental nature of the 'charge' was declaring itself wantonly to be at the very heart of everything, the engine of the universe. Every pore of him was soaked in bliss, as he seemed to dissolve in the love that informs the cosmos.

Pema

4 September

Despite the flood and devastation, the mystic masked dances at the Hemis Gompa, famous for their elaborate costumes, grotesque masks and sacred plays, were taking place this year as well, though much later than usual. The performance celebrated the birth of Padmasambhava, the founder of Tibetan Buddhism, and the victory of good over evil. This year it was also a thanksgiving. Usually, Ladakhis came from all over to attend the festivities. This year, it was rumoured that their numbers could be subdued because of the floods.

It was 8 a.m. Along with Anna and some monks from the monastery, Ajay had been walking for nearly two hours, and Hemis was still some distance away. Thankfully, the sun was a muted orangey glow. His thoughts drifted to the previous afternoon, when he had seen Anna in the abbot's room. He had walked up the stairs not knowing she would be there. The door was slightly ajar and he saw the abbot leaning towards Anna, her hand cupped over his.

He heard Anna's voice. 'Memories feel like shrivelled leaves. I can keep them or throw them away. Last night I asked myself: How can I account for my disowned life? I could die in an accident tomorrow. Then there would have been two unlived lives.' The words tumbled out in a rush. Then she smiled. A smile of great sweetness.

The abbot put his other hand over Anna's. No words were needed.

She bent and kissed his hands and then placed her head on them. There was gratitude in the gesture.

Ajay had felt an urge to step into the room and share the moment. But realizing he had been eavesdropping on a very personal conversation, he turned and went back to the greenhouse.

He sensed her presence as he bent down to pick up a large pot of petunias, ready to sing their special song of colour. The light caught the back of her head, so for a minute he could not see her eyes. When he did, they were as serene as the sunset hour. There were no lines of tension on her face, no sagging shoulders, no halting speech.

'Hello there. You are a stranger to these parts,' he said.

'But less a stranger to myself now. I have finally accepted that love does not mean hanging on but letting go. Thank you.'

He watched Anna's relaxed gait as she walked ahead in the slowly moving flow of pilgrims and monks, chatting happily with them.

Ajay mused that each of them had become the means for the other to revisit their past, a past with which they were still shadowboxing. All three of them had blurred the boundaries of 'faithfulness'—he with Swati; Anna with her memory of

John; and the abbot with his monastic vows. Little did he realize that the abbot's celibacy was an 'unfaithfulness' to Yodon.

Just short of the Hemis monastery, they were joined by more pilgrims making their way to the festival. The monastery was hidden by a huge projecting wall of rock, and the path to it was lined by long stone walls and white stupas. All of a sudden it came into full view, with its broad forehead of buildings, flanked by the monks' quarters built into the rock face. Somewhere here is the library that houses the rumoured Jesus manuscript, Ajay thought.

The air smelt of wild roses. The precincts of the monastery were a hive of activity, full of music, laughter and animated meetings between the pilgrims. Booths and stands selling food, tea and jewellery brought festivity to the occasion. For the peasants and nomads in the region, the annual gathering at Hemis was a godsend. They could stock up on essentials which ordinarily they would have bought in Leh.

Anna and Ajay walked up to the rectangular courtyard in front of the main door of the monastery. The open space had two raised square platforms, with a flagpole standing tall in the middle. Spectators massed around the courtyard that was already cramped for space and thronged the balconies and terraces; some even climbed onto the roof. They wove their way through the throng and found a place amidst a friendly assortment of people on the stone steps facing the closed temple door. The men clad in grey or brown long woollen frocks were a contrast to the women, who sported elaborate headgear or peraks, pink and emerald green scarves around their heads, bejewelled with turquoise necklaces and loops of gold nose rings.

Dressed in colourful bright brocades and wearing vibrantly adorned masks, some as high as one metre, of animals, demons, and spirits, the dancers in the middle of the courtyard moved with slow and rhythmic steps to the clash of cymbals and the beat of drums. On a raised dais was a table on which rested many ceremonial offerings like holy water, rice and butter tormas, and a semi-circle of incense sticks burnt steadily around them. Next to the musicians sat junior lamas; above them, the head lama sat cross-legged and impassive, as though carved in stone.

Over the noise, Ajay asked Anna, 'Is that the abbot of Hemis monastery?'

'Don't know. Never met him. Maybe.'

'Different, very different from our abbot,' Ajay murmured.

'Strange, our abbot has become the benchmark for everything,' Anna said.

Ajay smiled. It was the gentle smile of a man happy that he had found a benchmark at all.

The dancers wove this life's demons with the demons of the afterlife, the good here victorious again in the hereafter. The battle was grim and long, the victory sharp and decisive. The dance ended in the late afternoon, once the idol of evil made of dough had been destroyed by the leader of the Black Hat dancers. The audience rose triumphant, and cheered. The beating drums and the clashing cymbals seemed to join in the celebrations.

Slowly, people started dispersing. Near the monastery entrance, in one corner of the courtyard, there was a flutter of activity. People were milling around an old woman. Ajay asked one of the monks who she was, and what drew people to her.

'She is known as the Hidden Teacher,' the monk replied. 'Because she refused to preach with words, yet she taught by her sheer presence, beauty and example. Wherever she goes, she is surrounded by people, even if they don't know who she is. Just like you noticed her!'

Ajay tapped Anna on the hand and together they wove their way through the crowd and were finally facing the Hidden Teacher.

The Hidden Teacher

4 September: Evening

'She is Sangyum Pema,' Anna told the abbot later, as she and Ajay recounted the highlights of the fair.

'I've heard of her but never met her,' the abbot said.

'She is in her seventies. You cannot but be struck by her charm, her great gentleness of bearing. More than her attractive face, it is her eyes that catch you. Her contentment is her beauty. Perhaps a consequence of the life she has led.'

'She radiated presence, even I could see that,' Ajay nodded.

'Did you find out anything about her life? All I know is that she was the spiritual wife of Rinpoche Chokden, who was much older than her,' the abbot said.

'She was married to him when she was nineteen. He was in poor health, and his disciples urged him to take a consort to prolong his life. For the next eleven years, until his death, she served him as his attendant and devoted companion. Even though she was barely thirty when he died, she chose not to marry again. Instead, she quietly devoted her life to constant prayer in the presence of his stupa. They say she

274

walked the path of passion under the umbrella of devotion,' Anna said.

'I am amazed at the choice she exercised. After all, she had married an ailing old man for very unusual reasons. She must have been a very attractive woman when he died. I asked her why she chose not to marry again, and she replied, "When you have tasted true passion, that memory is enough to warm you for the rest of your life. One is very, very lucky to taste it even once. You no longer need to go from flower to flower. It is already within you. I tried to anchor myself around it." I wouldn't use the words "a happy person" for her. She is happiness itself!' Ajay smiled, reminded of the debate on his first day here.

Anna and Ajay looked at the abbot, but he had withdrawn from them. His half-closed eyes were looking towards the door, his eyeballs moving imperceptibly as if he was communicating with someone.

The wind blew outside as though there was still more dust to be raised.

Anna and Ajay quietly left the room to find Tsering waiting at the bottom of the stairs.

He said to Ajay, 'The road has opened. The airport is working.'

Yodon

4 September: Late evening

After Anna and Ajay left the room, the abbot rose and went to the cherry-wood desk. He took out a worn-out leather folder and opened it. There were three letters in it. One was from his mother; another was the reply he had never sent. He took out the third one, noting the creases deeply etched into the folds. The paper had yellowed and the margins had turned a dusty brown. He must spread it out and preserve it in a plastic folder or it would tear, never to be pieced together, he thought. He knew the contents of it by heart. Yet he wanted to preserve her writing, which was the only material memento he had of her, this poem of hers written for him.

It had been delivered to him on the night he flew to Ladakh. Her writing was on the envelope with his name on it. He had not read it that night for fear he would not make the flight the following morning, and arrive at her doorstep instead. He had read it on the first day of his arrival in the monastery, and the second and the third. He read it in the dead of winter, and when spring came and summer shone. He had read it until it was no longer her poem but theirs.

He opened the page for the sheer pleasure of it and read the once clear, crisp writing on the worn out page, in the house of memory, in the book of time.

What kind of freedom should I ask for?
For my beloved country occupied by Red Chinese
Or for the millions killed and tortured in detention camps
Or for that serpentine line of people crossing the border
Through snow, mountain pass, ill-equipped, shot like dogs by
the Chinese guard.
The first and the last in the line collapsed and in between more,
Leaving bloody stains in the snow as markers of one
kind of freedom.
What kind of freedom should I ask for?

For those of us who live borrowed lives in a borrowed land,
In ghettos of Majnu-ka-Tilla, where the Yamuna
breaches its banks,
Floods our closely built cramped houses and narrow bylanes,
Plunges us into darkness and dries our water supply.
Where we bravely create a Little Tibet with our momos,
Tankhas, prayer wheels and butter lamps
And live amidst wavering hopes of a dying nation.
What kind of freedom should I ask for?

From my tortured thoughts
That have little to do with my country but myself.
From my own heart searching restlessly,
Amidst endless uncertainties for something unknown.

If love is an expression
Of the fragmented part's desire to return to the whole
Then what is hate an expression of?
What kind of freedom should I ask for?

From the strange angst of existence
Where I bleed on many thorns
I hurt with every impulse.
I search for certainty in the flux,
And walk the catacombs of the mind
To find a handful of thoughts
Jingling merely between the pleasant and the unpleasant.
Should I ask for freedom from these?

Or should I ask for freedom from things yet to come,
Both the shadow and the sunlight,
From the rain that blesses and the sun that redresses,
From the unknown me and the little known me.
And most of all from this strange longing to visit this veiled,
secret place,
From my small, earthbound window of existence,
Called the great domain of Love.
What should I ask freedom from?

There is one heartbeat I cannot let go of where you and I
walked together
And left no trace to follow or find that place.
Yet I will always move through my memory of you with
insubstantial feet,
Reviving, thrilling, sorrowing, knowing I will not see your face
again.

Yet you are near at heart, always.
Whose renunciation was greater, oh monk,
Yours or mine?
You chose to relinquish, to forget, and I live only to remember.
That is the only kind of freedom I really ask for.

He closed his eyes and leaned back.

It had never occurred to me…you may not have returned to your marriage. I am sorry, Yodon, truly sorry for thinking myself nobler because I was the robed renunciate. I am guilty of believing that mine was the harder struggle as I had chosen an arduous path to follow. And why did I ignore the choice you could have made? So that I could live with mine? You chose and lived, I believe now, not in despairing and bitter renunciation but with a calm and lucid grace—a final benediction. Dare I feel reassured that, like with Pema, our love was a stepping stone and not a hindrance?

Slowly the abbot opened his eyes. They held the shimmer of tears.

He closed the letter and wondered yet again whose punishment was greater, his or hers? Yodon, I thought I could forget and you chose to remember with the freedom of choice. For me, flowing towards you and drowning were synonymous. In time, I learnt to exercise that choice without the fear of drowning. And when I stopped fearing, I no longer saw the difference between you and the path I had chosen. Now your remembrance is everything—the language of the flesh, the certainty of desire, my path and pilgrimage. No longer are you separate from my worship; I am seeing less and less of a difference between spirit and flesh, desire and renunciation. I created duality where there was none.

I saw you as my greatest longing and glorified myself in my capacity to renounce it. It was my grand gesture. But was it? It came upon me quietly without the beating of drums that my love for you helped me stretch my mortal arms towards some empty space I would never have dared to venture into without the courage of your love. If I dared not lose myself in your love, how could I lose myself in the great Void? You became the tangible proof of the intangible. Paradoxically, the sorrow of our separation became our secret bond, the signature of our union that indissolubly sealed you to my life.

Perhaps I now understand what Rumi meant when he wrote:

> *I do not know if I am a man and you a woman.*
> *But where once there was a man, now is a woman.*
> *Where once there were two, now is one.*

Airport

6 September: Early morning

A day later, his taxi came. A pause in the pendulum of time. In that one day, Ajay felt he had lived the essence of his life. He knew he was leaving behind as much as he was taking with him. His luggage had been taken down. The abbot and Anna were already in the courtyard to see him off.

He touched the abbot's feet. 'How inane to even try and thank you,' he said with an unsteady voice.

The abbot drew him up by the shoulders and embraced him. All three of them stood at attention to a moment, only their hearts speaking to one another.

Ajay turned to Anna. 'Will you be here when I return to visit?'

'If it is meant to be,' she replied, then added very softly, 'and the unspoken will always be there.'

In a daze, he walked down the steps and into the car. As they drove off, Ajay looked back and caught a final blurry glance of them standing there waving. Then the taxi turned a bend and the monastery disappeared from sight. He leaned back in his seat and closed his eyes.

He could not remember when he had last cried. His being felt saturated with the abbot's words, with the richness he had offered so unconditionally and generously. He fought the longing to go back to the abbot's room. Just to sit with him, watch his eyes shine, hear him throw his head back and laugh with deep-throated abandon; to come alive once more. What I have been given will remain even if I don't meet him again, Ajay thought. I do not know fully what has been passed on. What I do know with certainty is that he has sown a seed in the deepest chamber of my heart. I am afraid, for now I am its sole caretaker.

A month ago, Ajay had wanted to run from the monastery, horrified that this same Yeshe who was driving him now, had abandoned him. What had these four weeks been about? A working through of emotions that had not run their full course? Or a pilgrimage?

I am not sure which, he thought, sitting back and letting the emotions take over. All I know is I am not the same man who came here four weeks ago. My life has changed. I came to him with my heart barred with disappointment, ready for a life of inner deadness. The abbot sensed my troubles, put words to them, and then gave those words new meaning. Before I knew it, there was a path that led out of the bramble. Now I have hope. I am willing for the first time to take the risk of feeling, of flowing. I know nothing else defines one more than the capacity to love. Through Anna, a defunct ability was revived in me and that restored my faith in myself.

But how intertwined our paths are and how difficult that, at the height of desiring her, I renounced her. Will this renunciation hold as strong a power as it did for the abbot? Will it shape and weigh my days from now on as a memory of a bright mirror that reflected my face clearly, and something beyond?

They had crossed Hemis Gompa by now and were approaching the Indus at Karo. Life was limping back to normal after the devastation of the floods. The taxi crawled to a halt a few kilometres after the Karo crossing. They were caught in a snarl of traffic—long winding lines of cars, trucks and buses. Ajay relaxed when he saw the army handling it briskly. Work forces were deployed all over, restoring fallen electricity poles, repairing sunken roads, clearing the debris. The tents for the refugees had dwindled to a few. The valley was sunlit and the rising wood smoke held the hope of renewal. People were returning to rebuild their lives.

But what was he returning to? A life defined by carpet area and measured out in coffee spoons. Leaving behind nights of deepening infinity, full of stars polished by the breath of the high mountain air. Of waking to an ethereal dawn. Of fading evenings with the mountains as companions in stillness. When he thought of the monastery, what came up was a tone, a state, an inner configuration. Would all that he had received in the monastery disappear once he stepped out of it?

Ajay felt a moment of rising panic. Each kilometre increased the unsettling separation. He leaned forward, clutching the front seat, wanting to say something to Yeshe. Then he sat back, slowly releasing his breath. If the alchemy of the place lay in its evocative beauty and seclusion, then it would not be too difficult to find similar spots. But would those places make him pause on the carelessly lived, unattended moments of his life? Would they help him understand that an unobserved life was an unlived life?

Then again, was this only about a disciplined, monastic life? No. It was about understanding how a force between two people is greater than both. Was his journey, then, about Anna? If it was, then why was he moving away from her? Eventually she would return to America. If he went back, it would not be for more of Anna. After all, she was only the container, not the 'thing' contained. That point of joy happened without Anna. The rapture came when all was absent, including himself. Attraction was ephemeral but that state was not. That power was too vast to acknowledge any particularity, too big to permit any other. If he wanted to return, it would be only for the sake of a path that would lead him back to that joy. For nothing else.

A few kilometres before Choglamsar, the central focus of the second cloudburst, he saw for the first time the apocalyptic extent of the floods. Tin sheets and timber lay in a collapsed heap as the memory of a shed, its floor inundated with slurry of mud. Giant boulders wrenched from their firm moorings in the earth, trees snarled and looped into monstrous shapes shadowed the river. Jerked out of his thoughts, he stared aghast at how much had been wiped out.

For a moment again, his resolve faltered. He was leaving behind a place where every effort was directed towards a meaningful aim. In contrast, he was headed towards a city where he might lose everything he valued. Then, why was he not telling Yeshe to turn the taxi around?

Because of Swati. Can I abandon or forget Neha and her? Maybe Swati would like to meet the abbot. He dialled her number. It rang. 'Hi Ati...Yes, I know. You must have been so worried. I am all right. I took shelter in a monastery... I am on my way to the airport... Ati, before anything else, I want to say I'm sorry—' The phone got disconnected. He tried again but was unable to connect.

He wanted to tell her that he had not understood her because he so little understood himself. That he had come to see giving would have enhanced him while shutting her out had diminished him.

Ati, I now know there is no 'me' without you. He wanted to remind her of Mauritius, and of that moment of dissolution, so little understood then. He wanted to tell her it was she who had put match to wick and ignited the first flame. He wanted to tell her something has come full circle. Something big had happened in a mysteriously small compacted 'moment'. He became one with the world. It was as impersonal as it was sacred: unattached in its certainty, stainless in its radiance, joyous in its completeness. He wanted to share with her the hidden story of this flame and tell her that his whole life was the fuel for this moment; he was nothing before it and he would only count for something because of it.

That moment of epiphany doesn't belong just to him. Perhaps their misunderstandings were the catalyst for it. The fire between them, which had burned bright before smoke had dimmed its brilliance, could be reignited. So that, unburdened by the mistakes of the past, they could 'enter into the fire and rise with the flames'.

As they drove on, a thought, a name hovered at the back of his mind. Yodon. Why had she not gone in search of Rigzin? She must have found a way to handle her renunciation, or rather Rigzin's. What did she look like? Was her face like the path she followed, receptive, chiselled out of the certitude of silence, impregnated by love that clung to nothing, collected nothing? Like Pema, had she found that the ground of her being was the same as that which she sought in the 'beloved'? Had she ceased to grope without for the jewel within? For her, all this had happened in Delhi. Not in a monastery. Perhaps it was possible to keep the fire stoked there. I must search for Yodon, he thought suddenly. A spark of anticipation lifted him out of the dominion of polarities.

The taxi wound its way to Leh. He looked at the gently flapping prayer flags, bleached with centuries of prayers wafting from the monasteries, and the Indus with its whispering streams carrying their chants to the end of the river's journey. Wherever I go, I will remember these illumined moments that came from my true place of birth, he promised himself.

He closed his eyes, bowing to the abbot in thought. 'I have warmed my hands near your hearth. Maybe I have been presumptuous enough to do more. I have taken coals from your fire to light my own.'

After checking in at the airport, Ajay waited in the unpretentious lounge. A newspaper lay on the seat next to him. He had not seen one for a month. It was a Delhi edition of *The Hindu*, dated two days back. He glanced through the news, turning the pages idly. An article captioned *'Pay More Attention to Buddhists: Rinpoche'* caught his attention. It was about a statement made by Buddhist spiritual leader Kyabje Thuksey Rinpoche, the head of the Hemis monastery:

The Drukpa Order flourished in Ladakh because it received royal patronage and 70 percent of the Buddhist followers owe their allegiance to this lineage. Founded in the 17th century, the Hemis monastery is the oldest monastery of the Drukpa Order in Ladakh. According to the Rinpoche, the Hemis Gompa (monastery) has some of the most famous holy relics, which are thousands of years old. 'We have a handwritten manuscript of Jesus Christ in our secret library but we have not yet got the opportunity to make it public to the world,' he said.

Very slowly, Ajay folded the paper.

The first announcement to board the flight to Delhi had been made. Ajay did not hear it. Some journeys choose you. Another fifteen minutes elapsed and Ajay, sitting on the sofa, was only physically present. Another announcement to board the Delhi flight. Ajay did not move. With unseeing eyes, he just stared outside the window. Minutes ticked by and the last of the passengers were left to board the bus.

Finally, Ajay stirred and looked at the haversack lying next to him. He rose and picked it up. Then he turned his gaze towards the entrance, and to the taxis parked outside. He stopped and looked towards the last person boarding the bus. His name was announced, the voice urgently summoning him to board the flight. 'Final call for Ajay Kapur...calling Ajay Kapur...' It felt like a strident drumbeat in contrast to his slow and deliberate movements. Each step he took was not a step but a decision.

This time, too, the journey chose him.

Postscript

The New Delhi edition of *The Hindu*, on 23 June 2013, carried an interview with Buddhist spiritual leader Kyabje Thuksey Rinpoche, wherein he revealed that a handwritten manuscript on Jesus Christ is in their secret library in Hemis monastery. I have taken the liberty of telescoping time.

The article, written by Aarti Dhar, is available on the Internet at the following link:

http://www.thehindu.com/todays-paper/tp-national/
tp-newdelhi/pay-more-attention-to-buddhists-
rinpoche/article4844624.ece

I am grateful to Ms Rigzin Chodon for drawing my attention to this article.

Khandro Tsering Chodron or Khyentse Sangyum (ca.1929–2011) was a member of the *Aduk Lakar* family and lived more or less withdrawn in a small house in Sikkim. Sogyal Rinpoche, the author of *The Tibetan Book of Living and Dying*, described her as the foremost female practitioner of Tibetan Buddhism. She was known as a 'hidden master' because her life, full of grace and worship, eloquently exemplified her silent teaching. 'Khandro was such an enigma,' describes her caregiver, Australian nun Kunga Gyalmo. 'Wherever we went, whether a gathering in a common park or a hospital in France, inadvertently people would approach and feel the need to show veneration to this elderly Asian lady in a wheelchair, not knowing anything about her.'

The details of her life have inspired the character of Pema in my book. It is within the bounds of possibility that Ajay and Anna met Khandro-la when they had gone to the Hemis festival in September 2010. She passed on in May 2011 at Lerab Ling in France.

Acknowledgements

To Karthika who strove towards a vision of the book that had initially eluded me. Indefatigably she worked on it, again and again. If the book has reached anywhere near its potential, it is because of her.

Malashri Lal, my first reader, for her continued interest and support since the inception of the book; and to Maia Katrak and Jaswant Guzder, for their insightful comments and criticisms. Maia, thank you for the title.

Shefalee Vasudev, Chitra Sarkar, Ujwala Samarth, Vasundhara Bhalla, Neelini Sarkar, Prof Jasbir Jain, Nitya Mehra, Debasri Rakshit, for reading the manuscript at various stages.

Vipin & Shaila Sondhi, Nikhil & Natasha Mehra, Naveen & Alka Budhraja, Gautam and Kiran Kochhar, for conversations on the book.

Kanishka Gupta, for being more than my literary agent; to Rukmini Chawla Kumar, for her editing and her enthusiasm; and to Shreya Punj at HarperCollins, for her belief in the book.

The India International Centre library, where much of the book was written. To Rajeev, Kanchan, Hema and Shafali, for their warm cooperation in making books and articles appear on my desk. And, of course, the monastic cabin space, where all things were made possible.

And, as always, to Rajeev and Purnima, for the wrestle with thoughts and words, and being a mirror to my imprecisions.

Some books were especially useful in the writing of the book:

Beck, L. Adams. *The Garden of Vision: A Story of Growth,* New York: Farrar & Rinehart, 1929.

Eliade, Mircea. *Yoga: Immortality and Freedom,* tr. W.R. Trask, Princeton: Princeton University Press, 1969.

Harvey, Andrew. *A Journey in Ladakh,* London: Jonathan Cape, 1983.

Haule, John Ryan. *Tantra and Erotic Trance,* Vols 1 & 2, Carmel, CA: Fisher King Press, 2012.

Kersten, Holger. *Jesus Lived in India: His Unknown Life Before and After the Crucifixion,* New Delhi: Penguin, 2001.

McCullough, Colleen. *The Thorn Birds,* New York: Avon, 1978.

Mehrotra, Rajiv (ed.). *Voices in Exile,* New Delhi: Rupa, 2013.

Notovitch, Nicolas. *The Unknown Life of Jesus Christ,* tr. J.H. Connelly and L. Landsberg, New Delhi: Hachette, 2013.

Rizvi, Janet. *Ladakh: Crossroads of High Asia,* New Delhi: Oxford University Press, 2005.

Rosing, Ina. *Shamanic Trance and Amnesia: with the Shamans of the Changpa Nomads in Ladakhi Changthang*, tr. Jane Miller, New Delhi: Concept Publishing Co, 2006.

Shaw, Miranda. *Passionate Enlightenment: Women in Tantric Buddhism*, New Delhi: Munshiram Manoharlal Publishers, 1998.

Yalom, Irvin D. *Momma and the Meaning of Life: Tales of Psychotherapy*, New York: Harper Perennial, 2000.

Yalom, Irvin D. *Love's Executioner and Other Tales of Psychotherapy*, London: Penguin, 2013.